The Cascades Sanction
By

The Cascades Sanction

Mike Mason

Published by Mike Mason, 2025.

This is a work of fiction. Similarities to real people, places, or events are entirely coincidental.

THE CASCADES SANCTION

First edition. February 28, 2025.

Copyright © 2025 Mike Mason.

ISBN: 979-8230089704

Written by Mike Mason.

Also by Mike Mason

Exile
Webb
The Cascades Sanction

To my Wife Jenni and to our children. It is only through their patience that I have the time needed to allow these characters in my head to take shape on the page. It is for them that I do everything.

To the 12,000 +/- members of The OSS. The Office of Strategic Services. These men and women, selected and trained in some of the most creative and secret ways conceivable and led by William J. "Wild Bill" Donovan performed some of the most dangerous missions of World War Two. There work opened the doors for the creation of The CIA, British MI-6 and led to countless growth spurts throughout the world of special operations. They did their work with little recognition and they knew how to keep their mouths shut. Thank you is not enough.

> "The statesman who, knowing his instrument to be ready, and seeing war inevitable, hesitates to strike first is guilty of a crime against his country."
>
> Rudiger von der Goltz 1899

Northern Pennsylvania

The Pennsylvania sky had rapidly turned grey and angry. Taking a quick look upward from the speeding chain of his high-powered saw Matt Hauer frowned and shook his head with the knowledge that he could not avoid getting soaked. Despite the fact that he was standing near the middle of 4500 privately owned acres, he could not in good conscience walk away from the giant red oak with a cut through its heart. It had to come down before he could leave the woods.

The rain began with a simple patter of drops slapping on his face shield and the dry leaves on the ground, just one drop per second, as the chainsaw screamed away. The sharpened carbide bits threw chunks of wet wood in a ten foot radius. The slow pace lasted for a beat of twelve before a bolt of lightning lit the sky. The hair on his neck stood up. As if a giant door in the sky had been kicked open, thunder boomed and rolled down the valley below him. On the second echo the deluge came in earnest. He was drenched in seconds.

The great oak gave a shudder as gravity and a cut through its middle won out the battle. With a groan, a thump and a splash on the now soddened ground the tree was down. Green t-shirt, blue jeans, leather gloves, even the tops of his socks under his thick White's logger boots were soaked when Matt killed the saws engine trading its rattle for the tattoo of the rain and the bass assaults of thunder.

With no need to rush, haste kills in the mountains, he gathered his tools and slogged the hundred yards to his dented old Army Deuce and a half truck. The tools rode in the bed with a stack of logs while he sought refuge on the tattered seat in the cab designed for soldiers headed for war in Vietnam in 1968. What the truck lacked in creature comfort was made up for by being dry. Retrieving his Omega Dive watch from the rearview mirror he saw that despite the dark sky it was only quarter till five. The late September storm had ended his day earlier than he would have preferred. Just as well, he thought, as sore as he was.

The six wheeled trucks big diesel engine rattled to life with a puff of thick smoke and the lights and wipers came on while he cleaned himself with an old towel. At least partially dry, he sat back for a moment to take the first real break he had allowed himself in twelve hours. He was not so much tired as he was weary. He had fought doldrums all day by staying busy. For the first time in months, he truly, desperately wanted a cigarette. *Just that first mind numbing drag.* That evilly addictive drag. Alas, there were no cigarettes, not even a decent cigar in the truck. It was time to go.

The going was agonizingly slow as the truck crept over the muddy and rock strewn excuse for a road. On several occasions he had to drive through now rushing streams or over ledges only a foot or two from an edge that dropped off for three hundred feet. Finally, after twenty minutes of steady concentration and effort he was rewarded with a level gravel roadway that quickly arrived at a ten acre clearing of immaculate landscape. Stone walls and tall hedgerows separated the road and the lush lawn. Walkways of crushed white stone crisscrossed the lawn and led to double flagstone staircases at the base of an enormous granite and timber lodge. The American black granite of the foundation had been laid in massive slabs that had been hauled in on stone boats in the winter by long teams of horses and oxen. The walls rose twelve feet from the ground to meet a wraparound porch and the log structure of the lodge, all crafted with red and silver maple thicker than the man staring up at them. Cedar shingles covered the roof three stories above him. The black granite climbed up the center of the building in a castle turret so that the log structures spread from the center as separate wings, each accented with granite and fieldstone chimneys at their ends.

A few orange tinted lights shone in the big windows near the double front doors and long low streams of smoke rolled into the cool autumn sky from the chimneys. Hauer could think of few sights more inviting than this.

Entering the lodge through a back door in the basement he walked past an orange 1967 Tucker Model 342 Snowcat with a wooden stake pickup truck bed, a couple of zero-turn lawnmowers, ATV's and several snowmobiles to deposit his tools on a workbench for later attention. Here too were all manner of new and antique hand and power tools mingled with outdoor gear, canoes and several pair of short and long antique snowshoes and skis which had earned places on the walls. Shucking his muddy logger boots at the bottom of a long staircase he made his way up into the lodges center, the living room, a cavern with four brown leather sofas and six matching chairs over thick blue carpet with the round fireplace as the centerpiece. An ornate Holland and Holland double rifle rested over a six-inch-thick live edge slab of oak that wrapped the mantle. Under the rifle was an array of black and white photographs chronicling the lodge from the groundbreaking in 1898 through the 1950's. A long coffee table complimented the sofas as did an 80-inch television and a pair of bookcases. None of this interrupted the double doors to the patio. The carpet swept throughout the room ending only at the black walnut wainscoting at the base of gold and blue wall papered walls adorned with Remington sculptures, and Muir prints. At the back of the room hallways opened to each of the long wings and a staircase leading upward. He passed a long teak bar and took the hall on the right heading directly to his personal suite. In truth they were all his suites, after all it was his home, he thought with a smile.

His suite was decorated much in the same manner as the living room. The sitting room was simply an extension of the great living room but more intimate. This led to his bedroom and most importantly the bathroom and the waiting shower. The wet clothing, stinking of sawdust, chain oil and gasoline, went directly into a wicker hamper and he climbed into the heavy pulses of eight shower heads. Starting with hot water and a liberal dose of soap he cleaned himself and let the pulses massage his back and legs before gradually dropping the temperature until he had nearly icy water running over him for three minutes to wake him up.

Rid of the odors of labor and refreshed, he found new jeans and a black polo and a pair of black Salomon speed cross 6 shoes. He had caught the Salomon bug serving with the SEAL Teams in the rugged landscape of Afghanistan and had never looked back. His short brown hair needed no brushing and he could shave tomorrow he decided as he looked in the mirror. He, like his father and grandfather before him, had strong and handsome features that were complimented by hazel eyes. Though none of them would have done it, they could have gotten away with acting conceited about their looks. His friends had often told him that he was the only reason he ever left a bar or party alone.

Back in the living room he made his way around the long bar to pour himself three fingers of Single Barrel Jack Daniels and pulled a Churchill cigar from a teak and glass humidor. With the cigar lit he stood in the great bay window looking past the patio and lawn down into a wide valley. Lightning danced, creating a false daylight while the rain steadily beat the mountains. He was reminded of watches he had stood while a student at Annapolis. It hadn't been that long since he had worn the uniform, but it seemed so far away.

"I was sure that I'd heard you." A deep voice carrying a Scottish brogue came from behind. The man had entered through a door past the back staircase. The dining room and kitchen were back there. "Supper will be ready in ten minutes."

"What are we having?"

"John has done up some pepper jack steaks, sweet potatoes, a rye bread and salad. I believe he said cheesecake for desert. And what are you at Mathew Hauer? You have a rather serious look about you."

"Just thinking Carl."

"Not so fast boy. I've known the family Hauer for nearly fifty years and I know by now that look so don't try selling me on 'just thinking'."

"I guess it's a curse. It seems like every time something bad happens I can feel it coming, but damned if I know what it is or have any way of stopping it."

"Aye lad, it's a curse. I see it in you as I saw it in your dad and granddad. I imagine that some Norse ancestor of yours stood at the dragonhead of some longship with the same apocalyptic look about him. There are worse curses though."

"I'm sure there must be."

"McCafferty. The lad was one of my sergeants when I was a Sergeant's Major with the 45th infantry Black Watch. For seven generations this poor lot suffered. They would marry and have a family but, within the first year of their son being born they would lose their wife. Sergeant McCafferty had four sons and buried four wives. That my friend is a curse."

"I guess so." Hauer winced at the thought. "I just hate feeling helpless."

"Welcome to the human race. I'm sure you do. In time you'll settle with it. You are not God Matthew Hauer and be thankful for it." The tall man told him. "Now, I believe I have earned my whiskey and smoke for the day."

"Yes, you have." Hauer had to laugh and turned to face the big Scot Carl MacManus stood six foot six and weighed three hundred pounds. At sixty he was just beginning to show grey in his short red hair and goatee. He wore polished size 14 combat boots, jeans and a white wool Fisherman's sweater.

"Nights like tonight boy you think that not much has changed since these doors opened in 1900, eh?"

The lodge had been built as a retreat for the Pittsburgh and New York rich. The work was begun in 1898 and completed in 1900 when it was purchased in a private arrangement by Wilfred Otto Hauer from Theodore Roosevelt. This sale was never made public. Matt's living room had begun life as the lobby for the 110 room hotel that Wilfred Otto had named the Wolke Haus or Cloud House. Like so many other retreats along what had been called the Borscht Belt, the invisible line along the Adirondacks, the place had lost its clientele to the more exotic locals with the dawn of the jet age and was all but vacant by 1972. A one hit wonder band and a failing comedian played the last shows ever to grace the front lawn and bandstand. The Wolke Haus had sat empty until Matt came along to renovate the place.

After their supper Hauer and MacManus shared another drink and a cigar with their feet up reading, Matt from an old leather-bound journal and Carl from a colorfully covered fantasy novel.

"Let me guess." MacManus broke the silence as he sat down his drink. "You're reading of maidens, treasure and swift battle?"

"I believe that we would have to switch books to make that possible."

"Touché."

"I'm reading about my great grandfathers account of sailing around Cape Horn aboard the Kirsten in 1901."

"Quite a feat even today. How many hands were on that schooner?"

"Twelve."

"I don't suppose that with the fortune that there is that there would be a hidden Hauer treasure anyway."

"You're sitting in it."

"True enough." Carl smiled. "I'm glad that you save the old girl. A few more years and she would have been little more than a memory."

Three years earlier Matt, being the last of the Hauer family, had decided to undertake the restoration and remodeling of the Wolke Haus at a cost nearly ten million dollars. He had lost his parents and grandfather a year before in a tour bus accident in Egypt. The tragedy had ended his career as a naval officer and threw him directly into running the family business.

He considered himself fortunate to have a few friends like Carl to help him get through the worst of his pain. Feeling uncomfortable in his childhood home on Cape Cod he had quickly sold the place knowing that he could not bear spending time there, not even to rent the place to someone else. Though difficult in its own way, he kept his grandfather's mansion in Maryland. The old house made too much sense for accessing D.C. business, of which there was much. This left him with the Wolke Haus for much needed getaways.

Their peaceful silence was broken by the sounds of Matt's satellite phone chirping in his pocket. They exchanged a frown.

"Hauer." Matt spoke into the phone. He listened for a moment, still frowning, then said "Okay" and hung up.

"Visitors." Carl asked as he began pulling his big boots back on.

"Two. Non-monetary business."

"Right. I'll get coffee then. John is sleeping, I'm sure." John Eagan, the young chef/caretaker of the Wolke Haus generally followed the early to bed early to rise adage by beginning his day at 3 a.m.

A few minutes after placing the phone back in his pocket Hauer stood under the patio roof watching the single pair of headlights weave their way up the long driveway. A long Suburban from an airport rental agency pulled up at the foot of the lodge next to the two black Hummer H1 Alphas that Matt had chosen as lodge vehicles. The driver killed the engine and headlights as Hauer hit the bottom steps. The passenger, an olive skinned woman with long black hair to the middle of her back left the vehicle first while she wrestled into her waterproof pullover. When she stood upright, she was five foot seven. Despite the assistance of her hiking boots, she still fell short of Hauer's six foot two. The driver had three inches on her and looked like a linebacker dressed in jeans and a black wool sweater and black baseball cap over his bald head.

"Sar'n Major, Jax, get in here out of this storm." Hauer bellowed over the pelting of raindrops on the metal of the truck. "Shaw, I'm dually impressed that you managed to make your way around in this soup and you actually found your destination. I'd been informed by reliable sources that you army guys were afraid of the water."

"No, my amphibian friend, not afraid, respectful." Shaw said and gave a chuckle.

"Jax, a good evening to you. How about a cup of coffee? I'm sure Brett would prefer Kool-aide in a sippy cup."

"Yes sir. Thank you." Andrea Jackson Malone, ten years Matt's junior was known as Jax. She preferred this over the Doctor title she had recently earned through M.I.T.

"The look on your faces tells me that this is something other than a social call. What's up?" Matt asked.

"Matt we should do this inside." Shaw gave him a frown. Carl waited until they were seated in the living room before leaving to get coffee.

"Spill it, Sergeant Major." Matt said as he focused in on his friends' dark eyes. Brett Shaw, a few years older than the thirty five year old Hauer ran a big hand over his bald head and took a deep breath.

"Matt earlier today McGuire got a call at Langley. Because he's locked in meetings with the alphabet soup gang, he had to send us."

"Brett. What's up?"

"About three o'clock this morning Seattle time Deke Hassen was shot in the line of duty. He's presently in serious condition at Seattle General. Angela made the call to Mitch."

Deke and Angela Hassen had been Matt's friends since kindergarten. Matt and Deke had co-captained the soccer and ski teams in High School. They were the closest thing that he had left to family. When he had lost his parents and returned from Afghanistan in a daze the Hassen's had dropped everything to run to his side. They were a long way from High School, he thought. Deke was now a detective with the Washington State Police and he was in trouble.

"Thank you both for going through the trouble to come up here to tell me in person. That means a lot to me."

"Never a problem. Mitch has made arrangements to get you out there quickly. The screens are clear and we're still on break so get your gear and we'll give you a lift to your plane."

"I have a couple of planes in Pittsburgh and a chopper too."

"Not one like this." Jax said.

Hauer nodded and let out a low sigh as she took his hand and Carl and Brett both laid a big hand on his shoulder. After a long pull from his coffee, he stood up and left the room. When he returned, he was wearing a thick necked blue submariner sweater and black Origin logger boots with his jeans. He was carrying two heavy black duffle bags, one almost as long as he was tall. Jax was standing alone in front of the mantel looking over the black and white photographs of a man looking much like Matt standing with what was unmistakably Theodore Roosevelt. Another had the man standing next to a dead Rhinoceros. Both photographs showed him with the big rifle mounted above them.

"Is that an Elephant gun?" She asked.

"Yeah. Pretty much. It's a Holland and Holland Double rifle in 500/450 Nitro Express. Nasty tool." Theodore Roosevelt had gifted it to Matt's great grandfather after Wilfred Otto had brokered a deal between the U.S. Government and the German company Mauser to use their design in the creation of the 1903 Springfield rifle which would serve as a main battle rifle for several of the country's most difficult decades. Roosevelt had been so impressed by the Mauser rifles he and his Rough Riders had run up against in Cuba in 1898 that he had insured that the military would adopt something as stout. It had been reported that the then future President had used a captured Mauser in the taking of San Juan Hill and had quickly grabbed an inferior U.S. Krag rifle for a photo and morale purposes.

"Wilfred Otto only fired three rounds from that rifle. The kick is insane. The first shot was a standard factory round and cracked a four foot thick maple log. The second and third rounds were given more powder and were drilled to create hollow points in a solid brass bullet. The second round shattered another section of log and the third dropped that Rhino when it charged him. By then he had developed a Nitro Express Flinch precluding the safe handling and accuracy, unquote."

"Wow." She whispered. "Have you ever fired it?"

"Not yet. I have the seven rounds of doctored ammo from Wilfred and I bought a small lot of factory loads at auction last year. At two hundred to five hundred dollars a box I can promise you I won't be shooting it very much."

"You'll be taking my best with you for the Hassen's" Carl spoke up as he began cleaning away their coffee cups.

"Thank you." Matt said with a nod. "Tell John to just finish the wood that is down and get ready for the winter button up. I'll probably need you back in Maryland. Have Wilson get you when you're ready."

"And Matt." Carl spoke with the same command voice he had perfected in the Black Watch. "Above all, for the love of all that is Holy, get some sleep."

"Yeah. I'm sure that'll happen." Shaw let out his first sarcastic words of the evening.

"This really is a beautiful place." Jax offered in an attempt to crack the begging of a brooding mood more befitting a funeral parlor.

"I forgot that you hadn't been here before. You have to come back when the weather is more accommodating." Matt responded, flattered that she had a sense for the situation and thankful for her approach. "What did I rate for wings?"

"Something out of Skunkworks I'd wager." Shaw referred to Lockheed's top secret facility of the 1950's and 60's. From the secretive hangars of Skunkworks came such aircraft as the SR-71 Blackbird and the F-117 Stealth Fighter.

Pittsburgh International Airport
2145

SHAW AND MALONE STOOD in the unlit hanger that should have been housing tankers from an Air Force Reserve Fueling Wing while they watched a long and sleek grey plane whose entire body appeared as an arrow head. It was as long as a passenger plane but not as tall or as wide. The plane was towed outside where it taxied away onto the east/west runway. Despite their proximity to the large aircraft, they could barely hear more than a buzz. There were also no tell-tale flames as with other jets. Onboard the jet along with at least four other people that they knew of, was Matt Hauer and his gear. Although they had known for over a month that the plane existed, they had yet to see it. There was no surprise that the stops had been pulled out to get their boss aboard and get him to Seattle. After all, Hauer had had a large part in getting the design pushed through. Old Wilfred Otto would be proud.

Indeed, Hauer was accompanied by only four other people. Two of them sat side by side in an encapsulated cockpit that he shared with them. The other two, a second flight team, were in a separate spartan ejectable apartment where they would wait for their turn to fly a six to eight hour session.

The XB-88 Demon, experimental bomber, from the outside had a strong resemblance to the failed XB-70 Valkyrie bomber of the 1960's. Matt long held personal feelings that the Valkyrie should never have been cancelled, but allowed to serve out a long life in defense of the nation as a fast Strategic Nuclear Delivery Vehicle. Those feelings had worked heavily when he was shown the designs for the Demon stealth Scram Jet. The Demon was equipped with reconnaissance equipment, could cloak itself into invisibility and carried the bomb load of the venerable B-52. All of this was conducted at speeds exceeding MACH 8. Matt felt a slight jolt as the weight of the jet left the runway and the pilot throttled up. Once in the air he opened his laptop computer. The screen displayed the seal of the Defense Intelligence Agency before flashing to a video feed of a man with a decent suntan and short salt and pepper hair. The man looked uncomfortable in his dark blue suit. Hauer noticed that the tie was already missing and that two buttons had been undone. Matt knew how he felt.

"Matt. I'm sorry that I couldn't cover this myself. How are you?"

"A bit stretched out. I'm enroute to Seattle now. Anything new on this?"

"Only that he is in guarded condition. I've been in locked sessions with SOCOM, NSA, JSOC and the President all day."

"No sweat. I'll be out there soon."

"Priority one Matt is get out to your friends. Anything I can do, let me know."

"Will do."

"And don't forget to sleep."

The co-pilot turned around a short time later to tap his foot. He had, after all, fallen asleep.

"Commander Hauer we'll be on the ground in McChord in a few minutes. There's an MP on standby to take you to your vehicle. Local time is 1850. Weather is overcast with scattered showers and 50 degrees."

"Damn that's fast."

"Good luck sir."

"Luck and I aren't on speaking terms." Hauer told him.

"Roger that."

"Thanks for the ride. Safe flying."

Hauer mused that it had taken him longer to get his gear to the undercover government Tahoe and get off of McChord Air Force Base than it had to fly there. The nap had done nothing for him. In the short time it took to drive from Tacoma to Virginia Mason Hospital in Seattle he fought off the urge to buy cigarettes and the pressing desire to get good and drunk until he could forget it all. The urge was doubled when he stopped at a grocery store to buy a dozen roses for Angela. At a little after seven thirty he walked past two State Troopers into room 4183. The troopers had been shown an identity and a badge indicating that he was an FBI agent. Neither had so much as blinked.

A tall brunette in a recliner that had been pulled tight against Deke Hassen's bed shook herself from under a thin sheet and blanket and crossed the room to embrace him. She accepted the vase of roses, setting them on a small table with a multitude of others and a long display of cards. Under another thin sheet on a bed surrounded by a maze of tubes, wires and bandages was the pale form of Deke Hassen.

"Good. They found you." Angela whispered.

"I came as soon as I found out Ange."

"Thank you."

"Of course. How is he?"

"Fair now."

"What happened?"

"Lock the door." Deke rasped. This brought a frown but compliance from Matt.

"Let me have some water too, please." He asked. His eyes were now wide open in contrast to the bandages covering the right side of his face. A salve covered small bloody spots on his left cheek, chin, scalp and nose.

"Go ahead. You sure you're okay?"

"Yeah. I was wrapping up an investigation and was on my way back to Seattle." He began after a short sip of icy water through a bent straw held by Angela. "I grabbed a van that ran by me at 90 in a 65. As I started to get out, the back doors popped open and the next thing I know we're trading fire and I'm on the horn for help. I got off twelve shots, I know I hit someone. They machine-gunned me Matt."

"Why the locked door?"

"I just gave you the official line."

"Oh." Hauer said as he sat back heavily in the hard chair and sighed audibly. The machine-gun, the hit and the secrecy and paranoia regarding fellow officers was making Hauer think that his friend may have gone bad and there was a drug ring coming after him. The lack of sleep and the confusion were trying his patience. "What's going on Deke?"

"I got too close to something ugly and I got set up to get hit."

"Something that you can't tell your own people about?"

"No. I don't know who to trust right now." Deke wheezed. "I've got fourteen new holes in me and I don't think it was meant to scare me. Now I know that you aren't officially in the SEAL teams anymore but, you disappear right when weird things happen in the world. It leads me to believe that you might be involved with the kind of people that can handle this the best."

"We'll get to that. Give me the straight line though." There was more than a bit of discomfort at Deke's guesswork and the fact that he was no longer a member of an active SEAL team was a sore spot. The loss of his parents and grandfather had ended a brilliant career and robbed him of a life in the proximity of some of the best men he had ever known. His oldest friend was correct though, more than he could guess. Hauer's new position kept him on a far less restrictive leash than the Navy had afforded. Now he actually wrote his own missions, usually on the go.

Two weeks earlier, Deke explained, he had been approached in a coffee shop by a college kid with a fantastic tale of the disappearance of several friends and the suspected cover up by local authorities. Her friends had been hiking in the North Cascades National Forest when they disappeared. The local Sheriff had told her that his deputies had found the car of one friend along with a note that indicated his intentions of murder and suicide. That had been a week prior to her approaching Hassen. When asked why she did not believe what the Sheriff reported she produced a video on her cell phone in which he watched the accused murderer begging for help. There was automatic weapons fire and the image of a camouflaged soldier drawing closer from the trees. The video stopped abruptly. Disturbed by the apparent cover up, Hassen had taken the file out of circulation and took it upon himself to conduct an investigation in the mountains.

"I found what the kids must have bumped into. You'd either have to know where you were headed or hit it by accident. There's a compound up there. Concrete buildings, trucks and K-9 patrols that look a lot like military personnel. I got a couple of dozen photos before my nerve gave out. Two days later I got machine-gunned."

Hauer twisted his lower lip wishing that he had something to take the edges off of his mounting stress and the headache that was chasing closely behind it. He would almost take a cigarette right now if it were offered. He wouldn't shy away from a nice belt of scotch either. A full day worth of sleep was what he really needed. Those thought lines if given any steam would turn into a road with a bridge out sign that appeared too late. He could not afford them. Not now. Rubbing the bridge of his nose between his thumb and fingers he asked the question hanging in the air.

"What's in the pictures?"

"Firearms crates coming off of military trucks, fuel drums and mucho bio gear. All going into the buildings. The funny thing is there are trucks with logs coming out the other side."

"I guess that it's my turn then." Hauer spoke after giving his friends words and the look on his battered face some thought. He turned his cell phone over to stare at the back of it and the three green LED lights shining back at him. "No bugs. That's a great sign. Okay. My file sits on the desk of only one office in the DIA. This is a blanket appointment for an organization that we call the Fraternity. I am a Wraith. My work is a lot like what I did in Special Warfare but usually done outside of D.C.'s knowledge. My bosses don't always agree with the swamp about what is best for the country. Mostly, right now, I find and eliminate terrorist threats."

"You're a vigilante'?" Deke asked with a scowl.

"Not at all. I still wear a uniform and sometimes a badge. I am very much in the light of favor with the President and most of our ranking officials. Do you think that the people in your department or any other that you can think of are involved in this case?"

"I don't have any suspects but like I said, I don't trust people right now. These people are pros. They act quickly and I have to think that this is about much more than drugs which was my first suspicion or an illegal logging operation which is what drove the kids to the sight."

"Where are the pictures?"

"One set of prints and a thumb drive are in two separate safety deposit boxes. One key is taped under the dog tag in my old left boot. Another is under the passenger vanity mirror in Angela's Jeep."

"House keys?" Matt asked impressed with his friends' tactics. Angela handed them over and wrote the alarm code on a slip of paper for him.

"Write your sizes down as well. I recommend that both of you get some rest, we'll be flying out rather early in the morning."

"I can't fly in this condition man. And where the hell are we gonna go?"

"You can fly in a stretcher." Matt responded as he set the chart back on its holder at the foot of the bed. "Don't worry, your Uncle Sammy is going to take care of it."

Timberlane was a suburb on the northeastern skirt of Seattle. Dozens of streets in a maze like pattern of cul-de-sacs and cookie cutter houses had been built for baby-boomers in the late 60's as people flocked out to tech and aircraft jobs. It was, Matt knew, a quiet neighborhood where neighbors shared cookouts, pool parties and probably spouses on occasion. This was the land of designer coffee, big sport utility vehicles, high dollar sports cars, Botox and soccer trophies. It was late enough that most people were inside but not so far along in the night that his arrival was likely to wake anyone. Hauer pulled the Tahoe into the driveway next to Angela's pearl white Jeep Grand Cherokee. After Deke's ordeal and story Hauer made sure to take proper precautions and had clambered into a tactical Kevlar vest and plate carrier while still parked in the hospital parking garage. From his kit he produced a black tube that was no bigger than the center tube from a roll of paper towels. With the flick of a switch, he was given an X-ray view of the house and cars. The device was still having some kinks worked out and couldn't yet be used for targeting so he had not yet mounted it to a weapon but it gave a real view of what might be behind windows and walls at night. At least semi sure that he was alone on the property he slipped out of the truck with a short and suppressed MP-5K submachine gun in his hands and a Sig M18 pistol strapped to his right hip. With a black box the size of a pack of cigarettes held in his left hand at the front of the sub gun he waved over the Jeep twice as the device scanned for explosives. As with the x-ray he came up empty. For a moment when he opened the SUV's door his heart sunk. The interior had been obliterated by knives and hands. Seats were torn, the air bag had been punctured and door panels had been ripped off. But, from behind the vanity mirror came the little brass key to a bank safety deposit box.

The house and garage had been given the same treatment as the car but they looked worse. Drywall had been pulled away to leave its powdery residue everywhere. Appliances were kicked in and pulled apart. Clothing and furniture had been ripped to shreds. Not a single photo frame went untouched. It pained him to bear witness to the despoiled memories and shattering of a life, especially those of his friends. What he was able to extract from the house were a pair of photos of boot prints left in the drywall dust on the carpet and tile floor.

The pain turned to a seething anger which had to be reined in before he lashed out. Someone was not only stalking and terrorizing his friends but he was sure that they would try again to kill them. For what? Unlike the missions he had run in the past this presented a challenge. This was personal. He could not hide from that truth. He hoped that he could remain an objective professional throughout its course. To do otherwise could prove fatal, for everyone involved.

Outside of an all-night truck stop Matt typed away at his laptop and spent the better part of half an hour on his cell phone looking up the history of the North Cascades while raindrops danced on his windshield. Finally feeling like there was little more he could accomplish at the moment he went inside and at the red Formica counter and squeaky red vinyl stool he ordered an omelet and strong coffee. He felt like he was back in Hell Week and might stand a chance of falling asleep with his fork somewhere between his plate and his mouth. Looking around at truckers either ending or beginning a shift he realized that he fit in with this tired lot without a second look. Some of them wore beards or goatees, others made their statements to the world via a beat up baseball cap or a t-shirt or the old standby, tattoos running down their arms. Some wore flannel sleeves all the way to their wrists while others had no sleeves at all. It seemed though that they all wore jeans and boots. From the waist down all men are the same he could hear some angry women yell. It made him grin. In reality these folks all wore the road on their tired eyes and bodies. The other commonality of the night owl driver was the coffee and cigarettes. And, they all looked like they had given up on anything that might resemble a normal life. They looked like prisoners who had done too much time and didn't know how to get back to being right. He wondered how far removed from their reality he was. This restaurant was considered a private club and dodged all smoking laws and these people took full advantage of it. The smell was both alluring and sickening for him. The smoke burnt at his tired and bloodshot eyes and the acrid and somehow alluring odor called to his wounded psyche. He could see how easy it would be to start right here and knew how hard it would be to stop again if he allowed himself the slip. There could be no sanctuary here. It was time to move on.

0700

"At ten minutes after six this morning." The red raincoat clad news anchor spoke against the wet backdrop of the Emergency Entrance to Virginia Mason Hospital. "State Police Detective Lieutenant Richard 'Deke' Hassen passed away, the victim of a yet unsolved vicious roadside shooting early yesterday morning. Detective Hassen was a well-liked member of not only the State Police force but his community as well. He will be sadly missed. For Channel 9 at Virginia Mason Hospital, I'm Molly O'Shea back to..."

"Oh, that's real nice Matt." Hassen said from his stretcher looking away from the small television mounted to the countertop of the private jet.

"It has to look real. In another hour or so there will be a body found in a car at the pier, the distraught widow, then my team can get to work." Matt told him and winked.

"This is how it has to be?" Angela asked.

Matt could only nod in reply.

"What's the plan from here?" Deke asked.

"We'll be in the air for about four hours. At Reagan we'll transfer over to a Med Flight chopper and get you into a secure wing at Johns Hopkins. We'll play it by ear after that."

"I mean the investigation."

"I'll be taking that over. After we get in and settled my boss will meet with you and figure out what you want to do from here. The case I will see through to its end. Now, why don't you join me in some sleep."

As promised, Deke was admitted to one of the eighteen secure suites on a government only ward of the Johns Hopkins University Hospital. Four armed Marines stood guard at the wards sole entrance. The doctors had already received his records from Seattle. The chief surgeon, a short and balding young man in a white shirt over grey wool dress pants, assured the Hassen's that having reviewed his X-rays that Deke would retain his legs and arms as well as full mobility. After the surgeries necessary for the skeletal and muscle tissue they would work out where to begin the cosmetic work for scaring. First, especially after the stress involved with being moved across the country, Deke needed to rest for a few days and his immune system needed time to catch up.

Carl MacManus stepped into the room wearing a blue wool suit and carrying a pair of shopping bags from one of the areas upscale boutiques.

"I shan't say your names, but I am glad that you are now here and safe."

Angela jumped up and hugged him for that.

"Matt gave me your sizes and sent me shopping for you. Hopefully the clothing is suitable."

"Well thank you both. Now I can get cleaned up." She took the bags into the bathroom with her and headed immediately for the shower.

"You got a pen and paper while she's gone?" Deke asked. Matt produced a small wire wound notebook and a grey steel Mont Blanc pen from his jacket.

"The students name is Jennifer Beck." He wrote an address and phone number. "That's the best that I can do. Whatever you do keep that kid safe and be careful please."

"I will brother. My boss will be here to see you tomorrow. His name is Mitch McGuire."

"The same Mitch that used to visit your dad?"

"Same guy. He'll come with Carl so you will know who he is. I'll be gone for a while but Carl will be at your disposal. Whatever you guys need just let him know."

"Matt. Thank you."

"You'd do the same. Just get better."

"That's so much better." Angela declared as she reentered the chilled air of the room. She was wearing new khakis with a thin navy top and a pair of white cross trainers. Her cheeks were reddened from the heat of the shower and a light application of blush. Just enough to accent what she already had to offer. She smelled of the soap and perfume that Matt had recorded in her own bathroom. He decided that familiarity would keep her at ease. To Matt she looked as she had so long ago in high school, pretty and innocent.

We've seen the evil of the world and our innocence was the price we paid for the viewing, He thought.

The decision for Angela to accompany Matt and Carl to the Maryland mansion was Angela's to make, but it was an easy one. Her husband was on a large dose of pain killers and exhausted from the flight. He would be able to offer little in the way of company. There was no sense in her sleeping in either a chair at his side, he said, or in a hospital bed. After what she had been through, she deserved her own rest and pampering. She didn't agree but she listened. Deke was fast asleep before they had left the ward.

The Hauer Estate sat on 800 acres across the bay from Annapolis in Woodstream in the heart of Queen Anne's county. It was difficult to fathom that life could be so fast paced and intense on one side of the bay and be at the heels of the peace of the 19th century on this side. Carl managed to hustle the large blue Ford Excursion along so that they made the commute from parking lot to gravel and crushed seashell driveway in just under an hour. Stone and split rail timber fences separated the road from the grassy fields. Elms, oak and willows stood tall and majestic at the roadside, their boughs creating a soft canopy. On the opposite side of the fence were the horses, Morgan's on one side with Clydesdales on the other. After half a mile the driveway formed a wide circle fronting a four story stone castle complete with six perimeter towers, parapets and a central tower standing eighty feet above the car. Three levels of Vermont marble steps led up to a long and wide patio and the tall oak double doors engraved with the twin lions of the family crest. At an angle from the house the gravel road continued on, leading to a long and low timber and stucco garage and a twin building serving as the stable. Both of these buildings reminded her of Swiss Chateaus. Taking a closer look at the main house one would see that the stone gave way at the upper floor to the Bavarian design so that the upper floor was a chateau with a sharp mansard roof and many dormer windows.

Two young women in the traditional black and white uniforms of maids met them just inside the door. Monique, a tall brunette from Le Mans and Rachel from Cork Ireland, a red head just an inch or two shorter than her coworker. Angela was formally introduced, it would be noted, the girls had been forewarned, she was not a visitor but was to be treated as Master Hauer himself. She relinquished her bags to the young women and left in their company to see her new room.

"Supper will be in one hour." Carl spoke in dismissal as he looked at his watch.

"You'll give me the tour again I hope Matt."

"Directly after dinner."

"You look like you could use a drink sir." Carl remarked when they were left standing alone in the living room at the bottom of an ornately carved and red carpeted staircase.

"Very much so. Laphroaig in the armory. Do bring yourself a glass too."

The first floor of the castle was where the daily life took place. Here there was a great kitchen, a dining room, a sitting room for the entertainment of guests, a library larger than most people's homes and Matt's office and an armory set up as a museum which itself took up half of the floor. He had considered placing the office and armory in the enormous basement but had decided that for lack of natural light it would be better suited as a wine cellar, storage and gym.

His office sat behind a mahogany door that opened only through a code panel in the library. Starting at the door was a dark blue carpet that stretched out twelve by eighteen feet before the hardwood floor took over the room. The carpeted area was the office leaving everything else to the armory. Around an old Presidential desk, one of Theodore Roosevelt's personal desks, were three black leather swivel chairs. A large display monitor and a custom built Cray computer that rated their own modern desk sat adjacent to the main desk. He sat in his chair and ran his hands over his temples glancing at the wall that had been behind him before closing his eyes. The wall displayed almost fifteen years of service, a little less than half of his life. There were degrees from Annapolis, photographs from all over the world with members of the teams he had served on and the medals he had been awarded. At the top of the medals was the SEAL team trident, often referred to as the Budweiser, an eagle holding a flintlock pistol and the pitchfork-like trident of Poseidon. He had been awarded the silver star once, the bronze star twice along with the Navy Cross. In his course of service and time spent cross training with other U.S. units and foreign governments he had earned and been allowed to wear the U.S. Army Ranger tab and Army master jump wings. He had also earned master jump and master diver badges from the English, Australians, Greeks, Italians, the Thai's and the Norwegians. Held separate from these ratings were a pair of Navy aviator wings that indicated that he was qualified for any naval aircraft. Climbing the wall toward an American flag at the top of the display were his high school diploma, a degree from Annapolis, a Master's Degree in Maritime Design from Woods Hole and his commercial pilots license, all in their own frames underneath the flag and a wooden boat paddle with its handle wrapped in rope. On the blade of the paddle was another trident and a challenge coin from his last placement at Seal Team 6. He had just enough time to think about earning all of the pieces on that wall and the price and time he and his brothers in arms had paid for them to be there followed by the loss of his parents and grandfather before the double sets of footsteps in the library interrupted his thoughts. He sighed through his nose and looked up.

"Your scotch and a guest." Carl announced at the door.

"Come on in. Boss can I get you a cigar, a drink maybe?" Hauer stood to take McGuire's hand.

Mitchell McGuire stood just shy of six feet and even in his late fifties retained an athletic and tanned physique that was visible under his black pinstripe Ralph Lauren suit.

"I'll take the drink, please." He said as he took long look around before taking a seat and the drink from Carl. His eyes danced over the four double sided racks that made up the center of the wooden floor and the table displays that lined the walls. He knew that the display began with a short Chinese wick fired musket and wound through to the most cutting edge military testbed weapons. There were also all manner of swords, knives, lances, hammers, axes, maces, atlatls, a morning star and blow guns. The exotic 7.62mm General Electric M134 Minigun sat on a table at the end next to an M2 Browning 50. Caliber machine-gun. The display was as near complete as any in private hands had ever been.

"I'm always impressed when I come in here. The whole estate is incredible, but this museum is awe inspiring."

"I think it's sad." Matt responded with an exhale.

"That's sort of odd, coming from a warrior."

"Not really. Yes, I'm a warrior. I'm good at it, but I take no entertaining pleasure out of the acts of warfare. The tools of our trade are a sad necessity to maintain a level of enforced civility and safety that fewer and fewer people appreciate."

"Fair enough." McGuire conceded. "How's your friend holding up?"

"He's probably sleeping right now. He at least has a road back. Even if it might be kind of a long and strange one. I need a full recast on both him and his wife. Whatever it is that those kids found up in the park is guarded by professional shooters who don't want their principal found out."

"Is this personal?"

"Mitch, I'd be lying to you if I said no. I'm not looking to use the Wraiths as a vendetta force on a group of smalltime gang bangers. I would walk away and take care of it myself if I thought that that's what this was. I think we have a real op here."

"I guess that's what I'm asking, is can I keep you on this?"

"Absolutely."

"Alright then." McGuire said and laid his empty glass on the coaster. "Break it down for me."

"I want to head back out tonight. I'll contact my witness in the morning and we can bring the team up shortly after."

"Any ideas where this is going yet?"

"I'm going to look at the photos that Deke took. He talked about military hardware and chemicals being moved. Once I have something actionable, I will be on the horn with you. Can I buy you supper?"

"Hell yeah."

The full staff sat together in the main dining room. The was a place fit for formal dining and had been built back when men wore top hats and women wore wide girthed dresses. Now, everyone was dressed casually including the maids who had had time to change out of uniform in favor of jeans and shirts and the mechanic who had cleaned grease thoroughly from his big hands. They sat next to the mechanics wife Rita and their preteen son James, alongside a pair of chefs, the groundskeeper and a husband and wife veterinarian team as well as Carl. Angela was working overtime trying to collect and remember everyone's name. The mechanic she had known since she and Matt were in school but had only ever known him as B. Some people had called him Mac but it had gotten too confusing when McGuire was around so people had just left it at B. B was a big man like Carl. He had a bright smile in his heavy jawline that was accented by a shock of thick black hair. To Angela he looked like he belonged on a field lifting and throwing ogres more than he did holding a tiny fork in a formal dining room. After the maids served everyone with a plate piled with curry and rice complimented by thick cuts of moist chicken and served the beer in tall glasses, they took their seats and waited for Matt to ask a blessing and a hand over his friend Deke and his wife in their time of need.

"This is fantastic." Angela said after a bite of food and a sip of her beer. "I've had a lot of micro brews in the last ten years out in Seattle but, this is amazing."

"It's called Tail Dragger. It's an IPA from Ten Eyck. A bunch of local women who are prior service or first responders started it up and are really knocking it out of the park. We'll have to drive over to their place after Deke heals up."

"B can I borrow you for a few?" Matt asked after he had walked McGuire out.

"Anytime champ."

"Angela, you too please."

Angela and B followed him out of the main building and onto the packed gravel walkways overlooking the Corsica river where they could look down the stretch of lawn to a willow grove that lined the shore. She could hear the horses nickering in the field and in the stables as the night came on. Bugs and birds still danced and sang in the fading light. It was strangely unreal that less than a day earlier she had been on the other side of the country in fear for her husband's life and was walking here feeling as though all was right in the world.

She felt like she was at the beginning of a vacation and hated herself for feeling good while her husband was down.

"Carl will drive you back to Hopkins in the morning." Matt told Angela as he led the way. "Mitch will see you both sometime in the afternoon with new identities and accounts. I'd like and prefer if you were both to stay on here until whatever this problem is reaches a conclusion."

"How could we refuse an invitation to live in a castle with servants, horses and a hundred fine cars to go shopping in?"

"I don't have a hundred cars. There are seventy-one and fifteen motorcycles. But I'm glad that you haven't lost your sense of humor."

"It's a survival tactic."

"I know it is. Keep it. It works."

B opened the first of the four bay doors into the garage and turned on the overhead lights.

"The garage?" She beamed.

"Yes. The garage." Matt was smirking. "Can I really trust you with this?"

"For sure."

The interior of the garage was in complete contrast with the chalet facade of the exterior. The floor was polished concrete and the walls were lined with neon lights, bar stools, car advertisements and movie posters, car parts and hoods or grills of various automobiles throughout history. Cars, trucks and motorcycles were lined up in three rows with the motorcycles taking up the center of the big room.

"There are just a few rules." B announced.

"No drag racing, no sitting on the cars and no parties." She teased as she played at ticking off the points on her fingers.

"Pretty good." The big man chuckled. "Just a couple more. None of the racing stuff. They don't have plates anyway. That silver 1969

Charger goes nowhere unless there's a fire in which case, we move it and then the photo albums."

"It's that important huh?"

"It's an absolute one of one. A lot of trusted people believe that it never existed but we have the build sheet for the guy who ordered it. It's the only car ever to leave the plant with a dual overhead cam Hemi. Some might say it was a mistake and some might say it was another shot at making the Silver Bullet car which pairs it well with the first Silver Bullet, that 67 Plymouth GTX down the row.

"I bet that guy didn't want to sell."

"He really didn't. I had B lined up to play poker with him." Matt said.

"You're that good?"

"I'm okay."

She stood in silence for a moment to drink it all in, reading floor displays for the cars or motorcycles that she didn't know. A red 1940 Indian Four motorcycle, a maroon on tan 1931 LaGrande Cord L-29 Speedster that the late great actor Gary Cooper could have been seen in and an extremely rare Koenigsegg One:1 of which only six had been produced by the Swedish company.

"Okay, cool enough. How about that Charger Daytona, that's legal. And, how many Chargers do you own?"

"Six. I also have two Challengers, a Hemi Cuda, two GTX's, a Savoy, a 68 Dart A/FX, four Vipers and a 70 Road Runner. I'm putting some work into my Mopar lineup. That Daytona though, isn't ready yet and it's being built for a race."

"It's not restored? I'm shocked."

"See the supercharger sticking through the hood?" He asked. "No, it isn't restored wiseass."

"What's the race?"

"The Silver State Classic." B told her.

"Very nice. 90 miles all out. The best time is what 27 minutes. And you plan to beat that in a car built in 1969, right?"

"Absolutely. The record was held by a 1969 Camaro for a long time." Matt said.

"What is it exactly that makes this black beast so special?"

"Big brakes, wide sticky tires, a six speed transmission and about 2400 horsepower."

"What?" She nearly cried out. "How fast is it?"

"We should hit 275 out there easy." B told her.

"So, you are good at more than poker?"

"I'd like to think so."

"Matthew Hauer you are insane." She declared as she gave him a toothy smile. "What the hell. Let's hear it."

"Cover your ears." He said as he climbed into the carbon fiber racing seat. "It's loud."

"It can't be that..." Her words were cut off by the horrendous bellow pouring from the four three inch exhaust pipes that exited from under the car and shot into the air just in front of the rear tire. There were four more pipes on the other side. The high pitched whine coming from the massive supercharger was barely audible over the lumpy exhaust note that rattled her bones so hard that she involuntarily stepped back.

"Wow." She stammered when the noise died. "That's scary."

"I've never heard you say that about a car."

"Yes, you have. That black Hemi Challenger in high school terrified me. It still does as a matter of fact. I won't be driving that either."

"Good." He gave her a wink. "B will set you up with anything you want after you see Mitch tomorrow. How about some horses?"

"I love horses, but I've seen plenty to be able to say that for the moment I would prefer to sleep."

"How about a nightcap then?"

"You're leaving tonight, aren't you?"

"Yeah."

"Matty please be careful. This thing scares me."

"Me too. I will be careful." He said and took her in a strong hug. He held her there for a few minutes feeling her silent sobs. Her world had been utterly destroyed and she was lost. She needed to let her pain out so that she could figure the rest of her life out and this was probably her best avenue at the moment. "I need you guys to be careful too. Until Mitch gets you set up and we can put a weapon in your hands I want you to know that everyone here with the exception of young James is armed at all times. There are also several guards out there watching." He waved his hand at the darkening landscape.

Chapter Two

"No man is entitled to the blessings of freedom unless he be vigilant in its preservation."

General Douglass MacArthur

SEATTLE

The plane for Hauer's return flight to McChord AFB was a 747-400 from his own aviation division. The plane and crew belonged to a small fleet that he leased out to larger airlines and corporations. Before they left the ground at Reagan National airport in Arlington Virginia, he was asleep and stayed that way until an attendant woke him five minutes before landing. On arrival he reclaimed the unmarked Tahoe and followed a pair of sergeants from Air Force Security Force. He could not stop himself from thinking MP when he looked at them. They escorted him down the northernmost and lesser used runway to Hangar L-23 near the backside of the air base. The hangar had long ago been a maintenance facility for the air force's executive jets and was equipped with several air conditioned offices, a ward room and a small bunkhouse. It would be perfect as a staging area for his team.

At 800 a.m. he sat behind the wheel with the engine off while watching fat rain drops crash against the windshield. More than the rain, he was watching the traffic. He scanned both the vehicular and foot traffic in and around the Starbucks that he had agreed to meet Jennifer Beck at. A dark blue 1975 Ford Bronco eased out of the oncoming traffic and pulled into the parking lot a few spots away from him. The rugged off-road vehicle rode on tall aftermarket tires. A winch rode on the front bumper and it sounded to Matt like the little truck had been tweaked for more power. This vehicle was no show piece he decided as he looked over the pair of dented and scratched five gallon military gas cans on a back rack along with a full-sized spare tire. The driver, a tall and trim brunette woman with bleach blonde streaks in her long hair got out and zipped up her tight green jacket she must have picked from a hiker's catalog. Jeans and hiking boots filled out her outdoors woman look. Deke had called her grunge but had missed the mark. She walked until she was a few feet in front of the Tahoe, sure that she had his attention, and waved at him. Frowning and a bit embarrassed for having just been marked as a Fed by his vehicle he climbed out and caught up to her.

"Jennifer Beck, I assume." *My God, she's beautiful.*

"Matthew Hauer." She asked.

"Just Matt is fine."

"Jen." She said and stuck her hand out as he held the door for her.

"Nice Bronco Jen."

"Thank you. I'd say nice Tahoe, but it's not yours, is it?"

"No." He blushed as he gave his head a shake.

"What'll you have Just Matt?" Her light green eyes simultaneously invited and pierced.

"Same as you."

"Risky." That beautiful smile flashed his way again. She ordered two venti caramel macchiatos and stood to the side so that they could wait. Matt paid and left a five dollar tip. "So, Detective Hassen said that you two are lifelong friends."

"That's right. He's my best friend. I'm sure you can guess that he and his wife are in hiding right now."

"He did tell me that. I'm very sorry."

"Jen you've lost a lot in this too. I'm sorry for that. I need your help if you can give it."

"Absolutely."

He led her to the passenger seat of the Tahoe.

"Two weeks ago, now, four friends." Matt paused to look at his notes and sip at his strong and sweet coffee. "Erica Benoit, Dean Kamen, Mark Jannot and Brian Ash disappear in the North Cascades National Park. My friend goes up there with a camera and finds some ugly stuff. Forty eight hours later he gets gunned down. Do you know why your friends went up there?"

"Yes."

"Does the fact that they were all focused on Forest Resources, Biology and Marine Biology have something to do with their motivation? This wasn't random, correct?"

"No. This wasn't random on their part. My friends played the wildlife activist role pretty hard. Last year they uncovered and helped prosecute an illegal logging operation in Olympic National Park. They were convinced that they had found another in the North Cascades."

"Were you with them at Olympic?"

"Yes. I took most of the photographs."

"And The Cascades?"

"No. I didn't make either trip up there. The first because I needed to intern that weekend. The second trip I missed because Brian didn't think that my opinion on the logging issue was good for the group. I scanned their GPS plot over to my phone but I gave up the fight with Brian to be able to go. Anyway, they went up and they got to within a mile or so of the facility. There's a cliff that broke out of the trees and looks down and west. They snapped a few shots of two buildings. You know those prefab steel warehouses we used during World War Two? One of those and a huge one that looks like concrete. There were a couple of photos of people walking around too."

"Do you still have the GPS and the photos?"

"Yes. I can email them to you."

"Deke told me that you got the run around from the Sheriff's office up there."

"The Sheriff believes that there was a murder suicide and because of the size of the forest neither they nor the feds that service the park can easily find the bodies. None of my friends was the homicidal type. They were murdered to cover up whatever is going on up there."

"Jen. I'm not sure what Deke told you about me. I'm about to bring in a team to help me solve this. At present I have four missing and because of the time and weather in the area I have to assume dead students, one wounded police officer who is now hiding with his wife and then I've got you. In all this time nothing has come your way, but I'm about to stir this hornets' nest and I'm not sure what to do with you. I think we should start thinking about housing you."

"Mister Hauer, Agent..." She tried to slow herself down.

"Matt." He said softly.

"Matt, I agree. I think that my friends are gone. I want them found, buried and avenged. I want justice for Detective Hassen too. As for my safety, my dad was a Marine. He died in combat and left my mom and I to run a truck stop in upstate New York with a restaurant and a bar. The bar got more use than the fuel pumps. I've had my fair share of knock down drag out fights. I know that life itself is a risk, that's why I carry a pistol and keep a 12 gauge pump loaded with number four buckshot and slugs at my bedside, university rules or not. I want to be part of this any way that I can. Up to and including going up there on my own."

"You're a law and psychology student, correct?"

"I think I'm guilty of being a professional student, but yes. I'm working on my masters in law right now."

"What are your aspirations after that?"

"FBI."

"Alright." A thought was already beginning to plant a seed in his head.

"Anything else I can help with?"

"I just need to give you my number and email so you can send me the GPS and we can meet again to get the photos."

"I have prints and a topographical map, I could have them in an hour."

"I've got some errands to run. Tonight?""

"Sure. Thanks for the coffee, Matt." It was her turn to blush. It was ever so slight but it was evident right under her eyes as she smiled.

Hauer's next order of business was a pleasant surprise for a young real estate agent who showed him a grey Dutch colonial mansion in the Madrona neighborhood that had been a longtime sorority house. The asking price for the seven bedroom home was 3.89 million dollars. Hauer told her that he would sign off on that price plus five percent if she could arrange for an immediate move in with furnishings and power and water. He reiterated that the place would need everything from shower curtains to a leather living room set. He gave her Carl's number for bank authorizations. She was so overwhelmed when she realized that Hauer wasn't pulling her leg that she had to take a seat and catch her breath. She assured him that he could indeed move in that evening.

White Sands
New Mexico

Jesse Randall wore the Marine Corps digital desert camouflage BDU's he had worn in Afghanistan. Down his back from under his floppy 'boonie' hat hung his long black ponytail tied off with several lengths of rawhide. He lay prone on a black foam shooters mat, a standard issue M27 IAR carbine lay at his right side. A black stocked bolt action rifle nearly twice as long as the infantry carbine rested on a backpack laid out in front of him. The big rifles action was open, the butt sat in his shoulder. From an open ammo box, he grabbed a single round. The cartridge was nearly eight inches long and as fat as a cigar. The blue bullet was tipped by a grey needlelike nose that ended in a sharp point. Randall set the round gently into the open chamber under the fat telescopic sight and pushed the bolt closed. He pulled the rifle into the cup in his shoulder and drew a long breath as he set his cheek onto the raised carbon fiber comb of the stock. The image of an old army five ton truck came into view in the scopes reticle as he slid his hand over the pistol grip and let his pointer finger rest on the trigger guard. With a red dot centered on the void between the trucks front left tire and the hood Jesse knew a hit would enter the trucks heavy engine block. The scope had a digital read out in the upper left hand corner which told him in red numbers that his target was positioned exactly 2900 yards away. This was not a range that was unknown to many modern shooters who competed in ELR (Extreme Long Range) matches. But it was beyond the capabilities of most shooters in the world. Although this rifle would find itself in the competitive world neither the round he had or the scope would. Not even the American military had access to either. Another red dot appeared and flashed lower in the reticle and adjusted itself as Randall tilted the rifles barrel skyward until the light stayed steady.

There was a relentless vibration on his right upper thigh. He sighed and let the weight of the big rifle down on the mat to retrieve his satellite phone.

"Randall." He spoke.

"Gunny." Matt Hauer's voice answered back. "I need you to get to Hangar Lima 23 at McChord Air Force Base tonight."

"Washington State, correct?"

"Roger that Gunny. Dress dry and warm."

"Will do." He said with a frown. When the phone clicked off, he set it back in his pocket and returned his attention to the rifle and the truck.

When the rifle kicked it sent a three foot long flame from the muzzle. Just over a second later the blue bullet slapped into the side of the big truck, rocking it on impact. The slick blue polymer jacket shredded itself against the sheet metal of the wheel well leaving the spent uranium and explosive payload of the bullet to shatter the cast iron block sending white hot shrapnel throughout the vehicle. This shrapnel, some of it three inches long and razor sharp, pierced the pair of dummies in the cab and ignited the trucks fuel tanks. Randall placed the empty shell in the box and folded the stock of the rifle to place it in a padded Kevlar drop case.

Forty-five minutes later, in jeans and a black t-shirt Gunnery Sergeant Jesse Randall was in the cool cabin of a Gulfstream 550 headed for McChord with a cold and frothy beer in his hand.

The Monkey's Fist Bar and Grill
Panama City, Florida

Kevin Buhr sat alone on the patio overlooking the beach. He wore black Salomon Speed Cross 6 shoes over short ankle socks and a pair of khaki cargo shorts. His sun-bleached hair was a bit shaggy over his deep tanned skin. A pair of wraparound sunglasses covered his eyes and a blue Experimental Dive Team t-shirt rested over the arm of his deck chair. Taking the first break of his day he finished off a thick steak bomb sandwich with a sweaty beer bottle in hand while he watched the sailboats out in the gulf. There was little for him to do in his downtime besides caring for his now year old restaurant. The temptations to just kick back and get lazy were insane in a party environment like this. With that knowledge in mind, he drove himself to extremes on a daily basis. He began at four in the morning with a five mile run on the dry sand in boots with a fifty pound pack on his back. This would be followed by a three mile swim and then an hour circuit of weight training. At least three times a week he would pay a visit to his friends Brazilian Ju-Jitsu gym so that he could roll for a few hours. That drive had made him an all American running back, a swim team captain and after high school helped him pass the BUD/S (Basic Underwater Demolition/SEAL) course. Standing three inches over six feet and weighing two hundred and thirty pounds he was actually in better shape at thirty three than he had been at seventeen when he had joined the Navy.

"Buhr. Go ahead." He spoke into the phone when his call came in.

"Kevin." Hauer spoke on the other end of the line. "Time to put down the board and get back to work."

"The beer." Kevin moaned. "The much deserved ice cold beer."

"I'll buy you another. Hanger Lima two three on McChord."

"Mountaineering?"

"Very likely. See you tonight." The phone clicked off and went back into Buhr's left pocket. In two pulls the bottle was empty and he pulled on his shirt while a group of female dinners watched appreciatively.

Inside was a sports bar that was just beginning to come to life for the day. At the bar Buhr set his plate on a tray destined for the dishwasher and dropped his empty bottle in a cardboard case to be returned to the distributer.

"What's up boss?" His manager, Tracy Horton, asked. She was a tall bleach blonde, shapely and hot in black shorts and a white polo. She was also out of reach because she was an employee.

"I have to go back to work. Can you cover things?"

"Of course. It's in good hands."

"Thanks Trace." He gave her a hug. She wanted more, but she was not ready to push him yet.

"Be careful please."

Upper Peninsula
Michigan

Brett Shaw's hobby table was positioned in his cabin so that he could periodically gaze out the window at Lake Superior. A southern boy by birth he had begun visiting Michigan for the fall hunting while a young man in the Army. He still kept a home in North Carolina near Fort Bragg where he had spent much of his career, but found himself enjoying the cool weather on the lake more and more. At the moment all thoughts of the lake were gone. His complete focus was on the three inch tall piece of Georgia marble held in his left hand while his right controlled the tiny air driven grinder. The rock was slowly taking on the shape of a king complete with a beard and a staff and a six pointed crown. Several more bits for the grinder were set up on a wooden block for easy access. A chessboard formed of light and dark woods held the finished and polished pieces. Only the kings and a black queen remained to be made. The black king and queen lacked even the material to be made from. On closer look, differences from piece to piece could be seen indicating that they were not cut from the same stock, in fact not even from the same type of stone. Each piece had been hand-picked for its own significance.

The grinder stopped its air driven buzz as Shaw traded the tool for his satellite phone vibrating against his hip.

"Colonel Shaw." He answered.

"Sar'n Major." Hauer bellowed happily in his best southern drawl. "How'd you like to come out and enjoy the beautiful rainforests of Washington State?"

"Something tells me that I'd rather hire cannibals to guide me on a piranha fishing trip, so I'll go with that."

After a chuckle Hauer asked if Malone was with him. Indeed, she was. She was outside on a red Adirondack chair on her laptop. With that confirmed, he gave Shaw the hangar number at McChord and told him to give an eta as soon as he had one.

                              1630 Lake Washington Boulevard
                                              Seattle Washington
                                                        845 PM

 Jennifer Beck recognized none of the five S.U.V.'s parked in the driveway of the grey Dutch colonial mansion when she pulled in. She was sure that she had read the address wrong. She checked again before killing the Bronco's engine and walking to the front door where Jesse Randall was dealing with a pizza delivery driver.

 "You must be Jen." He asked her. His Apache accent was showing hard.

 "I am."

 "Come on in."

Hauer met her in the kitchen and introduced her to his team in the living room where Malone and Shaw were setting up their computers and radios to create a command center. Kevin Buhr and Jesse Randall were studying a large colored topographical map of the North Cascades that had been spread out on one of the rooms larger walls where in a normal world there would have been family portraits or several pieces of art.

 "I can have the Hooligan on line out here in about five hours." Malone was telling Hauer.

 "Whoa. Take a look at this." Jen spoke as she glanced over the photographs that Hassen had taken that Matt had affixed to a whiteboard. "This might help if you can scan it and get a better clarity." She was pointing at the picture so that her fingernail directed their eyes to a white blur on the side of a red tractor-trailer truck.

 "Oh." Jax beamed. "Nice." She took the photo and got directly to work on scanning it.

 "What do you have there?" Kevin asked

 "Trucks." Jen explained. "They have to display their company names, towns of the company's address and their registration numbers with the motor carrier commission and the department of transportation."

"Great call." He responded and when Jen turned her attention to Jax he caught Matt's attention and made a show of raising his eyebrows at his boss and longtime friend.

"Pontif Cartage of Seattle." Jax spoke up a moment later. "I'll run the numbers and get an address."

"Kev, I'm going to put you on that. Brett, I need you to work with the State Patrol for the evidence on Deke's hit." Matt spoke in rapid fire fashion as he looked over the monitor displaying the blow up of the photo and turned past Jen to the topographical map where Kevin and Jesse had placed a series of red pins indicating each of the GPS pings that Jen had been able to supply. "Jesse you and I have a flight in the early hours."

"What the hell is this place?" Kevin asked.

"The government owns the whole area. They haven't allowed a logging operation in the area in over seventy years. The site is on a rock pit that ceased in 1960. Whatever is up there is completely illegal." Jax told him.

"WELL." JEN SPOKE UP after sharing some pizza and going over her photographs and reiterating her story with them. She had been feeling that she was out of her element with these Fed's and that maybe she was in the way of their work. "I've got a test in the morning. It was nice to meet all of you."

"I'll walk out with you." Matt offered. He didn't really want her to go but wasn't sure how he could keep her.

Unable to sleep, Jen decided to make a pot of coffee and grab some time on the computer. She was barefoot in baby blue pajama bottoms and a loose white t-shirt. The PC at her study desk flashed on and was ready to go before she had stirred creamer and sugar into her University of Washington mug.

'Search or enter website name' The box on her search engine prompted.

'Hauer' She fired off the key strokes.

The top three entries listed were:

1) Hauer Industries Inc.

2) Hauer Aviation.

3) Hauer Accident.

She clicked on the third entry already thinking that this was a fruitless venture and that she would be destined to a long night of boring and mindless television or that maybe she could win some money in on-line poker.

She was shown a newspaper article dated June 22, 2021.

'Industrial, Aviation and Real Estate mogul Johnathan Hauer 74, his wife Adriane 70 and his father Curtis 96 were killed last evening in a tragic bus accident outside Giza Egypt. They are survived by Lt. Commander Matthew Hauer of the United States Navy.'

"Oh my God. It is him." She spoke out loud to the empty room. She stared at his Navy photo while she pulled her hair back into a ponytail with the help of a black scrunchie. Her curiosity got the best of her and she clicked onto the Hauer Industries site.

'Founded in Kiel Germany on the Black Sea in 1509 as a firearms manufacturer and shipbuilder the firm has since diversified so that the Fortune 500 company has its headquarters in Baltimore Maryland.' There were more headquarters as the holdings spread out to Hauer Nautical Holdings of Fort Lauderdale Florida, Phoenix Arizona for Aviation and Flagstaff Arizona for both a firearms division and a separate building for real estate. The owner of all of it was Matthew Hauer. The site showed a photo of Matt in a tuxedo next to a corporate jet on the assembly line.

She typed United States Navy and got herself into a search area for personnel. She typed Lt. Commander Matthew Hauer. 'File restricted', the site spat back.

"Thanks so much for the help." She sneered as she exited the site.

Her next search brought her to Cardell's Financial Magazine. She sought out a list of the wealthiest people in the world not expecting to find Hauer in the top five hundred let alone to see him in the number four slot just behind a couple of internet billionaire geniuses. Why was this guy out at a mansion on the shore running an investigation?

"Rich." She whispered. "No. Rich is millions. This is mega silly filthy stinking rich. I'm the heiress to a truck stop and I talk to myself. He's some super-secret agent billionaire. Sure, that matchup will work out." She mumbled and clicked off the site to spend the rest of the night on the poker tables where she cleared 3500 dollars.

"Catching up nicely Mister Hauer." She cracked when she cashed out.

Chapter Three

"Pain is inevitable, suffering is optional."
Buddhist Proverb

North Cascade National Forest
29 September
0740

MATT HAUER SAT AT THE controls of his green DeHavilland DHC-2 Beaver float plane. Jesse Randall had the co-pilots seat and ran a laptop computer while they flew. The computer was connected to an array of cameras and sensors hidden inside a false canoe that hung from the planes belly. From 4500 feet Randall was collecting high resolution video while the sensors probed away at the compound below. All of the collected data was bounced via satellite back to one of Malone's computers. Hauer caught the silent Marine squinting at the computer's readouts several times and heard the muffled grunts that often accompanied the man's frown when he disapproved of something.

Were it not for the seriousness of the job at hand Hauer would have lost himself in the beauty of the high peaks surrounded by old growth Hemlock and Douglass fir stretching to the horizon in every direction. He was tearful that they had technology at their disposal to research this problem rather than have to put people down there in the wilderness to hunt blind.

"How long of a delay before have with getting a Hooligan on station?" Hauer asked over their headsets.

"It looks like we're down to an hour for sight and another hour for actually loitering. The first went to Utah for repairs and they sent another." Randall told him.

"Do you have enough video?"

"Bring me over that western access road real quick."

Hauer banked the small powerful plane until they were over the winding gravel road. When the road met the tarmac of the state road Jesse shut the systems down and closed his computer.

"All good?" Hauer asked as he watched the man stare through his sunglasses and the Lexan side window into the mountains below them.

"Yeah. Wrap it up. It's contained." Randall replied. "But, there's a hell of a lot of yellow and orange flagging down there. All of it inside the buildings and underground from what I can tell. The Hooligan will get a much better peak and maybe give us an identification on whatever it is. Beyond the chemical trace there is a triple fence system. All electrified. Video is every hundred feet. This security force can't possibly be bored."

"Fantastic. What kind of a head count?"

"A buck fifty three plus sixteen dogs." Randall answered.

"Any ideas?" Hauer asked as he began a slow climb and bank to get in a flight path back to McChord.

"Yup. It looks like a prison but it's most definitely a chemical weapons depot. I bet they mix it and ship it from here. I need to get down there to have real eyes on and we can utilize Hooligan for the analysis."

"When can you do that?"

"I'll load up as soon as I'm back on the ground."

Hangar L-23
McChord AFB
29 September
1045

Shaw and Buhr were seated at a long beat up picnic table in the air conditioned wardroom when Randall and Hauer entered. Both men had a manilla folder and a series of plastic evidence bags before them. In the hangar, parked on a blue tarp was the bullet riddled white Ford Interceptor SUV that had been Patrol 63, Deke Hassen's truck.

Buhr looked up from the long thin brass shell casing held in his light blue latex gloved hand at his boss.

"What's up?" Hauer asked. "Car first."

"You've got three 40 caliber shell casings inside. All police issue. Your buddy damn sure nailed someone good because there's blood and grey matter splash back on the hood and in the grill. That lets you see how close they were when this went down. Say inside ten feet." Buhr told him.

"Damn." Randall winced as he imagined the close proximity gun battle.

"We've got a couple armor piercing five five six NATO bullets pulled from the back seats and pillars. These probably made the life and death decision because they buzzed straight through rather than go hydrostatic or tumble. First thing for the outside of the vehicle is the cases. 1999 Frankfurt Armory head stamps, but." He paused to flip the rifle case over to show Hauer and Randall the bright silver primer in the base. "They're reloads. Judging by their performance, I'd say somebody did some grunt work to reload military brass and they made magnum loads. We'll get an analysis on the propellant but it definitely contributed to the over penetration of the bullets."

"Number two outside." Shaw took over and held up a piece of bent black sheet metal between his finger and thumb. "We narrow the weapon down."

"Disintegrating link code M27 for five five six right?" Randall asked.

"Yup." Shaw replied. "FN M249 probably, could be an old Stoner 63, an H&K 23 or even an ARES Shrike."

"Hang on a sec. It's not a Stoner. The 63 doesn't work with M27 links. It had its own link style. The H and K's chamber flutes would have torn the hell out of the side of the case. I doubt it's a Negev, maybe a South African Mini-SS, but it's most likely an M249." Hauer told them.

"Dead end?" Buhr asked.

"Well at least we can bet against AK carrying gang bangers. These guys appear to be at least semi pro. They definitely wanted to give the illusion of a gang hit but, whoever was on that SAW had incredible fire control. Being that close and rolling out five round bursts is astounding. Until your buddy tore out his brain case. These guys are or were more than familiar with firefights. I'm betting on Merc's." Shaw told the room.

Matt nodded as he stared at the truck and played out in his mind how the ambush had happened. It was a wonder that Hassen had survived. It was miraculous that he had gotten off three accurate pistol shots in return.

"Any tire track photos?" Randall asked.

"Yeah. Staties got a cast too. FBI database says Bendren Light Truck 275/65R17. Cheap and common aftermarket. No factory applications." Shaw told him. "We have a single footprint in blood and dirt as well. This popped as a British Altberg lug pattern. Analysis said it belongs to a MK 3 'Tabbing boot.'"

"SAS style kit. Either a player or a wannabe with a wallet." Buhr commented.

"How about video?" Hauer asked.

"White van. Probably 1985 Ford Econoline." Shaw replied and gave his own frown. "No plates and there's the dead end for now."

"And what about the folks at Pontiff Cartage?" Hauer asked.

"Jax pulled them up. They look like a clean company. They pull a lot of logs and Conex boxes on and off the ships at the docks. Twenty two trucks all told." Shaw read from a notepad. "Jax is still working on their records. Please tell me that these kids and a police officer didn't get attacked over logs."

"It looks like chemicals." Randall answered.

"Kevin." Matt spoke up after a gulp of coffee. "Get with the attaché' here, scrap the truck and incinerate the evidence. Jesse and Brett go car shopping. We need four wheel drive. All local camouflage. So, look around and see what people are driving and duplicate it for me. We need to cover us with a swap and we need Chapter Psi for the backup team."

"Are we going live?" Kevin asked.

"Not yet. Tonight, we're going to put transponders on Pontif's trucks and bug the offices. I want Hooligan's analysis before we go kicking in doors." Hauer told him.

"Who's running Team Psi now?"

"Brian Tindall and Strike Bravo."

Seattle
4PM

JEN BECK AND JAX MALONE were having coffee in the living room turned command center when Hauer returned. Jen was showing Jax the way around online poker rooms where the money was good. Matt gave them a quick wave on his way to the coffee pot in dire need of a recharge.

"You look wrecked." Beck said when he opened the sliding glass door to the patio and the salt air of the bay before taking a seat at one of the free computers. "When's the last time you got any sleep?"

"Early this morning, how about you?"

"Between ten and one today."

"How'd your test go?"

"I don't know how I could not have aced it."

"Even on sleep deficit?"

"I'm always on sleep deficit. My mantra is work, friends, sleep pick two."

"We were given the same options at M.I.T." Jax offered.

"Doctors and soldiers, right?" Beck asked.

"Constant sacrifice."

"Busy day?" Malone asked Hauer.

"After the flight things dragged. I got rid of my wheels and found something more appropriate to the task."

"Yeah. Like what?" Beck asked.

"1986 GMC K-5 Jimmy. A guy I know built it. How about our friends over at Pontif Cartage Jax?"

Malone gave Hauer a look, indicating that she had concerns for dumping information in the Beck's company.

"It's alright. She's clear. Go ahead."

"So far, the paperwork looks legit. None of the IRS stuff indicated a payment from a company in the vicinity of the park so I started with Department of Transportation and bills of lading and worked backward. The only pickups within twenty miles of the sight were listed as Riverton, this went to Yuma Arizona. The other two were said to have come out of Clark and supposedly went to the Seattle Seaport."

"Who was the receiver?" Hauer asked.

"Dalton Cargo."

"How about a shipper in Clark?"

"Nellis Enterprises New York. Also, a real company dealing mostly in textiles. It looks like they have shipped six loads of logs to mainland China."

"Don't buy it." Randall spoke up as he, Shaw and Buhr returned. Randall and Shaw looked at least semiprofessional in jeans and polo shirts while Buhr wore torn shorts and an Iron Maiden t-shirt with a red and black flannel wrapped around his waist. "I'd say it's clever cover for containers of weapons grade material."

"Terrorists?" Beck asked.

"One of the potential end users for sure." Shaw conceded. "Stateside we're looking at an arms dealer. We are going to find out where that stuff went and get at both ends of this." He found a seat next to Jax, grabbed up his own coffee mug and after putting a microphone headset on he began typing at his keyboard. He caught Matt's eye and gave a subtle glance at Beck before looking back to Hauer with a frown on his face. Hauer nodded and turned away.

"How was the shopping?" He asked Buhr.

"Fair. We all have vehicles and now there are a bunch of pickup trucks at the hangar."

"Tindall's team will be here in a few hours." Randall told him. "I'm just gonna grab some food and gear and I'll head out there to get them up to speed."

"The Hooligan is fully on line and running the analysis." Shaw announced to the room. "Another hour or so and we should have a better idea of what we have up there."

"Why don't we break and get some chow then." Hauer suggested.

"Maybe I can buy the Agent in charge a burger?" Beck offered him.

"Sure." He was trying to keep a straight face knowing that there was something involved with the offer.

"Enjoy." Jax said and smiled at both of them.

"Run her for me." He whispered at Jax and Shaw as he leaned over to look at Shaw's screen. "The full press."

"So, you traded in the wheels and went native." She teased as he held the door to his Blazer for her.

"All part of the plan Miss Beck."

"I thought that we had established Matt and Jen."

"After the Agent shot, I just figured that we were back on purely professional terms."

"God no." She paused for a moment. "Can I ask you a question?"

"Fire away."

"It's personal."

"I'm good with that."

"Are you really a Special Agent?"

"That's difficult for me to answer. I don't want to lie to you and I'm trying to work on some ideas I have for you. I'm going to tell you that I can be if the situation warrants it and hopefully, we can leave it at that for the time being."

She stared back at him with a furrowed brow and moved her closed lips around.

"Are you official or a billionaire vigilante?"

"Ah." He had to smile. "No. I'm not a vigilante. I am official. The agency that I work for is very old, very quiet and powerful."

"You used to be Navy. I had originally thought Army Special Forces or Marine MARSOC. But now that I know Navy, I'm thinking SEAL teams."

"That's right. How do you know about MARSOC? They don't get a lot of press."

"My dad was a Marine. After you lost your family, you left the Navy and now run or own Hauer Enterprises." She declared. "That is you, right?"

"Yes, it is."

"What does your agency usually do?"

"I can't tell you that right now. I shouldn't even be doing this."

"What is it called?"

"Same answer." He laughed and shook his head.

"So, let's say anti-terror."

He gave her a nod as he pulled the truck out of traffic in front of a neon lit pub.

"You are an enigma." She said with a sigh. "You are a multi-billionaire. I know a few rich people. They aren't anything like you. They are comfortable and pampered. They expect reverence or something to the effect. You don't even act rich. I can't understand why you were in the military at all, never mind sticking your ass out in the wind with special operations and I don't get why you are doing whatever it is that you are doing now."

"Come on. I think you do. When I was a kid, I got all of the history and footage of terror attacks like 9/11, the Marine Barracks in Beirut, Lockerby Scotland and on and on. I wanted to be part of anything that would fight people who target the weak and defenseless. I felt and still feel honored by this nation and the people to be able to be here and be rich. I feel like I can repay that freedom through service. I joined the Navy with the Teams as a goal. I ran a section of Development Group or SEAL Six for a year and a half before I lost my family. Now I do this."

"Rich or poor this is what you would do?"

He gave her a wry grin and a nod. "Let's get some food."

"Do you have any openings?" She asked after they had been seated in a dark corner.

"For what?"

"An agent. A friend?"

He cocked his head and looked at her as he intertwined his fingers and stretched backward.

"I was hoping for a friendship. A chance to get through this and ask you out on a date. The agent part I honestly wasn't ready for.

I've been toying with recruiting you since we met. What about your degree?"

"I'll still get it and probably another one after that."

"Professional student, right?" He had to smile "Let's talk. But, for now let's eat."

"So, I get it?"

"The date? Absolutely"

Matt's phone vibrated in his pocket. When he looked at the screen and the text from Jax telling him that Jennifer Beck was not only clean but an incredible pick as a team asset he had to stifle a smile.

"The job. How do I get picked?"

"You've got some pretty intense company to keep on my team. They aren't simply door kickers."

Following the deaths of his family Hauer had begun working as a security consultant and had considered starting a contractor company. He had been approached by his butler Carl MacManus and a longtime friend of his father's Mitchell McGuire. Matt had looked up to McGuire from childhood. The man was one of the first Team Guys that he had ever known. It was easy for McGuire to recruit him over to the fraternity once the details were laid out. The position allowed Matt to hand pick his crew. Brett Shaw had been in the 75th Rangers before the 5th Special Forces and then became a Delta Force operator. He spoke Russian, German, Greek, Chinese and Swahili. He also held a master's degree in Political Science.

Jesse Randall was, in 2020 when Matt recruited him, one of the best Sniper's that the Marine Corps had ever seen. He too was a linguist with superior written and verbal scores in Arabic, Apache, Navaho, French, Japanese and Spanish. At only twenty six he had made Gunnery Sergeant and earned a masters in History.

Kevin Buhr, a personal friend of Hauer's before selection, had been a platoon leader with SEAL Team One after graduation from the Naval Academy at Annapolis, where he had earned a degree in Nautical Design and Nuclear Science. Following Team One he had been one of Hauer's junior officers in Team Six. He was fluent in German, Russian and Swedish.

Andrea Jackson 'Jax' Malone had been a late addition to the crew. She had just a little over a year on board. She had come directly from the Massachusetts Institute of Technology with degrees and honors in Electrical Engineering and Computer Science. She was twenty four years old and already held fifty-three patents.

"Jax is the smartest then?"

"By far. Her I.Q. is 192. She's the youngest and continues to research and study, so I imagine she will only move up."

"Who's the best?"

"The best what?"

"Just the best."

"Unlike some comic book super agent, we can't all be expert at every facet of the job. So, we have specialists. Over all my best agent is Kevin or Brett simply by time in service, real world experience and all. The favor there probably leans toward Brett with age again being a factor."

"Who's the best shot?"

"Jesse. Although everyone has gone through sniper school, Jesse has some extra gene coding that has him so dialed in its ridiculous. I don't believe that he knows how to miss."

"What do I have to do?"

"Pass some tests."

"Like what?"

"You're sure about this? Everything about your life changes after this starts."

Chapter Four

"Have you ever been hurt and the place tries to heal a bit, and you just pull the scar off of it over and over again?"
Rosa Parks
Pivotal Civil Rights Activist

Hangar L-23
McChord AFB
1930
29 September

THE STRIKE TEAM ARRIVED aboard a pair of the Air Force's venerable gargantuan slate grey C-5M Super Galaxy cargo planes. In the same manner that the Secret Service loads everything from toilet paper to the Presidential limousines and calls it the 'total package', so do the Wraiths. Jesse Randall sat on the hood of a five year old Dodge Ram pickup truck and watched the big jet taxi closer to the hangar where Air Force ground crew began unloading the plane from both the front and rear ramps. Sixteen men in all manner of attire deplaned and with backpacks and duffle bags in tow headed for Randall. The lead man, a tall dark skinned black man that Randall knew as Brian Tindall, waved his crew into the hangar to direct the delivery of their gear and find their billets.

"What's the situation?" Tindal asked in his deep Alabama drawl while he shook Jesse's hand.

"I always thought that the hot zones were supposed to be hot, but I stand corrected." He went on to tell him what was known thus far while they watched a pair of black MH-60 Blackhawk helicopters from one plane and a pair of RAH-66 Comanche attack helicopters from the second plane get unloaded and towed into the hangar. The second set of passengers were the helicopter crew and were led by a tall and lanky well-tanned man in jeans, a white dress shirt, anaconda skin cowboy boots and a black calvary Stetson. He chewed gum, swaggered when he walked and wore a permanent smile.

"Look at that Tindal. It's either Chuck Yeager or Turtle." Randall said with a big smile of his own directed at his newest guest.

"How ya'll doing Gunny?" Captain James Fowler had been among Hauer's first recommendations for recruitment. The name Turtle had come from his days as a Boy Scout. His pack had been so over stuffed and heavy that it made him look like a cartoon image of the tortoise from the old children's story. The son of Wyoming ranchers, he had been flying crop dusters since the age of eight. Not that he should have been. After West Point, he flew first with First Air Cavalry where he had earned the privilege of wearing the Stetson and later served with Special Air Wing 160 "The Night Stalkers." He had earned himself the reputation of being the quintessential helicopter and VTOL (Vertical Takeoff Or Landing) pilot.

Slightly behind Turtle came Wade "Nappy" Napolitano, an ex-Navy Captain from the HSC-85 "The Firehawks", the U.S. Navy's special operations capable helicopter wing. Napolitano was another of Hauer's choices because of his reputation for flying through anything to get support to people in need. Napolitano and Fowler headed up Air Wing One under Hauer's direct authority. As a basic package they traveled with a compliment of eight pilots, four door gunner/medics, eight combat medics and two cargo master/Flight Surgeons. If, as it rarely did, the mission called for a large number of aircraft the additions would fall to one or the others command.

Like fighter pilots, these men and women looked cocky and confident. In their cases they had earned both.

"I'd rather be on a horse getting ready for Elk season in Montana." Randall replied.

"Could still. Looks like we got a long season ahead."

"Yeah. I doubt it'll be for me though."

"Bigger fish?" Napolitano asked.

"Toothy ones." Randall answered and offered the tall New York pilot his hand. "Good to see you Nappy."

"We'll be mission capable in fifteen." Turtle told him.

"Don't rush. We just wanted you on station. We are still working this, but it may take a rapid insert and extract."

"How's terrain." Napolitano asked.

"It's Hindu Kush with rain and trees. Let's get everyone into the ward room and I can do this brief one time."

The operators of Strike Team Alpha looked like they were still on active duty in the special operations units they had been recruited from. These men and women for the most part, save for Master Sargent John Gamache, a thirty year old Marine Recon guy, were not the Hollywood stereotype of Special Warfare. They looked more like distance runners and soccer players than linebackers. At six foot seven and two hundred and eighty-two pounds Gamache was the biggest on the team. Lam Nguyen, an Army Special Forces man, stood five foot six and one hundred and forty pounds for the shortest straw. Everyone else created the average of five foot nine. Like the pilots, this was a cocky and swaggering group, and deservedly so, but professional. When Randall spoke, they shut up and listened. When he was done speaking, they began working out ideas and tactics on their own initiative.

1630 Lake Washington Boulevard
Seattle Washington
1138 PM
29 September

SEVEN COMPUTER MONITORS exclusive to the Hooligan system were set up in the living room. The Hooligan was a six hundred foot long GPS guided blimp that hung 120,000 feet above the Cascades compound. Two of the monitors displayed green overhead images of the compound. A third ran an X-ray camera. The forth, Malone explained to Beck, was chasing electronic activity including computers, radios and the electric fence. Unit five was dedicated to tracking life, specifically heartbeats. The computer had already separated dogs and humans from all other wildlife.

"What are six and seven doing." Beck asked as she pointed at one monitor running through a slew of numbers and letters that could form no vocalized language. The last monitor showed only blacks, grays, light greens and faint oranges."

"Six is a laser chemical analyzer and seven is a hypersensitive infrared device." Malone told her with deep sadness etched on her face. Beck thought that Jax must look like she had back in her days in her dorm at M.I.T. She was barefoot in her grey sweat pants and a pair of white and blue tank tops.

"You're searching for decaying bodies." She asked. "The same way the FBI would with a helicopter and FLIR."

To this Malone could only nod. Beck returned the nod and gave her attention back to the six pages of questions and problems that Hauer had asked Jax to produce. She had worked through a series of trigonometry problems and several brain teasers made up of boxes of dots with the goal of finding patterns. The last question on the page read 'disregarding oaths such as the Hippocratic oath are you able to kill another human being'. There were only two boxes, a yes and a no. She circled yes and handed the papers back to Hauer.

"Hooligan is incredible. So, is it solar powered?" Beck asked.

"You haven't seen anything yet." Malone told her. "The initial tech is a bit dated but it was easy to upgrade. The program was set up as a backup to a program from the eighties called Rods from God that would launch tungsten rods from satellites for kinetic energy on a target. It would work from Hooligan as well. Today we have a few more tools available. We've got all you see here plus a pair of laser microphones that can be intense enough to destroy buildings or low enough to move crowds. There are also a pair of laser weapons that will eliminate targets. We are fine tuning a sonar." "Check this out." Malone pointed at a green dot on the second monitor. "See that dot right there north west of the compound? That's Jesse." She touched the dot with the tip of her stylus and clicked a few keys on her keyboard. This isolated the dot and expanded it to fill the screen with a green blur. She then held down a button for the microphone in her headset.

"Gunny take a look up and give me a nice smile please and thank you." Another key stroke cleaned up the resolution so that Randall's green-lit face stared back at them.

"Thanks Gunny." Shaw took over on his own microphone. "How's the ground view?"

"I've got a straight shot at the west building."

"Okay." Shaw ran his fingers over his keyboard. "Let's do camera one there."

"Camera one will be at four hundred and eighteen yards." Randall answered as he took a pen sized camera from his backpack and placed it in the moss covered slice a logger had cut into a Douglas fir stump decades earlier to set a springboard inside allowing them to cut work a saw to cut the great tree down. He packed moss around the tiny camera to further camouflage it and crawled forward along the steep terrain. Shaw was already fine-tuning the view on his computer. "I'm moving closer and east."

"No closer than three hundred yards Gunny."

"Roger that."

Malone was focused on screen seven while she sipped at her coffee and tapped points on the screen, changed resolution, squinted, enhanced, frowned and repeated the process.

"Matt." Buhr spoke up only a moment after he had taken a seat at monitor six. He was in tiger stripe camo cargo shorts and a Black Sabbath t-shirt gulping coffee and rubbing sleep from his eyes. "I've got a spectrum."

Malone was the first to move her chair to look over the surfer's shoulder.

"Whoa." Shaw said. "You've got an extremely ugly chemical shopping list there bro."

"Underground facility." Buhr stared. "Six floors down and three top side. Almost seven hundred thousand square feet. There are four labs. One is making drugs, really high grade meth. One is Glanders, one is a designer biochemical, and the other is explosives. A shit ton of PETN."

"The nuke booster?" Jen asked.

"You've been doing your homework." Buhr gave her a smile.

"It looks like they are also making the tooling to manufacture nukes as well. Small scale stuff like B54 SADM back pack harbor masters." Shaw said.

"That's the bad news." Buhr said.

"There's good news?" Beck asked.

"It's designer. It'll be easier to trace." Jax told her. "We have a rough idea where to start looking and I've already tasked the equipment. Now I just tell the computer what to look for."

"As soon as you have it isolated send the chem data to Benedetti and Quarrels." Hauer told Buhr. He frowned and held his coffee close to his chest as he stared away from the room and across the Lake at the lights of Bellevue on the opposite shore. He wanted to be appalled that anything like this was happening inside a National Park, hell anywhere in America, but nothing surprised him anymore.

People seemed to be all too ready to profit from harm and fear. Those people needed to meet people like Matt at his angriest.

"Matt." Malone called out. There was a sad desperation in her voice. Hauer had only been sitting in the chair for twenty minutes and had fallen fast asleep when she called out. Beck, in the chair next to his had awakened with Malone's call and watched him sit up. She knew what was coming and could not speak. Hauer glanced at her and swallowed hard as he placed his hand on her shoulder and closed his eyes before walking over to Jax.

"What have you got Jax?" Hauer asked as he searched for the cup of coffee, he knew was going to be cold.

"Three sights. They are sixty yards apart, a little over two miles from the compound on the opposite side of the access road. There is a single, then three and then four." She was using her stylus to point and looked back at Beck who sat curled up in her over stuffed leather chair.

"Time is double O twenty." Hauer spoke up as he looked at his watch. "Jax, get me a GPS plot ASAP." Once into his own headset he hit the microphone button and waited for a response. "Colonel Tindal load up for recovery. I'll be there in fifteen." "Sar'n Major get Jesse into a covering position. You talk Nappy in. Kevin, let's move."

"Good luck." Jen said and gave him a hug. He forced a smile for her and left with his black backpack in tow.

North Cascades National Park
30 September
0205

There were eight black clad men in the darkened cabin of the lead Blackhawk. One man sat at each of the M134D miniguns in the doors while six sat on the floor among coils of black rappelling rope. Captain Fowler used the enhanced night vision on his helmet to look through the rain covered windshield at the tree tops that he was hugging in his slow twenty knot flight. Every now and again everyone on board could feel a tall pine scrape under the fuselage. Lieutenant John Cabral sat in the co-pilot seat for the ride and concentrated on the computer generated world inside his helmet. He had no view of the outside world, only a digital terrain map and a green line that was the path Malone had created for him.

The Blackhawk, even the MH-60S, the latest in Special Operations choppers, is an ungainly aircraft at low speeds. This truth was made more painful in foul weather. The stress level in the cockpit was understandably elevated. Despite the forty degree temperature Turtle and Cabral were visibly sweating as they flew.

"Sixty feet." Cabral's voice came over Hauer's ear buds. "Sixty feet to sight one." "Forty, twenty, ten, hovering."

"Green light." Hauer spoke into the microphone hanging in front of his lower lip. In seconds the six man team was out the door and fast roped to the wet moss covered ground.

"Razor One moving north for standby. Bring it in Razor two."

In another minute Nappy had deposited another six men on the ground for the second and third burial sites. Thanks to Jax Malone's work with the GPS the strike team was able to drop directly on top of their targets. All the while Rachel Brown and Joe Tobin hovered in the Comanche gunships ready to unleash havoc on anyone that attempted to interfere with the team. Turtle and Napolitano stood second string security and Jesse had primary ground overwatch with his big SWORD International MK-18 SA-ASR rifle and it's devastating 338 Norma rounds. With the knowledge that all of what was out there in the night the silence was eerie. None of the helicopters, even when hovering above, gave off any sound signature to the ground.

Despite the rain and mud the commandoes made quick, albeit dirty work of their task. As Malone had advised them, the bodies were found in military body bags and at only three to four feet below the surface. The operators worked in silence both on the ground and once back inside the helicopters for their return to McChord. Wet, muddy and cold Matt Hauer sat at a table in the ward room waiting for the coffee to brew and stared at his boots. The strike team first cleaned their rifles and the helicopters then split up to clean themselves and find sleep.

"Thanks Turtle. Nice flying." Hauer told the lanky flying cowboy as he came into the room alongside Rachel Brown, a short red head woman with a closed mouth and shy smile. "You too L.T."

"Not a problem boss."

"You need anything else Commander?" Tindal, still in a wet flight suit, stuck his head in to ask.

"Nah. Come back for coffee after you clean up."

When Tindall returned, he was wearing jeans and a West Point sweatshirt with leather sandals. He was now in company with Buhr and Shaw, both wearing green medical scrubs.

"I take it you're gonna need us here for a fair stretch?"

"If we reach three weeks, I'll stand you down and get Bravo up" Hauer told him.

"The objective will be that compound then?"

"For now."

"I take it from the scrubs that ya'll are going to get the autopsies tonight." Tindal checked his Rolex GMT. "Actually, this morning."

"I don't think we need autopsies. But we do need identification." Shaw said as he readied a tripod mounted video camera. Buhr was adjusting a digital single lens reflex camera.

Each of the eight body bags was placed on stainless steel tables under bright lights. A smaller cart with an array of surgical tools sat next to each table. The men moved into the workspace and waited for Hauer to take the lead.

"North Cascades National Park Sight one. Single body bag." Hauer spoke into the video camera as he unzipped the bag. They recorded a male in his late thirties dressed in British multi-cam fatigues and Altberg MK 3 'Tabbing' boots. "This would be our wayward shitbag." He said as he pointed at the custom hiking boots. The man had balding brown hair and no visible scars. The man also had no wallet, no dog tags and not a bit of money. There was just an empty man in clothing he no longer needed. Three closely grouped 40 caliber holes sat at the center of his brow ridge. His face and clothing were covered with the now rotting mess resulting from the instantly fatal shooting.

"I'd say that that's the asshole your buddy nailed." Kevin spoke up.

"I'll get his prints and start searching." Shaw declared and moved in.

The next four bodies had all been shot in the back and head at close range with a rifle. These were in three shot bursts followed up by a single contact shot at the back of the head. Mark Janot, Dean Kammen, Brian Ash and Erica Benoit were identified by their drivers' licenses left intact in their wallets. Kevin also took a pair of cameras from Kammen and Janot.

The victims at the third sight were a young couple and their young son. The boy had been about nine years old. The adults were identified as John and Amy Grendel of Fair Hope Colorado. The boy had no identification but had embroidery on his backpack that read Isaac. They had been murdered in the same fashion as Beck's friends and appeared to have been in the ground for a few months longer. Hauer stared hard at his teammates when he looked up from the tables of innocent dead and their evil companion. He sighed and tilted his head back to look up at the ceiling before he could gather himself and pull the bags closed over the lone family who took a wrong turn.

Once done with their grizzly work, the commandoes cleaned up and sat in angry silence over a cup of coffee in the wardroom.

"Brother. What about Jennifer?" Shaw asked.

"I'm on my way to talk with her."

"I'll get the cameras powered up and download the pictures." Kevin told them, checking his DOXA divers watch twice to ensure that it really was already seven o'clock in the morning.

Chapter Five

"Everyone thinks of changing the world, but no one thinks of changing themselves."
Leo Tolstoy
Russian Writer

1630 Lake Washington Boulevard
Seattle Washington
30 September
0730

"I WANT TO COME TO WORK. Now." Beck nearly growled the words to Matt. She was looking at him through tear-filled eyes as he hugged her. He hadn't known anything else to do but hug her when her silent tears began. She had only to look at his face to know that her friends were indeed gone.

"Are you really ready to consider this?"

"I've considered it ever since I bought the information to your friend. I want vengeance for my friends. I want to hunt the kind of people that my friends ran into. I'll have to make peace with their deaths in time, but if you let me get my stuff back to New York and take a few days I'll be ready to do whatever it is that you need me to do." Sensing his doubt, she locked eyes with him. "You decide if I qualify. But, those kids, my friends should no more preclude me from this than officer Hassen and your family should bar you from being where you are."

"Okay." He conceded and put his palms up.

They were sitting on the front porch watching the rain when Jesse Randall's battered but tuned green Jeep Wrangler pulled into the driveway.

"Sure. Leave the Apache out in the cold and wet all night." He said as he took a seat next to them.

"You're a tough Marine. Nothing you can't handle." Hauer gave him a smile.

"Yeah. Jen I'm really sorry about your friends." He said and looked at the puddles forming in the cracks between the cobble stones. "When do we go tactical?" He asked as he turned to Matt.

"Not soon enough. I think this is bigger than what it looks like on the surface. We need to take a breath because once this thing starts, it's going to be insane."

"Boss." Jax called out from the door. "Mac is on the horn looking for you." She tossed him his cell phone.

Hauer spent the next few minutes listening and repeating the word 'yes' a few times before a final 'will do' and ending the call. After a shower and shave and a change of clothes into tactical cargo pants and a black polo shirt he ventured back into the command center.

"We have some company intelligence on the table regarding this case. Mac is on his way to Langley to play nice and I'm going out to help tie up some of the ends with him. Sar'n Major you are up. Keep a watch on those cameras. I should be back here in two days. Jen why don't you come with me and get a jump start."

"Tonight?"

"Right now."

"Ah. I need some clothes."

"We'll take care of it."

"Alright." She nervously laughed and looked to Jax for some reassurance. Jax smiled at her and nodded.

The Pentagon
30 September
1430

Hauer and Beck both wore black pin stripe suits and arrived in Hauer's grey Bentley Continental GT. They had been carted across the country on a Demon flight and met Carl MacManus and Jim McCarthy at Joint Base Andrews. MacManus told them that the tailors were already at work on Beck's ensemble. It was ready shortly before they needed to make their meeting. Hauer authorized Beck's access to the Pentagon an hour before they arrived. Her photograph had been taken along with scans of her eyes, voice and finger prints and a blood sample. Once the identification had been handled and she was issued a pass they rode an elevator to deep subterranean levels that she had only heard tales about. Instrumental music and the sounds of falling rain played over speakers staged throughout the hallways creating white noise that was meant to thwart listening devices. Matt found the door marked McGuire and gave it a solid rap.

"In." Came the bellowed answer.

Mitchell McGuire wore an identical suit to theirs and sat at a presidential style mahogany desk in an otherwise empty white room. The only other furnishings on the black carpet were a computer and a pair of leather chairs.

"Good afternoon." McGuire said as he came around the desk to take Jennifer Beck's hand. "Mitchell McGuire. Pleased to meet you, Miss Beck. Welcome aboard and call me Mitch."

"And don't mind this mop closet. We have one at Langley and one at FBI as well." Matt told her. "I'll show you his real office later."

"You might consider dumping the ash tray this time too." McGuire raised an eyebrow at him as he returned to his seat.

"So, what's the skinny?"

"We have a good line of intel on the Asian side of this. Great work on this thing Matt."

"What's the catch?"

"If this is in fact good, we take it over and clean it up."

"Does the old man know about this?" Matt asked and cocked his head to the side and pushed his tongue against his cheek in a deep frown.

"At this point it's us, him, a handler at the agency and of course a deep cover agent."

"And the company wants out?" Hauer squinted with the idea that the CIA wanted to let go of something. It wasn't like them to not stay involved once they started.

"I'm not sure that I understand it either, but yes."

"Hang tight a sec." Hauer said and picked up his phone. "Outstanding. Thanks, Jax."

"What was that?"

"There are three Asian sites with this designer biological and Glanders. So, what is the old man saying?"

"He is hoping that we'll take it. He doesn't have all of the facts. When we have them, he wants to have a sit down with you and me."

"Any other catch?"

"We inherit a deep cover agent." Mac told him.

Hauer sat back, closed his eyes and rubbed his temples for a long moment.

"He doesn't have to be a team guy. Put him to work in analytics or something."

"Where is this guy now?"

"No idea." Mac had his own frown. "They are tight lipped about this until we accept."

"They aren't supposed to pull this shit." Hauer rubbed his palms together and stared at the wall behind his boss. "Alright. Take on the agent but, I want a sample of this biological. Get their files downloaded to Jax, Benedetti and Quarrels. Let the good doctors know that I'll be out there in the next twenty four hours."

"You're sure?"

"Let the heads, the old man and the handler know that the Agency is done with this. I will direct this op."

"Umm… Who is the old man?" Beck asked.

"Brian Connolly." McGuire told her.

"President Brian Connolly?" She stammered. "You're telling the President where to get off." She almost laughed in disbelief.

"I'll explain it later. But, pretty much." Matt told her.

"Oh my God."

"As soon as I have a chance to go over this with the team, I'll get back to you to call the meet with Connolly." Matt said.

"What else do you need?"

"A year in Bora Bora without my shoes on would be nice. You got one of those?"

"Right after I get mine kid."

"How's the board look?"

"Light stuff."

"I do not want to act on this compound until I know where the pieces are. I do not want to tip someone off. There's money and power involved here and I want to know where that is."

"That was my next line of thought."

"That's where I'm at now. I'm going to tie up some things out here and get Jen out to Utah to get started."

"Fine by me. Just be ready to brief Connolly in a couple of days max."

"What about Jen's pay grade?"

"Somewhere around Brett Shaw makes sense to me with her qualifications. And do keep in mind that her dad was a Marine yeah."

"If you insist."

"I do. Jen." McGuire stood up and offered his hand. "Once again, welcome aboard."

"We flew out here at God knows what expense for that?" Beck asked as they walked across the parking lot.

"Our flight wasn't made exclusively to meet Mac. But some conversations have to happen in person."

"I have to admit that I'm a little scared." She said as they cleared the guard shack. "You talk about telling the President what to do and you deal with the CIA like some cheap flunky."

"I don't usually tell him how to do his job. He doesn't tell us either. And the CIA, I'm a little upset with how they approached this. As a whole it's just a sibling rivalry thing. They do an awesome job. We just do it with less restrictions."

"Is that a good thing?"

"You'll see for yourself."

"What was that that McGuire was saying about my dad having been a Marine?"

"As a field agent with us you are going to find yourself in need of credentials appropriate to your mission. Like when you met me as Special Agent. In homage to your father, we will be assigning a Marine Corps rank."

"You're serious?"

"Very much so. And Mac gets a kick out of it when I recruit Marines. He was a Marine before he got into the Teams and his heart still pumps Paris Island and Ton Tavern. It's incurable, but we try to treat it."

"Sibling rivalry again."

"Why not?" He smiled.

"How black is this agency?"

"Nothing darker."

"So, what's my rank?"

"You are young for it but your level of degrees and the training you are about to receive tells me that I should make you a Major."

"Is Brett Shaw still a Sergeant Major?"

"On the books he's an Army Major and getting ready to move up to Lieutenant Colonel. He'll always be Sar'n Major to me. It's a joke, but a respectful one if that makes sense."

"You've known him and worked with him for a long time huh?"

"In some bad places."

"How much…" She began.

"What do think you would make as a lawyer or a doctor?"

"I was going to ask about vacation time."

"Usually sixty days a year."

"Money. You'll recall that I wanted to be an FBI agent so I'd say about a hundred grand."

"Oh." Matt said with a frown as he drove onto the highway.

"Why oh?"

"Because we've already paid you more than that this morning alone."

"What are you talking about?"

"We can't have our people in debt and possibly vulnerable to coercion so we paid off your loans on school and for the truck stop. Consider it part of the hiring bonus. I'll offer you three hundred for now. We can renegotiate next year."

"Three hundred thousand dollars a year. Get out of here."

"Tax free. I also helped Jesse and Kevin open their businesses so we can work that out as well."

"I'm overwhelmed and dizzy right now."

"Jen. I'm impressed and it's not easy for people to impress me. That's not me being a cocky frogman. It's just my realistic view of humanity. I'm confident in your ability to do this job and be an asset to this team or you would not be here. I'd have you in a safe house."

"I believe that and thank you."

"Now we need to do some shopping so that you have something to wear and things to do during your off time in training."

Wendover Utah

Newly established Marine Corps Major Jennifer Beck's second Mach 8 flight in the XB-88 Demon brought her to a desert landing strip in western Utah's barren great salt lake. The SCRAM jet throttled down and was towed inside a hangar hidden inside a giant butte. As she climbed down from the cabin, she watched two sets of four foot thick blast doors slam shut. The hangar was larger than a pair of football stadiums. She could see five more of the Demon aircraft, all but one of them painted in desert tan, that one was matte black. There was a plethora of aircraft surrounding her, helicopters of all sizes, a few old OV-10 Bronco turbo prop observation planes and several modern fighter jets. Every bit of usable space was taken up. There was an insane order to everything. Signs near ramps leading downward warned to watch for traffic exiting the motor pool. This made her turn to stare at Hauer with her jaw dropped.

"I thought that the Pentagon was huge."

"Down there we have a motor pool, a bio lab, a pool, water treatment and a power plant as well as storage. Above us are six floors for research and development, machine shops, armory, and life activities to include gyms, cafeterias, a hospital and dentist, barracks and a command center."

"This is crazy."

"It's a crazy world. These are Cold War implements that we constantly adapt. As long as they make sense, we will be using them."

"They will probably always be necessary. It's just incredible to see it for real."

"Let's get out of the way and head upstairs."

"What about my things?"

"They'll be taken care of. Fortunately, the heads of the Fraternity are here today so you'll get to meet the bosses."

"Bosses?"

"Three. They get all of the information and make decisions to give to Connolly, Congress or anyone in need of some direction. Sometimes we don't take it out of the group at all."

They stepped out of the elevator onto thick blue carpet lining the space between rows of cubicles and a long glass wall. The glass allowed them to look out at a brightly lit cavernous laboratory. In stark contrast to the hangar at the desert floor this place was clean enough to perform surgery in and modern enough to be confused with any of the big tech companies. Hauer led Beck along the glass wall so that she could peer out at people in white anti-static suits working away at projects on stainless steel tables. Drills, air-driven wrenches and grinders throwing their showers of orange sparks all offered little more than a low hum on this side of the wall. As her glance began to focus on what looked like a very large rifle Hauer kept her moving toward an office at the back of the room.

"Is this all weaponry?"

"It's mostly equipment to make our operators more efficient and effective in the field. We do make and modify weapons but, this facility has produced some of the best rescue and medical equipment in the world. For instance, these techs have developed a self-healing stent and they are replicating that healing ability into a Heart Valve Replacement with a three hundred year service life."

"Matt, that is all wonderful, it's amazing that a place inside of a mountain could look like this rather than some 1950's fallout shelter but, why are we here? How does any of this move our mission forward?"

"A doctor who works for me is on loan here and I need to see him. I thought that this might be an interesting stop for you."

"Matt Hauer." A black haired man with a tan only attainable by spending a lifetime outside stood up from a computer monitor on a polished and spotless desk to look at them with bright blue eyes. "And company."

"Doctor Kurt Thoma meet Jennifer Beck."

"A new recruit?"

"She's actually the first one to ever ask for, actually demand, an opening." Matt told him.

Thoma stood back from his desk after shaking Beck's hand. He pondered her face and eyes for a moment as if she were a complex machine of gears and springs too complicated for a simple mind to understand before he shifted his gaze over his right shoulder to the only wall in his office adorned with personal decorations. Jen followed his eyes until she could focus on photos of him mixed in with a print of M.C. Escher's Relativity, a black and white print portraying a world of walls and staircases that made absolutely zero sense to the mind but dared the viewer to solve the maze. She saw him in and around huts among tropical vegetation, in older phots near a gigantic red barn. There were others taken in schools and near old French and Swiss buildings. There was no display of awards or degrees. No trophies and no rank insignia. Above the photographs, in bold black stenciled letters was painted "Nothing will work unless you do. - Maya Angelou" Jen unconsciously nodded before she realized that it had happened and caught Thoma's eye again.

"I assume that you'll be a member of Matt's team."

"I'm hoping so." She began to blush. "There are still some tests and a meeting that I have to do."

"Given that you have ventured this far into the sanctum I fail to see an issue." He gave her a bright and toothy smile. It was so genuine that it was shocking to behold. She had never seen a person of his stature and authority broadcast such a childlike purity. "Keep those words in mind as you embark on the career path. Do not lose sight of yourself." He glanced over to Hauer as he said the last.

"I won't."

"We won't let her." Matt declared.

"You're a doctor?" Jen asked. "Isn't R and D usually an army of Engineers?"

"I'm a Doctor of Engineering."

"One of Cal Tech's finest." Matt told her.

"That's a stretch."

"We could go ahead and list his credentials but we lack the time."

"You're ready for an update on the Owl." Kurt asked as a way of changing the subject.

"Sure. "Hauer took the hint and allowed his friend to remain humble. Thoma knew that Matt would drop a litany of his accomplishments on Beck before they made it to her meeting but he did not have to be present for it.

"Right out here in my garage." The Doctor moved from behind his desk so that Beck could see the green hiking pants paired with black and olive Salomon tail shoes below his white lab coat. He led them back into the hall where he pointed them to a row of short steel benches and a series of white anti-static suits hanging on the wall. Once they were covered, he led them through a negative air pressure chamber and into the lab to steel prefab garage complete with a rollup door.

"Miss Beck meet The Owl. This is perhaps the most advanced and assuredly the most secretive glider ever built." Thoma said as he opened the garage door and switched on the overhead work lights.

"It's done?" Matt asked

"We did the maiden flight two days ago. It goes for speed and altitude tomorrow."

They stared as t long flat rectangle running down the center of two stacked triangles. The entire matte black affair sat on three short legs and tires and only came to waist height above the polished concrete floor. Hauer tapped the nose of the aircraft with the tips of his fingers.

"Did you fly it?"

"You bet. I'm not slated for the speed and altitude run though. I'll leave that to an experience test pilot. I will say that it handled like a dream."

"It looks like the back end of a dart." Beck said as she recalled throwing darts in the bar of her parents' truck stop.

"It sails through the air like one too."

"You like it don't you?" Matt asked Thoma.

"Man, I really do." Kurt smiled. "It's been such a rush since we drafted the first lines. I had to change the ratios of carbon and Kevlar a few times to get what we wanted but, this is by far one of my favorite projects. I wish I could take it to the Andes"

"I'm used to seeing gliders have much longer wings." Beck cut in and pointed at the rather stubby wings on the aircraft before her.

"They are retracted for storage and for the initial drop that will give it speed. The negative dihedral droop you see there is shared with the old F-4 phantom, one of Matt's favorite aircraft, and serves to mitigate roll." Thoma told her. "When extended the wings will keep that angle to assist with lift."

"You said drop?"

"The Owl will be dropped, not towed like a traditional glider." Thoma told her. "The mother bird will most likely be a high flying bomber like what you came here on. For rapid deployment."

"To what end?" She asked.

"Up until now if we needed to get an operator into a restrictive airspace, we had to parachute them in from airliner altitudes and often far out over the ocean. That comes with a litany of risks and a monumental amount of time. That operator pops silk at or above 25, 000 feet at high speed and hopefully can drift in the dark and frozen air into the target area." Thoma explained. "This is the HALO or High Altitude Low Open technique. It is extremely expensive to train someone to this level of aptitude, taking years. The aircrews also require several hundred hours of training for delivery in this manner. A twisted ankle could effectively end a mission and we risk that and more with each jump. Give them the Owl and even with rudimentary training we extend their range and probability of success."

"How are we doing with a training program?" Matt asked.

"Doc Quarles has everything we've gathered thus far and will add tomorrow's findings to the cycles."

"But," Jen spoke up. "Now we have a delivery vehicle that we're leaving behind in and ostensibly hostile country at what I'm guessing is an exorbitant expense." She argued as she looked over the rough surface of the glider.

"We thought about that when we started the program." Matt told her. "There was a lot of kickback on the issue."

"So, The Owl can fly itself home." Thoma gave her a smile.

"How?"

"There is technology in used today in light aircraft which allows them to auto land at the rush of a button. If the pilot is incapacitated a passenger pushes the button and the computer will fly to the nearest airport to land safely. We took cues from that tech and adapted it to what we've learned with drones. The Owl has four electric fans that will lift it before two electric pusher type propellers engage and allow it to fly at 180 knots to a safe haven for retrieval."

"That's pretty impressive." She said. "Still pretty expensive though, right?"

"The prototype, from design to function, ran a little over two million dollars. The remainder of the order should be around ninety thousand dollars per unit." Kurt offered. "In today's dollars it will cost the taxpayer upwards of two million dollars to train soldier to the Tier One level and have them ready to deploy. That's a hell of an investment to have dangling in the frigid air over hostile territory and the Owl is a small price to pay for a bit of insurance."

"Well." She smiled. "I think it's freaking awesome. I hope that I get the chance to try it out."

"If that were not on the table Matthew Hauer would never have brought you here." Kurt gave her another gleeful and toothy smile. "Jen, when you're done training come back here for some tea and a chat."

"I will." She turned back to the glider. "Would any of this work with something like a small submarine? Something that could navigate rivers."

"I can see why you recruited her."

"That is definitely some RKS." She said getting a smile from Hauer in response.

"What's RKS?" Thoma asked.

"Rich Kid Shit." She told him, garnering a raucous blast of laughter from the genius engineer.

"She fits right in." Thoma finally said. "Matt, a word if I may." When Jen had stepped away Kurt leaned in to look Matt in the eyes. "Please, tread ever so lightly on both of your hearts my friend." With a pat on his shoulder the doctor smiled and walked back to his office.

SHE GAVE HIM AN INCREDULOUS look as they stepped back into the elevator. The selection panel marked buttons for destinations rather than floor numbers. Hauer hit the button labeled 'Control'. At the end of their ride Matt led her down a bright and well-lit hall that made her think of a luxury hotel. A gray-haired man of about sixty in a well cut black pinstripe suit like her own greeted them at an open carved wooden door.

"Major Beck. Welcome to Utah. I am Ian Ashworth. Good afternoon, Matthew."

"Ian Ashworth of Ashworth, Delaney and Hamilton? The Law Firm?"

"The same. Please, come in and meet my partners." He smiled for her and then shot a wink at Hauer. "How pray tell do you know our firm?"

"One of my professors, Doctor Emily Blackwell speaks highly of you. She places your firm in the dream job club."

"That is high praise. And, she was an incredible litigator."

Robert Hamilton and Joseph Delaney were dressed in the same expensive tailored black and grey pin stripe suits and stood at the conference table as Beck and Hauer entered the room. Hamilton had not gone completely grey but had more salt than pepper in his hair and beard. He stood tall and carried a barrel chest. Delaney was closer to forty years old, Beck thought, and was suffering from pattern baldness and was not yet ready to lose his black hair that still grew around his ears. He was shorter than his partners and a bit on the thin side. Beck and Hauer were directed to leather chairs and accepted mugs of rich coffee. Ashworth took charge of the conversation.

"I'm sure that you are feeling rather lost right now." Ashworth said to Beck. "Please allow us to present this world in the best light that we can. The Greek fraternity of Delta Sigma Omega began life with law students at Notre Dame University in 1846. To this day we house chapters at only Notre Dame, Yale, Harvard and Stanford. Now we are open to women and many fields of academia. The three founders, Curtis Ashworth, William Delaney and Oscar Hamilton were men of wealth. The Ashworth in Ship building and shipping. Delaney's fortunes came from livestock and coffee and Hamilton's came from Timber, Real Estate and Construction. At the outbreak of the civil war and with the assassination of President Lincoln our predecessors decided that it would take the initiative of private citizens and personal funding to protect and lead this great nation.

With that belief in mind and very much in secret Delta Sigma Omega has been hard at work ever since. Many of our members were heavily involved in spying and fighting throughout the Spanish American War and both World Wars. Matthew's great grandfather and his friend Theodore Roosevelt were both members of this fraternity of warriors. His grandfather worked with us and the OSS during World War Two and was instrumental in the maintained relationship with what has become the CIA." He winked at Hauer as he said the last. "Our largest fighting capabilities have come about in this and the tail end of the last century. You met Mitchell McGuire today. Much of what we do stems from a document that he wrote in 1996 while observing the lack of action with regards to the Genocide in Rwanda. It was his belief then that there should have been a force at the disposal of the United States government to intervene in such matters and not be exposed. It took the beginning of yet another war. Two actually, in Afghanistan and Iraq, for that idea to take hold. As I'm sure that Matt has explained, we fall under the guise of agencies of our choosing to maintain open doors and to maintain our anonymity. For your part, Matthew's team, known as Wraiths', operates predominantly in a bubble of the United States Navy that technically does not exist. During the buildup of Naval Special Warfare numbers, the number Nine for team designations was purposefully left out. It does not mean that nine does not exist. It just means that it does not get discussed. Welcome to Nine."

"The three of you run the country?"

"Not exactly." Hamilton coughed in way of interruption. "We make sure that nobody jeopardizes the country. Most recently we have taken on the role of terrorist interdiction. Elimination if you will. In some cases, before the terrorists have a chance to act."

"We do still fight the battles of old enemies. Espionage, treason and organized crime." Delaney told her.

"And the law firm? I actually have an application I sent out to you two weeks ago."

"We read it after Matthew informed us of his choice. You received the same votes that you did for sitting in this room."

"What did I get might I ask?"

"We only act unanimously." Hamilton told her and gave her a smile.

"Gentleman, I'm sold."

"You do understand that as a field agent, most likely as a member of Matthew's team, you will be called upon to eliminate threats to your fellow citizens and your country."

"I do."

"Major Beck, make no mistake, as an FBI agent you would have stood a very real chance of never having to fire your weapon in anger. As a Wraith you will walk right up to your target and you will feel them die. You will kill Miss Beck." Hamilton declared as he prepped his fat cigar. "And painful though it may be, It will not bring your friends back." He said after the first exhale of grey smoke that was quickly pulled skyward and through a vent in the ceiling.

"I understand that and I accept."

"Then." Delaney spoke up as he filled five glasses with dark whiskey." Welcome to Delta Sigma Omega Sister Jennifer."

"Welcome." The others declared and all gulped down their drinks.

"Now. Where are we with respect to the sleeper agent?" Ashworth turned to Matt.

"Malone is due to make contact with them in the next few hours."

Chapter

Six

"Three may keep a secret, if two of them are dead."

Benjamin Franklin

America Statesman, inventor and philosopher

Ulan Bator
Mongolia
1 October
0700

AN EMPTY AND DENTED Coca Cola can adorned with Chinese characters sat on the short and battered table next to a bowl of rice that had grown cold. A laptop computer and a satellite transmitter took up the rest of the space. The only other furniture in the single room apartment was a dirty bed which the man in tattered pants, scuffed boots and course shirt that looked like burlap and felt like wool sat at as he typed. His black hair was down to his shoulders and greasy to match a shaggy beard and mustache. In his lips was a foul smelling cigarette. Outside of his third floor room he could hear children screaming in their play and cars beeping as they competed for space in the growing Ulan Bator traffic. Once he was finished with his typing he sat back and exhaled while watching the computer screen.

'Total Download transmission received. Scrub Order Acknowledged. User Tan Ting Kim. Please enter Emergency Wipe Code Now.'

Kim typed his code and hit enter. Twenty five seconds later the laptop was a useless piece of metal and plastic that would not even turn on. Next, he removed a pair of cheap pocket flashlights from a rolled up shirt. He gave each of the devices the care he would afford to broken glass as he moved them from the shirt into the foam beds of a pair of aluminum cases that had once held expensive sunglasses. As a precaution, he threw the dead laptop into one of the pit fires in the alley when he left the building carrying his worn out Chinese Army backpack. In another hour he had switched his identity in the back room of a store where his work clothes and pack were left in a secret hole in a concrete wall. When he left this place by the back door, he was clean shaven and wore a blue suit and carried the identity of Jim Leepan, a businessman selling farm equipment from Vancouver Canada. In thirty more minutes, he was ordering his favorite Japanese beer, Kawaba Snow Weizen, in a first class seat of an Airbus bound for Tokyo. Though he relaxed his muscles after a few sips of the wheat beer tasting of citrus and bananas he could not shake the memories of all he was leaving behind. Things he had been unsure that he would survive. Neither could he rid himself of the idea that someone may want him dead soon.

1630 Lake Washington Boulevard
Seattle
1945

Hauer was fighting exhaustion when he walked into the mansion to witness chaos as Malone, Shaw, Randall and Buhr worked at computers. Malone and Shaw were running two monitors each. Matt's head was pounding from the flights and meetings and the research on the compound. He desperately needed sleep and was no longer willing to fight it.

"What the hell is happening?" He asked as he threw his bag down.

"The sleeper just dumped his files and we're still running a chemical scan." Shaw responded. "This guy was deep cover man. Multi-role deep cover for over two years. In Ulan Bator Mongolia."

"No shit. What's he got?"

"It reads like a terror cell." Malone spoke up.

"Al-Qaeda?" Hauer asked.

"Maybe worse."

"Don't tell me that." Hauer shook his head.

"Nazi's" Buhr told him.

"What? Shut the fuck up."

"Nope. Ultra-Nationalists. Neo-Nazi's. At the very least this guy our sleeper was watching has an in with them and will use them as a tool for his own gains." Buhr continued.

"Hitler targeted Mongolian's specifically. Why the fuck would they go ultranationalist?"

"Chem Check is complete." Randall spoke up.

"What's that look like?" Hauer asked.

"Seven more sites, one in transit at sea."

"Including the Cascades?" Malone asked.

"No. All China and two in Mongolia."

"Everyone take a break. I'm going to make some print outs and we can try to do this in an organized manner." Malone told them.

"They call themselves The Sons Of Temujin." Malone said twenty minutes later when they had regrouped on the leather couches in the living room. "Temujin is the birth name of Genghis Khan."

Tan Ting Kim had been sent to Shang Hai China to work his way into the underground in the search of Chinese Uighur terror cells. Having made friends with two brothers who were ex-Chinese infantrymen he was led into Mongolia where their ancestral people 'the Bourchikoun', the grey eyed men, lived. The brothers told Kim of a new brotherhood striving to bring back the old ways and the old power of Mongolia. He was given a job at the Temuchin Foundry in Ulan Bator where he worked for six months under close scrutiny before being taken to a meeting in one of the offices. Here an enormous man with bright green eyes and long reddish brown hair and beard in a black suit sat above a crowd of several dozen gathered men. The man sat in a high backed chair of white horse skin.

This man spoke of restoring the Mongol Empire beyond its once great stature. He spoke of Mongolia taking its rightful place as the world super power. He wanted to rid the world of China's brand of communism and to ride into Moscow Russia flying the standard of Nine yak tails. The man referred to himself as Temuchin, finest steel.

Temuchin promised that his Mongols had kept a silent faith and maintained order awaiting their time to rise again. That time was drawing near. Now was the time to become sworn soldiers of the horde. The men in the room accepted a long knife and cut a gash under their left breast to let the blood run together into a copper bowl. From that bowl each man took a handful and smeared it over their face.

Before that day was out Kim was on a flight into the mountainous north country. Here the would be soldiers were equipped with Chinese uniforms, a pair of hardy horses and a pair of Russian AK-12 rifles. Over the course of the next month, they were trained in weapon craft and horsemanship. Some days they rode for eighty miles across terrain one might think impassable. In addition to this they trained daily in Bokh wrestling and the Russian martial art Sambo. They ate better than most of them ever had before while training. At the end of the month, they were returned to their work and now moved the foundry closer to Lake Hovsgol on the Siberian border. They were paid handsomely each week and lived in an Urdu yurt village full of five hundred men. Most of them had two wives and several children.

These people lived in giant yurts and handled the jobs of farmers raising wheat, potatoes and barley. Others were cattlemen, shepherds and goatherds. The foundry workers lived in small wooden houses as did the miners and the fishermen. Tan Ting Kim wrote that he had thought the Urdu and Temuchin's rich influence were on par with an overzealous mid-western militia in the U.S. He had thought that this was just a cultish survivalist community. His mind was changed when a pair of curriers arrived from Siberia carrying gold bars on the backs of a dozen horses. This gold was melted into smaller bars weighing several ounces and sent out with four teams also carrying heavy weapons. The foundry became a weapons manufacturer making machine-guns and ammunition that Kim began to believe were being shipped out by horse to multiple Urdu's throughout Mongolia, China, Siberia and possibly into South East Asia.

"This is unbelievable. This is the blueprint for Al-Qaeda all over again. If these people have chemical weapons, it'll be catastrophic. If they have multiple coordinated attacks, we are talking about an Armageddon event." Shaw declared.

"Exactly. The cells start multiple wars and are never suspected. They fall back to the wilds and let it play out and then steal the spoils." Buhr added. He ran his hands through his hair and then over his face as he stared at the wall. "How long are we going to be quagmired in this war?"

"How long before we can get a Hooligan on site?" Matt asked.

"Four hours to get to the central site. That should give us visual on four of them."

"Solid work guys. Let's get some rest and start working plans. When is Kim due in?"

"He is leaving Tokyo on the midnight flight. He should be here around nine in the morning."

Kevin Buhr met Kim at the airport with an exchange of prearranged dialogue and rushed him back to the mansion to meet with Hauer, Malone and Shaw. He was informed that he no longer had ties to the Central Intelligence Agency and that the information and assistance he rendered here would dictate the career he had with this organization. He reiterated the files that they had poured over but, his spoken word conveyed a level of fear that the printed word could not. Temuchin truly believed that he was the Khan and through his fortune had amassed an army.

"Talk among the Hovsgol Urdu was that there were six Tuman. A Tuman is ten thousand horsemen. The Khan only counts men. Most women and children are armed for battle as well. With the average of two wives and four children that equates to roughly three hundred and sixty thousand fighters."

"One of the sites is Lake Hovsgol." Malone broke in. "There is a site in west central China that mimics it."

"You say that Temuchin preaches for a restored empire. How does he intend to accomplish that?" Hauer asked.

"He is prepared to feed the people after creating the war that would starve them. He who has the food has the control."

"You ever see Nukes?" Shaw asked.

"No. Chemicals and high explosives, but nothing as advanced as nuclear devices. Hovsgol had nothing that could facilitate that kind of manufacture. I would not say that he does not have assets elsewhere though. I'm sure that ability would interest him. There were a lot of Chinese and Russian trainers, possibly there are scientists as well. This organization is very old and deeply rooted. There is a sort of pony express. Older that the one we had and spread across the continents of Asia and Europe. There are Paladin insurgents practicing at war within other organizations like

Al-Qaeda and there are sleeper agents inside Russia and especially the Chinese military and government."

"They've been playing the long game." Buhr said.

"Why did the company keep you in?" Shaw asked.

"They thought that the sons would be useful like the Montagnard were in Vietnam or the Northern Alliance in Afghanistan in the event of a war with China."

"Why the change?"

"Because it's Mongol for Mongol. Temuchin will make no affiliations. The British tried and lost an agent. We cannot be tied to this guy."

"Are the Chinese aware of these people?" Malone asked.

"Not to my knowledge."

"Why don't we tell them?" She asked.

"We would spark an incident for sure. What negations we do have would become nonexistent. We are not supposed to spy on China and that's exactly how they would see it." Hauer said.

"Very true." Kim assured Malone.

"You said that you knew of chemicals and conventional munitions. Did you ever see any?"

"I did, on a daily basis. I personally made more than a thousand PKM machine-guns. My friends made ammunition. The most common munition outside of small arms stuff is the sixty and the eighty-two-millimeter mortar. I never saw howitzers, but I did see the shells for seventy-five and one hundred and twenty-two millimeter. We made these at the new foundry and shipped them out in wooden crates on horseback. Last year we started getting the chemical delivered and would break it down into two gallon canisters to ship out. Never both chemicals together. When we started loading shells with it there were two canisters placed inside the shell and always observed by the Russians."

"Do you have any idea what it is?"

"No. Only that it is horrible. I have some of each in two ounce canisters. A year ago, there was an accident in the foundry laboratory. Seventy men died. The chemicals come in fifty-five gallon barrels of each compound. They were mistakenly loaded on the same truck and two of them broke open. The crew unloading was not dressed in the right gear and I was told that only several drops mixed. The gas that formed when the compounds met ate their flesh to the bone in minutes. It is said that each man in the Mangudai will have a canister of this chemical if the cities are to be invaded. That man will take fifty thousand souls with him when he dies."

"What is a Mangudai?" Shaw asked.

"They are God Belonging. They are the enforcers, death squads and when necessary …"

"Kamikaze." Hauer finished for him. "With all of the honor and prestige that go with Samurai."

"Oh. That's fucking perfect." Buhr said.

Hauer looked over Malone's shoulder as she positioned the Hooligan blimps cameras to afford her the best views of the sites. She was presently able to catch two in China and two in Mongolia. Matt stared at the chemical traces and frowned as he scratched at the stubble he desperately needed to shave.

"Get me another Hooligan above Hovsgol and a third over Western China." He said.

"What about the ship?"

"The ship, Clara, operating under at the Panamanian flag is still about 1300 miles off of Seattle. Final destination is Tianjin China." Jax said.

"That's far north of Shanghai." Kim told them.

"Call up Robbie Williams, Bravo and Charlie teams. And get the Chem team prepped. Kevin, take Mister Kim to his stash and get him and the stuff out to Benedetti and Quarrels. I want CIC ready for guidance on this."

Shaw was rubbing his face as he stared at the screens observing the Cascades site while Buhr grabbed a gear bag and headed out. He made a series of key strokes on his keyboard and watched the box around a human head grow on his screen until it was enhanced enough to see eyes and facial structure. Once that was accomplished, he sent a capture of it into a facial recognition program and let it run. Hauer, still sitting back in his chair, watched what his second in charge had thought of on the fly and attempted and smiled when the man felt like he was being watched. If it worked, he knew that they had a game changing development not only for this mission but anything else that they used the Hooligan on. Malone watched as the facial recognition program began running the faces against every open database on the globe.

"You just established that Hooligan can and will recognize a face from that high up. It has not let go of that face." Malone told Shaw. I'm going to create a program to catalog them all and run them individually. As soon as I have it, I'll duplicate it system wide."

"The guy's name is Trevor Whitelaw." Shaw said. "Ex-SAS. Wanted for aiding and abetting the enemy in Syria as of twenty twenty-two. Missing weapons from a capture showed back up in the field. He traded out to a South African Merc unit and disappeared."

"How do we know he traded out?"

"He showed up six months later at a group involved with CIA and they should have grabbed him but didn't realize it was him until he was gone. We got a solid photo of him entering and exiting the building. He hooked up with someone down there though."

"Outstanding Shaw. Damn, I love how your head works. He has to have friends."

Some of the things that Kim had said had been muddled in with the minutiae of Mongolian living and had gone unquestioned while they were in the same room. Now that he was gone, they were coming back to Matt as he began to breathe and think clearly. The mention of gold which was not a regular commodity in the vast tundra struck him. The man had said that the gold had come to them out of Siberia which shared the same lack of need or availability. Now curious, he grabbed his laptop and typed in 'missing Russian gold.' Several stories popped up. Most of them told stories of fortunes that had gone missing in the breakup of the Soviet Union and further back to the time of Tzar Nicolas. There was however a story of a military train derailing in Siberia the year before. The story, only available in Russian, showed several photographs of the train derailed and run off the side of a mountain and resting at the shores of a river. It also showed the photographs of Yelena Burkowska age 38 a Nuclear Physicist from Moscow, Zydrunas Klokov age 61 The Commissar for the Ministry of Gold, Stephan Kravchuk age 36, Gregor Balabanov age 45 and Dmitry Shaposhnikov age 40. These people were listed as missing from the dead or survivors of the wreck.

"Hey." Hauer spoke up to break his teammates away from the hypnotic flicker of faces on the right side of their computers being flashed in comparison to their captured images. "I think we just figured out where a bunch of this assholes money came from." He turned the computer to face them. While they read, he picked up his phone and called McGuire.

"This better be epic."

"Who is our best Russian expert?"

"A guy named Thornton. John Thornton. What do you need with Russia?"

"Our wannabe Khan has a couple of links I think, and I want to unravel some shit. How do I talk to this guy Thornton?"

"Fantastic. He was at Langley. He's probably penned up in the hills of Vermont at this point. I'll find out for you."

"Nice. Thank You. I could use whatever you have for a jacket on him if you can get it over to me."

"Yeah. Right here. He's in East Montpelier. It's really a place called Adamant. I'll go up with you. He has a tendency to not be very friendly."

"Meet me at Burlington Airport then."

"No. There's a quieter place called Edward F. Knapp. Code KMPV. It's regional, so no Demon flight. Transfer over to one of your planes somewhere. We aren't knocking on this guy's door before eight a.m. I'm telling you; he can be a son of a bitch."

"No worries, it's just the fate of the free world hanging in the air."

"Read the file." The phone went dead.

Utah
1 October
1800

Doctor Michael Benedetti had graduated at the top of his class at Annapolis in 1998 and gone directly to Medical School at the Uniformed Services University in Bethesda Maryland. For the first few years of his career, he had been in general practice before specializing in chemistry and biology. USAMMRID (United States Army Medical Research Institute of Infectious Diseases) had recruited him to work with virulent diseases at Fort Deitrick in late 2013. Here he was one of three Navy Doctors in a predominantly Army club. When McGuire had been given the green light to build up the action groups within the Fraternity Benedetti had been the first name he offered in the search for medical staff. Michael had not abandoned Fort Deitrick easily. The Doctor was a stickler for duty and was admittedly distrusting of what he had thought was a thinly disguised CIA operation to manufacture biological weapons. When he had finally sat down with McGuire, Matt Hauer's father and the Three as he referred to Ashworth, Delaney and Hamilton, he had only agreed to sign on if they could woo his co-worker Doctor Leslie Quarrels.

McGuire and John Hauer both could appreciate the benefits and dedication of a team and chose to vet her and get both Doctors on board. Quarrels proved to them that she alone would have been a perfect pick for the Fraternity. The young Doctor had excelled in every academic venture she had ever undertaken. Despite the challenges of life and education in inner-city Philadelphia, Leslie had decided at an early age to become a doctor. She had witnessed a husband and wife team of Doctors jump from a Porsche in their fancy dinner dress to aide and ultimately save the lives of a young man and woman who were the unintended victims of a drive-by shooting that claimed the lives of a pair of gang members and one of the members younger sisters at a barber shop. Watching them work, she knew immediately that she needed to be able to do what they were doing.

On the first day of freshman year, she sought out her guidance counselor and explained to him that she was a straight A student, she was not a disciplinary problem and she was not a star athlete. With that established, she needed him to produce a map for her to get into a University and a Medical School. The guidance counselor had become more than jaded over their last eighteen years in the school system and had barely been paying attention. He now looked up at her and had to smile when it became clear that she was not a punk kid destined to become a statistic or a teacher pulling a prank to get the year started.

The former Marine had asked her if she had ever been given the opportunity to skip a grade. She had not. He took a moment to pull up her records and asked her when she would be available to take several tests. Her answer was that she was ready immediately. He then asked if she had any interest in military service. Her grandfather had been in the Marines in Vietnam and her great-grandfather had been a tanker with the 761st tank battalion, The Black Panthers, an all-black unit, in Europe during World War Two. She said that she felt duty bound to make them proud. The guidance counselor again had to smile.

That Saturday while the new batch of trouble makers were serving their first Saturday detention of the year Leslie took a battery of tests. That night she had dinner with her mother Rita, who was pregnant again at age 29 with her sixth child. They were in the company of the guidance counselor, Mister Dickson, a captain from the United States Naval Academy and Laurie Devers, a midshipman from the school. It was established that Leslie had incredible academic scores and student leadership skills. Both of these were attributes that the Captain said would be selling points at selection.

What she needed and what midshipman Devers was willing to offer her was coaching on how best to reach out for recommendations. After all of that, Leslie knew that the slot was hers to take. Convincing her mother was the easy part. The woman was overwrought with a son already in jail and a bunch of mouths to feed. Rita also knew that Leslie was a shining star and she could not take the idea of that star being extinguished by the life that the city had to offer her. Getting the recommendations on the other hand would take monumental work.

Monday morning, when the test results came back, Leslie had made believers out of her new principal, the board of education and already had letters from three state senators, a congress woman and the Governor to add to her application. The tests indicated to everyone that Leslie should at the very least be moved to a senior class. This was not a problem. Leslie's next real problem was her age. She was going to graduate from high school at 15 and would not be eligible to start at Annapolis for another two years. The principal sat in conference with the board of education and proposed that upon graduation she would qualify for a full scholarship to a state university and could continue to prepare for the academy. For everyone involved this was a slam dunk. Upon graduation she would begin pre-med at the University of Pennsylvania's Perelman School of Medicine.

These steps went off without a hitch. Leslie spent the next three years between her senior year and the University studying and working a part time job. When she went to the University, she took advantage of the dorm room. Here she was able to focus without the distractions of her neighborhood and her siblings. At the University she became excited by both Neurology and Chemistry and pursued both fields. Annapolis was another slam dunk. She was the first candidate accepted in 2000. By 2007 she was through USU (Uniformed Services University Medical School) and had been hand-picked to move into USAMMRID serving beside Doctor Benedetti.

By then she owned an apartment building in Fredrick Maryland where she kept her home on the third floor while her mother and a few of the kids had the second floor and rented out the first to pay the mortgage. Her single luxury prior to accepting the fraternity's offer was a red Corvette. With Benedetti and Quarrels, the Fraternity had two of the best doctors that the world had seen. The pair had not only brought with them the ability to identify and mitigate problems with biological weapons but to drive medical advances and research within the secret agency.

Benedetti looked through the lens of his Bio-Chem suit and thought of how many times at Fort Deitrick and in the laboratory that they labeled 'The Sub' in Utah that he and his partner had gone into confinement with horrific substances. He smiled at her as he thought there was nobody that he would trust as much as her to go in with.

The funding available within the Fraternity allowed the Doctors to expand their safety protocols. The medical world had yet to establish a Bio-5 Laboratory. If they ever did, The Sub at Utah would be the model that they would want to duplicate. Once suited up in blue rubberized suits and breathing on scuba gear on their backs, the team nodded to each other and checked their radio communications. They entered the lab proper from an air lock into the airtight stainless steel room. Part of their protocol was that there were never more than two people in the room at a time. This kept the necessary workspace down and lessened the chances of a mishap. The lab was just a few feet larger than either of their kitchens but equipped with the absolute best tools and computers available. Although not a contagious disease, the Doctors had agreed that this chemical agent was best explored within the confines of The Sub. Each of Kim's sample containers were moved to shielded vials and placed within the Biological Hazard Library, a frozen room where locked boxes held cataloged samples.

A table surrounded by a glass enclosure and large enough to house a gorilla was positioned in the center of the room. Inside this box were a pair of rails suspended from the glass ceiling and holding the steel structure that each held a pair of near perfect recreations of human hands. As Quarrels set herself up at a computer facing the glass Benedetti worked at his own station on the opposite side of the box. Benedetti typed the words 'Unknown Substance 310-A'. A robotic arm within the library extracted the sample from its locked box and placed it inside a plastic vacuum tube much like those used at a bank drive-thru. In a moment the hissing of air stopped and the sample was deposited into the box. Before proceeding any further, the doctors conducted a voice cataloging of the contents of the box to include tools and glass sample slides for their microscopes that had all been prepped prior to their arrival. Next, they accessed the Bluetooth tabs on their computers so that the robotic hands inside the box would interface with the sensor packages within their suits. Both doctors put their working hands through a series of test movements. Once satisfied, they split the sample into three vials. Two of the vials were immediately isolated and sprayed with a decontaminant before being sent back to the safe box. From the last vial Doctor Quarrels used the hands to extract a one milliliter sample which she brought under her microscope and a laser chemical spectrum analyzer. The green laser swept over the glass tray six times while she looked into the yellow liquid.

"Hmm. This is synthetic." Quarrels said into her radio headset and looked over at the video camera that was recording her before reviewing the computer. "There is a polymer and a defoliant."

Benedetti looked away from the lab box to his own monitor and winced.

"This is 2,4,5T mixed with 2,4-D and Dioxin. Do you know what this is?" He asked.

"Dichlorophenoxyacetic Acid and Triclorophenoyacedtic Acid is none other than Agent Orange." She answered.

"Yeah. And this is a thick mixture."

"It's mixed with a synthetic naphtha and peroxide. Why?"

"To make it sticky."

"This in itself is bad." Quarrels said. "But I can't see it creating the level of immediate destruction that Kim described."

"I agree. Let's lock this down. Grab another millimeter alongside this one and get this all isolated. I'll send the vial back and when the box is clear we'll proceed with 310-B."

Once they had isolated the chemicals, the box was filled with a mist of water and chemical cleaner from small nozzles in the corners of the glass. After a full minute a vacuum system pulled all of the air out and sent it into an incinerator and finally into the desert air outside the Butte.

Six green lasers swept every surface of the table seeking traces of contamination. Once clear Benedetti called for Unknown Substance 310-B. When the sample was opened it revealed a clear liquid that looked like jellied water. As they had done with the first compound this was split into three vials with two being sent back to storage. Quarrels moved her 1 milliliter sample under her workstation and allowed the laser analyzer to work.

"Alright." Benedetti spoke up. He fought against the urge that still hit him after all of his time in the suits to wipe his forehead. The constant flow of air into the suit negated that need. "This appears to be the more volatile of the pair."

"This is so corrosive that it is etching the glass slide." She said.

"Hydrogen Chloride, Chlorine Dioxide and Sodium Hypochlorite and another polymer. The computer is reading the hypochlorite in a concentration I've never seen before."

"What's high?" Quarrels asked. "One hundred parts per million is deadly."

"This is sixty thousand parts per."

"I think we are ready."

Benedetti ordered a bullfrog specimen to be introduced to the box. The animal was alive when it entered the enclosure and sat still in the center of the box without prompting. Even when the slide was moved to within an inch of the frog it remained still.

"No change in air quality and no change to the specimen." Quarrels said after a minute.

"The frogs heart elevated momentarily and returned to forty five beats per. Let's introduce 310-A."

"Proximity test?"

"Start at one inch if we can get it. If not, we will go to mixture."

When the compounds were placed an inch apart there was no change to air or temperature. The frog remained still and stared at its surroundings.

"No change." Quarrels stated.

"Mark time as 0932 and three seconds. Compounds 310-A and 310-B mixture commencement."

Under Quarrels' direction the robotic hands lifted the slide holding 310-B and let the liquid run off the glass and into the contents of 310-A.

"The polymers are bonding agents. They are magnetized." Benedetti said as he alternated views of the box and the computer. "Chlorine gas is present."

"It started at two seconds." Quarrels told him.

The bullfrog spasmed on the table for a second and went still.

"The gas is barely visible but, it has engulfed the box." Benedetti said. Before he was done speaking the bullfrogs' green body was covered in a film of grey ash. The Doctors watched in silence as the skin and flesh disintegrated over the next five seconds. In ten more the bones were gone and a tiny pile of ash was left on the table.

"This is the definition of a WMD." Quarrels said.

"It is hyper activated."

"Hyper Chlorine BQ?" She asked.

"QB Hyper Chlorine."

"You don't think it'll be confused with quarterback?"

"I'm hoping that with Hauer on the prowl it'll never really get to become a topic of conversation."

"The box it still as volatile as it was when the frog flatlined."

"Water test. Give it a rain ph level of five."

Eight jets of mist came from throughout the box. Tiny beads splashed over the surface and rapidly collected into puddles. Inside thirty seconds the computers read that the air quality had returned to normal. The vacuum pulled everything out to the incinerator again. They ran a cleaning solution again and incinerated the air a second time for good measure.

"How difficult is this to reproduce?" Quarrels wondered.

"I think it's an issue of the chemistry. It's not a solution that is easily accomplished in a kitchen or a cave. I would imagine that the compounds are manufactured at separate locations."

"What is the largest cadaver that we have available?"

"We have a guinea pig."

"Let's run that with a five milliliter mixture. This is a weapon and will obviously run a larger mix. Let's see if there is a noticeable difference."

Seattle

Hauer sat at the patio door on a leather and chrome chair he had pulled across the room to watch the rain with the door cracked a foot to allow the air to flow. With a cup of coffee, his pen and a leather-bound notebook he read through all of the intelligence that Jax had collected on Pontif Cartage, Tan Ting Kim, Jennifer Beck and the Russian defectors. He was reading about Beck's father when his phone vibrated with a message from Benedetti. 'We need a video chat with McGuire post haste.'

"Jax, Shaw. Meeting time. Jax pull up the CIC feed for us please."

Jax had the video feed opened so that they were looking at Benedetti and Quarrels in one of their offices a moment later.

"What do you got guys?" Hauer asked.

"When these compounds are mixed, they create a horrific Weapon Of Mass Destruction. We're now calling it QB Hyper Chlorine." Quarrels told everyone. "This video demonstrates the effects of one milliliter each when mixed. A warning. It is devastating."

Everyone watched with curious expressions as the robotic hands tipped the slide to let the liquids mix. Their eyes widened and mouths dropped as the air turned toxic and corrosive for the bullfrog. When it was done the meeting was silent. Hauer took a deep breath through his nose and rocked his shoulders back. Having seen the movies and read the stories of battlefields of world war one and the devastation of gas attacks had left him terrified by the idea of biological and chemical weapons. Stories of the Nazi's use of gas in attacks and their efforts at genocide built on that terror. When he had begun training for the possibility of Nuclear, Biological and Chemical warfare he had done so with what he thought of as a higher level of fear than he had of being shot or blown up. He realized now that despite training and equipment that fear had never really dissipated. Perhaps it was healthy. Perhaps it would translate to caution.

"There is intel indicating that this was loaded into sixty millimeter mortars and five hundred pound bombs which would most likely be triple stacked and vehicle delivered." Hauer finally broke the silence. "What would that look like?"

"Based on the test that you just saw and a series of increased exposures we've modeled that." Benedetti told him. "A single 60 mike mike cannister in a stadium would likely produce ninety percent casualties."

"Any attack conducted with bombs and mortars would be as destructive as a nuclear device." Quarrels said. "At that level of concentration, we would see material disintegration as well."

"What else should we know?" McGuire asked.

"It is neutralized by water and it is partially thwarted by cold air."

"Does cold keep the gas cloud down?" Jax asked.

"Precisely." Quarrels answered.

"What about explosions or fire?" Shaw asked.

"It would create a corrosive fireball." Benedetti told him.

"Are we still on for the morning Matt?" McGuire asked.

"Most definitely."

"Why don't you get out here and meet me at six so that we can discuss what we are doing."

Matt sat quiet for a moment while he rubbed at his lips and contemplated the Luke warm cup of coffee sitting I front of him. He looked at his watch before looking up at his crew and the map on the wall. He looked from his team of confident warfighters to the tortured face of Jennifer Beck as she tried to navigate all that was happening to her life. Thoughts of how dangerous this chemical and the people processing it were and how to best end the treat raced through his head until finally he tapped the table.

"Get Robbie Williams and SEAL 6 Grey Squadron out to that damned ship. Shut it down and don't let anyone know that anything happened to it." He said it to no-one in particular but Jax and Shaw got on the task immediately.

Chapter Seven

"Demons run when a good man goes to war."

River Song from Doctor Who

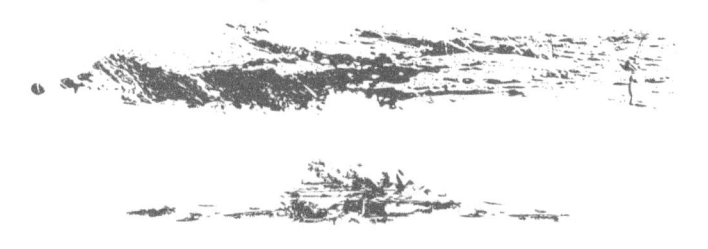

0300
Cargo Ship Clara
500 Miles South of Adak, Alaska

CAPTAIN THEO BOSKALIS was tired of sipping his coffee and staring into the night at an empty ocean. It was too cold and windy to stand outside as he would have done when he was younger. Truth be told he wasn't that old at forty-two and he knew it, but twenty years at sea on freighters had been taking its toll lately. He told himself that he should have taken the day shift and let his capable second in charge have the nights, next time he decided. For now, his watch told him that he had a few hours to go before he was relieved. He was making great money, especially for a boy from Nea Kios Greece, a small town on the northern edge of the Argolic Gulf. He owned one of the nicer homes in town and had three of the nicest cars, all of which he wanted to get back to as soon as possible. That would take another two months and a long flight out of Seattle if all went as he hoped. The time at sea seemed to run longer now than it had even ten years ago. Perhaps he should read more or workout like some of his crew to get through his days.

Boskalis had no idea that below and behind him scaling ladders had gone over the rails of his ship and that men in black salt soaked fatigues and boots were racing up the blue hull to take over his deck. Whether he knew or not didn't matter. There wasn't a thing that he or his crew could do about it.

Robbie Williams was the first man up the ladder on the starboard side of the ship. As soon as his boots were flat on the deck he had his short MK-18 rifle in both hands and covered for his teammates as they ascended and gathered. The team had mobilized out of Utah and Dam Neck Virginia where they gathered and refueled at Kodiak Island. Once on the island Charlie Team, a bunch of Wraith strikes linked with the Hatchet Troop of DevGroup / SEAL team 6's Grey Squadron, the reputed masters of maritime operations. Men and a pair of 60 foot CCM (Combat Craft Medium) boats were loaded onto VC-160 Eagles that brought them close enough to unload them directly into the water. SWCC operators held the long range boats against the hull of the cargo ship long enough to unload the assaulters before pulling back a few miles.

Williams had trained for ship takedowns several times in real life and had been told by Doctor's Benedetti and Quarrels that he had done it another hundred or so while he was sleep-training but he wasn't convinced that he was the best suited for this. None of these shooters could see his doubts, he thought as he shrugged the weight of his backpack and rifle against the freezing spray of the North Pacific and turned to the hatch on the bridge where the team would split into groups going after the bride, engine room and berths. He took a deep breath as he slipped inside the dim lights of the stairways and kept his back to the steel walls as he shuffled his feet up the grated steel steps. Three seasoned Seals and Wraiths followed close behind. The rest crept silently into the bowels of the great ship.

Less than two minutes after hitting the deck of The Clara Rob Williams pressed the tip of the suppressed chopped down M-16 into Boskalis's left ear, winked at him when he recoiled and called over his lip mounted microphone the Jax Malone.

"Clara is secure."

"Awesome Rob." She cheered. "Cut the engines and hang tight for a couple of ships coming to help at daybreak."

"United States Navy." Rob told Boskalis after one of the assaulters frisked the man and had him in handcuffs. "As you can see, we're taking over your ship for a piece."

"Why sir?"

"You've got something aboard that you shouldn't have. I need your manifest and crew list. Right now, would be good."

"I have twenty one crew."

"Twenty one accounted for. Clear. No weapons aboard sir." The leader of Hatchet Troop called out.

"Anybody brand new for this run?" Williams asked the captain.

"No."

"Jax." Williams called out after flipping through the manifest. "These guys were due in Tianjin in two weeks."

"10-4." She told him and looked over at Hauser. "I have all the links to their coms, radios, computers and phones. Anyone who had contact with these guys will pop up. We'll know shortly if we have a monitor aboard."

"Keep them all separated and cuffed until the hazmat is offloaded." Hauer told Jax who relayed the message. "Outstanding work Rob."

Montpelier Vermont
2 October

Edward F. Knapp State Airport stood atop a massive hill overlooking Montpelier. When Hauer climbed down from the confines of his dark blue Gulfstream G650 Mitch McGuire was waiting for him in the driver's seat of a black Suburban borrowed from the FBI's Montpelier field office. Hauer admired the view of the sun rising over the brilliant reds, golds and oranges of foliage mixed with evergreens along the autumn skyline. Mountains as far away as Canada and New Hampshire poked into the sky.

"I don't know why you never bought anything up here." McGuire said while watching the smile and childlike awe on his friends' face.

"I have a bunch of stuff up here. All over New England. I just don't have a home of my own here yet. We'll see. Something lakeside I think." Hauer shut the door behind him. "Thornton's file reads like fiction. What's the real story?"

"You know how some guys run 1911 pistols and you can't convince them that powder has improved ballistics across the board. That's Thornton. He was in West Berlin for a year or so before going to Vietnam with 5th Special Forces."

"I saw all of that. Recondo School. MACVSOG as a recon and Hatchet team leader." Hatchet teams were raiding forces of the Special Operations Group. "Laos and Cambodia then the CIA after Nam for trips to Angola and Afghanistan. Some legit shit for sure. Then he's back to West Berlin and the Russia desk. What I don't see is what's up."

"Who do you think they called up to talk to Charlie Wilson back in the day about how to really fight and win against Russians in Afghanistan?"

"Thornton."

"And one other guy."

"Okay awesome. So why is he the expert?"

"Because he went behind the Iron Curtain with more success and didn't come back turned more than anyone we ever sent in. He did marry a women from Russia that he had to sneak out. The Russians waited almost ten years before they sent a sleeper cell after her and her parents. He disappeared for a few years after the funerals. We would get back reports of a dead mobster or dead agents or someone up high in Moscow. Then he came back with a pile of files and got back to work at Langley and the Pentagon until we went into Afghanistan and he came up here. To Thornton Russia will always be Russia."

"He was married three times."

"Special Warfare challenges the threshold of marital bliss. By the time he had married Elizaveta he worked a regular schedule with an office and a house. Regular shit. They had the opportunity to nurture the love and keep it alive."

"Did they have kids?"

"A boy and a girl. The girl is a doctor working in Africa with Doctors Without Borders and the boy is with the agency."

"Do they know about their mother and grandparents?"

"They do now. They were kept from it back then. They were very young when she was killed."

The Suburban rolled through the small capital city and its rows of historic houses to break at a traffic circle and head north in to the colorful hills on a state road. In a mile the speed limit changed to fifty-five miles per hour and the built up area gave way to country life. Hauer had visited very few places in the country where that dramatic change happened in so short a distance. Especially on the east coast. Here abject poverty and avarice lived next door to each other. A broken down trailer covered in fiberboard and tar paper surrounded by piles of junk and dead rusted cars fit for a hoarder king sat directly across the road from a sprawling farm with a tall handsome cabin and a yard full of new boats and off-road toys. He watched both neighbors' wave and smile as they collected their mail.

"Why is Thornton up here?"

"He grew up north of here. He was going to buy a mountain where there was an old Air Force site. Cold War nostalgia maybe. But the mountain was so contaminated that it wasn't worth the hassle. This place tickled his sense of humor somehow and he found a decent spread. I guess in his own way he has enjoyed it anyway."

"What tickles an angry guy still mentally at war with Russia?"

"I think he was angry. I think the anger played itself out over those missing years. He's too smart to stay angry. Self-contained is how I'd put it. The name Adamant tickled him I think."

"I'll bite."

"So, it was first named Sodom. It wasn't even really a town but an area where people lived to work in a quarry. It was never incorporated and there's all of this debate over where lines are and all that madness. So back in 1905 this preacher stands at the pulpit and says 'I am Adamant that this town must change its name.' So, the people petitioned the state to change it. As it has no defined lines and no charter, people say 'Adamant is a state of mind'. To me that is perfect Thornton."

The Suburban turned off of the pavement and onto gravel roads for a few miles, climbing past fields and cliffs until reaching a long and winding dirt two track that brought them to a red ranch next to a new timber frame barn. A blue and white classic Chevy Blazer was at the foot of a stone walkway and well-tended shrubbery.

"Not what I was prepared for."

"Open your mind then young man. You'll see."

The man was already standing at his door as they approached. He was still tall and healthy despite being over seventy years old. His face behind a bushy grey beard and short almost white hair still carried a tan from a lifetime spent outside. His blue steel eyes cut through both men as the center piece to the scowl of a man thinking his way through a person based on sight alone. Hauer knew that this man was determining who he was by his profession. He watched the way Hauer walked and how his head moved. Hauer was sure that if his body language was not broadcasting 'operator' to this man that he would have no use for him. Matt knew the type and respected most of them. These people had earned their station in life the hard way. Just from what Matt had read in Thornton's file it was rather miraculous that the man had made it into late adulthood with the ability to walk, talk and think. If he was selective of his company there wasn't a soul who could fault him for it.

"Good morning, John thanks for seeing us." McGuire called out.

"I had a choice?" The man somehow managed to grin and still look angry.

"John Thornton this is Matt Hauer."

"I know it is. Come inside."

"Matt is one of..."

"Save that shit. I don't need to hear some title. How do you take your coffee Kid?"

"Black, two sugars sir."

Inside the house was an arraignment of plants, mostly bonsai, that looked as if they had grown under professional care for more than a decade. Surrounding the plants were tall bookcases and tables stacked with tomes in English, Russian, German, Vietnamese, Cambodian, Chinese and Japanese and reams of paper, stacks of photographs, rolled maps and a few pieces of what Matt thought were memorabilia. He saw also that the man had set out several firearms and knives in places that he could access quickly. Hauer knew that there had to be more that he could not see. Although the man had two computers that were turned on, he had no television.

"Something tells me that you know more about me than most people. I don't know much about you though." Thornton passed

Hauer a black mug of coffee that read in gold letters 'You were here. You Know. Don't forget to keep your mouth shut. Desert Place 1975.' He pointed to a living room where they all took seats around a battered steamer trunk serving as a coffee table. Hauer looked at the cup and back to the man and smiled.

"Yeah, something like that." Matt pointed at the cup. "You know that I work with Mitch. Mitch says you are the best guy to ask about all things Russia and I think I might be looking for a bear hunting license."

"How much do you know about Russia?"

"I speak and write the language as if I attended Moscovski Fiziko-Teknicheskiy Institut but that doesn't help me here."

"So, you are familiar with Peyotor Turgenev?"

"Fantastic Professor. A bit of a weirdo but quite the brain."

"Just tell him John."

"I know who you are Matt. I worked with your grandfather and your father a couple of times. I don't get visitors so I like fucking with the ones that I do get. Playing in Russia is a deadly proposition. You think you are hunting them but it's the opposite. It's like a cat toying with a mouse it ain't ready to eat just yet. Always remember that these nasty sons of bitches use winter and starvation as weapons. So, you play a masterful game of chess to draw them in. Make them think that they have you. What are you after?"

"Go ahead Matt." Mitch told him.

"I have five Russians and a bunch of material that are missing from a train wreck in Siberia, and I believe that they are all now in Mongolia. I want to find out all that I can about them."

"Mongolia? Like the cold as hell tundra Mongolia?"

"That one."

"Okay. That train you're talking about derailed in the winter last year. Siberian winter. Your dad ever tell you about Siberian winter?"

"No. But, I've been to Siberia in the winter."

Thornton stared into his eyes for a minute as if there were a legitimate roadmap or topography of life trials printed in his iris. Hauer wondered if the man could see Siberia somewhere between the intersection of his time in in the Korengal Valley Afghanistan and the death of his parents and grandfather.

"Of course, he didn't tell you. Your Dad was a stellar agent. You guys say operator now. That's him. Nothing but professional. Here's the problem. Materials either were eaten by the two and four legged Siberians or were lost to the elements. The people? That wreck happened at three in the morning local. You're talking about a place that has routinely recorded ninety-six below zero Fahrenheit. It was likely forty below that night. Those poor bastards were piss drunk and sleeping. They were not ready for the wreck and they died of exposure in minutes. And, they would have been bear and wolf bait."

"This is a photo of Yelena Burkowska and Zydrunas Klokov taken less than twelve hours ago. They are in good health and are not captive. That reads as suspicious enough that I believe my initial problem now has a Russian component."

Thornton sat back and rubbed his index finger under his nose as he looked at the photograph and then at the two men. He squinted hard as he looked back down at the photo.

"What about Dmitry Shaposhnikov? He's one of the missing as well."

"He is there too." Matt told him.

"Now this is some shit." Thornton said and got up to walk among his books before bringing one back. He set it on the trunk and turned the page to face Matt. "That is Dmitry's father at about nineteen years old in North Vietnam. Remember we were told the Russians were never there?" Matt was looking at a tall and muscular man in a tank top and green pants holding a Mosin-Nagant Sniper rifle. Thornton flipped the page. "That is him in Afghanistan in 1987. Upper echelon Spetznaz. His son followed the footsteps.

These people are closely tied to old Russia, the mafia Bratva, all of it. Like I said, You don't fight one, you fight ten. If you get the drop on him, put two in his brain and call it a day. You are not going to interrogate him. Yelena Burkowska is your link in all of this. The knowledge that she is alive tells me everything."

"There are two other Spetznaz hitters with Shaposhnikov. What do you know about them?"

"Yeah. You're talking about Kravchuk and Gregor Balabanov. Kravchuk is loyal to Dmitry because Dmitry has always given him assignments where he can make money and kill at will. He was for a few years 'the white death' of Central Africa. He liked to terrorize workers in the mines. Balabanov is something different." He stuck up a finger and turned to face one of the computers where he went to work on the keyboard.

"That's a Be-12 Chayka." Matt said when he saw the photograph of the airplane sitting in water on the screen. "We called it the Madge and they called it the Seagull."

"That's right. Cold War amphibious plane, anti-submarine warfare stuff. Kind of reminiscent of the Catalinas that were flown in World War Two. So, this guy Shaposhnikov is a jack of all trades in the Spetznaz world. He's a shooter, a demo guy, a mechanic and a master interrogator. Here he is in the far north three years ago." He scrolled down on the screen. "CIA picked him up in Africa about a year and a half ago. Same plane?"

Hauer looked at the photograph and sat back. The plane was the same. The numbers were the same but, the paint scheme had been changed from a grey over white to a dark green and tan pattern. Pylon fuel tanks and weapons racks had been added under the wings.

"When did this plane crash?" Hauer asked.

"Damn smart boy." Thornton said as he turned back to the two agents. "That plane went down on the edge of Wrangel Island." He produced color photographs of the wreckage. "Six men died on board. Being a federal nature preserve the pieces were cleaned up and taken away. You can clearly see the numbers 81 and the red Star. No Balabanov on that flight. This was a few months prior to the train wreck."

"That wreck is a cover up for something right?" Matt said. "He swapped planes. For what though?"

"Probably why they moved the wreck ten miles off shore and dumped it." Thornton passed over a grainy photograph of another aircraft the Hauer could see by the boats around it was significantly larger than the Be-12.

"This thing is still in the experimental stages. I'm looking at Russia's new search and rescue Ekranoplan right? Who did the recovery?"

"That's correct, that would be the new Caspian Sea Monster. We think that this one is bigger and more capable. There was a Russian research vessel working the area with a heavy lift ability and a helicopter. Dmitry Shaposhnikov was fortunately in the area and was sent out to supervise. Now, the funny thing is that this experimental plane is the craft listed as lost at Wrangel Island and not the Be-12."

"Convenient."

"Convenient enough to take off from a frozen lake somewhere between the crash and the Mongolian border with four metric tons of gold."

"What about Burkowska? How does she play in, besides being a nuclear weapons tech?" Matt asked.

"You ever heard of an organization called Oprichniki?"

"Sure. Old School pretorian guard. Disbanded in the 1500's"

"Nothing ends in the Russian Empire." Thornton smiled an evil and deadly smile.

Hauer stared back at him and had to wonder if the man before him had been younger if he still would be inside what he had known as the Soviet Union hunting people.

"What would their purpose be in modern Russia?"

"Russia is and was everything that the British Empire was. The sun never sets on the empire, right? Same here. They are pushing into the arctic. Then look at them in Central Africa. They'll never leave if someone doesn't make them. Just Afghanistan should tell us that. Oprichniki has been involved in everything Russian since its inception. As near as we have been able to tell they have also never left power. Even when the governing bodies changed. I'll give you a package of stuff I compiled on them but you don't have time for it now. Yelena is what the German's would have called 'wunderkind'. Child genius in a family held in high regard in Russia. We have tracked her since she was a baby. Not always on purpose, but she was often very close by. She even came here and to Canada to study, which made it extremely easy to keep tabs. Until she died, she was being groomed for the Kremlin. If she didn't become their president, she would have been some sort of minister. There was an actor a while back that people played a game with, seven degrees of. You get it. This is Yelena. Pick someone. Inside seven people that they know you have a pathway to Yelena. The concerns here are with who represents the number six."

"The actual link."

"Exactly. She's in Mongolia. That lets us drill down on some shit real quick. She had Klokov in her pocket. There's no doubt in that. Because she was a nuke physicist, we watched her hard. We watched her rendezvous with Klokov many times. Shaposhnikov served as guard leader for several state gatherings and we tracked her to him on several occasions. That's how they connect." He grinned at his own double entendre. "Chuluunbaatar Nyamdorj." He tossed down a photograph of a tall man in a grey suit standing next to Burkowska. "He was calling himself Chu back then. This is 2002 in Canada while they were in school together. She is five foot seven and you can see that he dwarfs her. Big fucker. Mongolian. Chu goes back home to

Mongolia and starts buying shit up wholesale. He also starts keeping company with Neo-Nazis. Strange shit considering that Hitler had a special interest in killing Mongols. Like Alinsky said and this guy quoted to an agent, 'useful idiots'. He had already been big in the steel industry and was sending better steel to Canada at a fraction of what the Chinese could produce and he made himself rich. We have an agent inside his organization. You should talk with that guy. Real deal shooter."

"Tan Ting Kim. He's with us now." Matt said.

"Oh." Thornton pushed his lips out and looked over to McGuire. "The Company gave him to you?"

"Yes." McGuire told him.

"What was the caveat?"

"That we take on the whole case."

"Fuck. Of course, it was. The common thread between Chu and Yelena as far as I can gather, is Maureen Collins-Roth."

"Senator Maureen Roth?" McGuire. "House Armed Services Committee, Trade Commission. Bell of the ball."

"That one. She's been up to no good for a while. They all went to school together at I'm betting she led the charge on pushing Chu up in status with the Canadians."

"There is Glanders Burkholdera at the site where Yelena is at and there is a chemical weapon with origins stateside. We're tracking the company that made the stuff right now."

"Roth's' husband was the heir to a few chemical manufacturers. She turned it all into holding companies after he died. There are several CEO's and an ex-Army General that now oversees the works and then confers with her so that she can figure out how much money she made that week."

"She's on your radar why?"

"They all are. Her though, I've been curious about for a little bit. A while back we had a State Trooper go rogue up here. You might have heard about that."

McGuire and Hauer continued to stare back at the man. Hauer turned the coffee cup so that if he so chose, Thornton would be able to read it again.

"This trooper, real pipe hitter, and his wife are among the missing." Thornton smiled and winked. "He was an Air Force Combat Controller. Documented badass. He took down a network of drug dealers that had initially killed his brother and eventually killed his parents and his wife's family."

"What's that have to do with Roth?" Hauer asked.

"I think she's again the puppet master here. I think so because there is a girl who was here in Vermont during all of this chaos. She was a student at UVM. Prior to the troopers troubles she wasn't doing very well and was rather close to the poverty side of life. Admissions gets a phone call from a secretary's office down the hall from the widow Roth. Then the girl starts spending money. Not Hollywood money but, substantially more than she should have been able to. She also shows up at a few state dinners. A friend of mine tagged her with a dead attorney at a quiet private club in Albany. She got tagged again on Myrtle Beach in company with Roth shortly after the Trooper is suspected of taking out a Cartel boss down in Texas. Funny shit is that the General was there too. Strange doings."

"There as in Myrtle Beach?" Hauer asked and sipped from his coffee. "I think we might have to take a hard look at that. Was Roth ever in Russia?"

"Roth has been behind the curtain several times. Before and after being a senator. And yes, she met with Burkowska and with Klokov."

"Do we have any intel on her being in Mongolia?"

"She's with the trade commission. She's there a good deal."

"Does anyone have her with this Chu guy during those visits?"

"That you'd have to dig for."

"Fortunately, we have a big shovel." McGuire said.

"More coffee?" Thornton asked. "Let me help you with the digging. There's a woman you need to talk to. She is deadly as a rattlesnake, so tread lightly. She's also one of the most naturally beautiful women you could ever meet, so there's that problem. She's good intel though. Karina Aminoff. Codename Nicky. She is FSB among other things. In my opinion she belongs to a section of Oprichniki known as the Leib Guards."

"The life guards." Matt said. "Like the emperor's own secret service. They were the elite until they were disbanded with the Revolution of 1917."

"Not so much." Thornton smiled and shook his head. "Russia is still Russia after all. I'll arrange a meet. She can tell you about Burkowska and probably about Roth and Chu. She won't tell them, but she is going to want something too. I have something else I need to show you. Well, give to you."

"Please." Hauer said and looked from Thornton to Mitch trying to figure out what was coming.

"If you are anything like your father and grandfather and I get the feeling that you are, I would say you are preparing to end something. I would caution you on Mongolia. You are going into a country routed in tradition and allegiances, far deeper than even the Russians. These are a people who still hunt wolves with eagles from horseback in weather that we won't venture outside in. When you give those same people rifles, heavy machine-guns, anti-air and anti-tank weapons you have asymmetric warfare on the scale the Soviets found once we gave the Mujahideen Stinger Missiles to hunt the Hind helicopter."

He produced a cardboard tube.

"Don't open that here if you please. I promised your father that I would not and I never have. I will tell you the same thing that I told him. Stay the hell out of Russia. If you disregard that warning and you go once and live, take it as a blessing. Napoleon learned the lesson hard. Do not take your war to them. Let them come to you. Yelena is a tricky and resourceful bitch. She's surrounded by real shooters. Larger than that problem is that she has no clue that she is a pawn in Chu's ancient game. He loathes her existence and he will kill her right when he gets where he wants to be. None of these people are the type that you want to hesitate on once the blades are out."

"What's in this tube?" Matt asked.

"Your dad said to give it to you when you came for it or make sure it got to you when I passed. Every day is extra now and here you are so it's in your care now. I will tell you that if it is what I think it is, it's right up your alley. You probably will want to confer with your friend Doctor Eric Bishop down at Woods Hole. I heard you were a treasure hunter."

"You hear a lot for a guy that is so tucked away in the hills."

"The internet is an amazing weapon ain't it?"

"Yeah. How did you know my dad?"

"Oh, we go back. He got me out of Russia twice. Once with a Mig 25 Foxbat that may or may not have landed out in Nevada. Or maybe Utah. That might be where I got that coffee mug." Thornton winked. "Come back up when you're done with that tube. I reckon you'll be busy for a bit. Let me know if you find a spider inside a double headed eagle tattooed to any of these people." Thornton got serious. "You tell me right away."

"What did I tell you?" McGuire said back in the Suburban. "What's in the tube?"

"I'm not ready to open it yet."

"Okay. When is it?"

"When is what?"

"The wedding?"

"Wedding. What the hell are you talking about?"

"We're all running bets on when you and Beck will tie the knot."

"We haven't even been on a date."

"Oh. I guess the burgers at that bar in Seattle don't count?"

"No, they don't. Since when did you become little miss gossip?"

"All the time I spend around Langley must do it to me." He laughed.

As soon as Hauer's jet was in the air he was on the phone back to Seattle. Although he felt that Thornton had given him solid intelligence, he found what he had said about Karina Aminoff and Yelena Burkowska unsettling. Even if all that Thornton had filed on his knowledge of Russia was considered speculation by the CIA someone should have at the very least forwarded the files to the Fraternity for review. Had they done that there could have been an opportunity to stop Burkowska before she left Siberia. That oversight now had Hauer and his team hoping that they could catch up.

"Matt what's going on?" Jax's sleepy voice answered.

"I'm sorry Jax I totally messed up on the time difference. When you wake up can you please do a deep dive on a Russian organization known as the Leib Guard. Give me everything, especially what they are up to now and how they interact with Russian intelligence and government. I'll be back in a few hours."

When he hung up, he held the old cardboard tube that Thornton had given him and gave it a sad frown before moving it to the seat next to him and trading it for a cup of coffee and the file Thornton had given him on Aminoff, Code Name Nicky. The codename was Thornton's sense of humor regarding the word Oprichniki at work.

Washington D.C.

THE BLUE FORD POLICE Interceptor parked on the street outside the brownstones and completely out of place made Moreen Roth sit up in the back seat of her chauffeured Mercedes as the driver approached her in-town apartment. As she got closer, she read the license plate and registered that the vehicle was not a police car but belonged to a government agency and had to wonder who would be coming out here rather than meet in her office. It agitated her when people thought that they could approach her in her private life. As far as she was concerned, she was off duty.

She recognized the man in the black suit the instant he exited his car. The tall and fit young man stood on the sidewalk under one of the maples that lined the old street and waited with his hands crossed at his waist. At least the bottom two buttons of his jacket were buttoned and he wouldn't be pulling a gun on her.

"Thank you, Earl. I may need you later. I'll let you know in the next twenty minutes."

"Of course, ma'am. If I don't see you, I hope you'll have a good evening."

"You too."

"What in the hell are you doing here Conrad?" She seethed as she pushed past the man and headed for the stairs to her door.

"We need to talk. There are some things you need to know."

"And you chose here?" She squinted in disbelief as she reached in her purse for keys. "I thought that you were smarter than that."

"This isn't exactly a topic we want to be discussing on the Senate floor and I think the timing dictates attention."

"Fine, come inside. Why the police car?"

"It's what I had at the moment and it isn't a police car."

"Everyone on this street sees a police car right now. Technicalities do not always win the day."

"At least it can look official."

Inside the apartment she tossed her purse and attaché case on a Victorian sofa and took her heels off letting them fall by the door. Conrad watched her stand on the toes of her bare foot while she pulled off the second shoe while she steadied herself against the wall. He admired the athletic tightness of her muscles and skin, thinking that it was exceptional that a women of her age could still look better that some women in their twenties. She caught his eye and both smiled and scowled at the thought of what he could be thinking about her.

"A drink?" She asked.

"It might be appropriate."

"I've never faced an occasion where it wasn't." "You're one of those piss warm beer navy guys or is whiskey more your poison?"

"Whiskey, I'll be ending my night with a bottle of tequila."

"The whole bottle?"

"If sleep comes before the bottom that would be a welcome surprise."

"There must be all kinds of fun in the in-between."

"Depends on if I'm alone or not."

"Ain't that the fucking truth." She poured two rocks glasses with twelve year old scotch and handed one across to the younger man. In the time it took the glass to move from her hand to his she looked at his eyes and the tension in his body and wondered what it was that kept him around her. How did he not kill her and her friends? How did he not walk away? This was a man who by all accounts had lived an honorable life until he met with her and her devious ways. Money was the only answer. Sex he could have nearly any time he wanted. He was one of those guys who could leave a bar with a woman on any night of the week almost as reliably as a woman could take home a man. He was good looking, in incredible shape and presented a picture to the world that he had his life together. So, he wasn't staying for the sex. Especially with her. She hadn't had sex with him. She hadn't really ever come on to him. It wasn't the way to lure him in. Money had sold him and money kept him. She had to wonder what had brought him to her tonight. She had had too many of these forced conversations before with people who got cold feet after facing what they were involved in. There were threats and ultimatums. Usually these ended with sex with her which is what they had been after in the first place, a little bit of hush money and for them a sunken car or a bullet in the back of the head. Looking at Conrad she realized that they were not about to have such a conversation. "What's on your mind?"

"I ran the agent imbedded with Temuchin. I washed his intel and kept him inside so that the Agency never sent anyone else, someone I couldn't control. We were solid in that aspect."

"Okay? What does that statement preclude?"

"Someone pulled him out last night. It wasn't me and it doesn't look like it was the agency." He told her and let the information sit. "Further than that I will tell you that someone started doing a real search into the happenings in Washington State. You know those assholes out there killed a State Trooper and may or may not have helped his widow commit suicide?"

"Come on." She tried to smile in an attempt to cover the fear and anger that his words dropped on her. "Does anything link the killings back to the operation?"

"Probably. Someone would likely have to do some serious detective work but this country has some of the best investigators ever to draw breath."

"I thought we hired professional soldiers to watch this."

"So did I. I think that was a bad bill of goods."

"What about these looks into the operation?"

"It's not just the operation, it's all of your holdings. Someone did a deep dive on your life. I caught the trail and managed to see what files they saw, accounts, acquaintances and then they were out. They left no signature. It had to have been someone with some astounding computer power. Something called a server hopper so that in the cyber world they never sat still for more than..." He squinted to recall the words he was given by a tech at Langley. "A femtosecond."

"What the hell is a femtosecond?"

"One billionth of a second. The kid said it's about the time that it takes light to move across a virus or it equates to what a second is to say thirty-two million years. It's fucking tiny and that means the person who looked at you cannot be found because they effectively didn't ever stop to look at you."

"And who can do that?"

"Up until about thirty minutes ago I would have told you CIA but we can't so I'm here thinking that we need to be considering some possibilities regarding how we plan to live out the rest of our lives."

"Right." Up until then she had been thinking of what sex was like with this man. He was something different than the toys she had spent time with. Something more possibly than she had ever known. Maybe the male version of Casey. What would she wear? Surely, he was a sucker for lingerie, he was still in that age bracket of men who had spent hours as boys looking through their favorite stack of magazines and catalogs full of fantasy. Then he struck her with the revelation that someone was going to pull back the curtain on what she was doing and they were going to try to stop her. Someone with computers apparently more powerful than the CIA meant that they would likely kill her and everyone around her to make it possible to solve the problem. "You mean an exit strategy?"

"Where I come from, we say 'Get the fuck outta Dodge' but, yeah that's the case."

"Tell me about this agent of yours. Not the back story on who they are. Tell me what happened."

"He scraped his hardware and vanished. And I mean gone. I'm not even sure that I could go ghost the way that he did. CIA has no idea what happened to him. We looked."

"These computer people, they grabbed him up?"

"That's the only way I see it." He finished his drink. "I thought that maybe the Mongol did it but, I see the surprise on your face and I know that's not it."

"So, who the fuck are these people and how do we make them stop?"

"We don't. We either do what we plan to do, whatever that is, and I now hope it's truly world changing or we cut bait and run."

"What do you mean we don't? You're the CIA damn it, super trooper Navy Seal and all of that shit, what do you mean we don't?"

"This is darker than the agency and I'm thinking that it's obvious that we aren't on their side."

"Is this Russia?"

"No way."

"It would have to be extremely dark to not show up to any of the subcommittees. For instance, where does their money come from?"

"Maybe a lot like your money. Maybe it's private and hidden. We've learned a lot of lessons in the spy game."

She poured another drink for both of them. Across from her she looked at this man who believed that someone was looking to stop what they were doing and was so concerned about it that he was advocating for running, yet he stopped that thought line long enough to come to her. The fact that most of the people involved in this would save their own skin and let the others worry about themselves did not eluded her. She had to wonder why though. Why the blind loyalty, if that is what it was. He wasn't here for money. She doubted whether or not she would have done the same for him.

"Joel the move we need to make here is to stay the course. I imagine that you have some place to be if you were to go to on the run, maybe multiple places. I don't think that we're there yet. The Mongols will, at the very least, make the world a different place and once this starts it cannot go back into its box. We are close enough to this that if someone does come knocking it'll be too late to stop it."

"The greater mission is outstanding, I'm all for it. But I have a strong feeling that if and when these people come knocking, we are going to be tried in the dark and will find out more than we wanted to know about secret prisons."

"That was always a risk." She passed over the drink. "Any idea who?"

"Not a fucking clue."

"What about your little network, people you used to work with?"

"There are a few guys who came over to work like mine after the service, some drifted out of the light and some just went back to normal life, some just fell off the radar completely." He scratched the back of his neck as he thought. "It's really hard to keep a secret and I can't believe I've never heard a word about whoever this is. Just the brainpower on their computer tells me that they have to be big. It's hard to hide something that big for very long. I heard a tale that the general public knew about the CIA almost a full year before we opened up shop. How has nobody heard of this?"

"Maybe they live within another agency. Maybe you have heard of them but the wrong name is used."

"Nope. I checked with a bunch of action groups and they come up dry."

"Ever been to France?" She asked.

"Twice."

"Did you like it?"

"I could get used to it. I didn't get to play tourist much. Why?"

"I'm not sure what you had in mind for your escape plan but I would put out there that France offers some nice alternatives."

"Really?"

"One of them being companionship. One should not have to suffer homesickness alone."

"I'm thinking it might not be suffering." He offered a smile and watched as she undid her blouse allowing him to see a black negligée and waved him to her room. He sipped at his drink as he followed. A short list of names of men who had ostensibly returned to normal life after their military service ran through his head. In that list he ran through who might qualify for this ultra-secret agency and again who might be interested in such a venture. Two names kept whispering at his mind. Matthew Hauer and Kendall Pierce.

When Moreen let her clothes fall away to show him a tight and tanned body all thoughts other than sex left his mind.

Chapter Eight

"Why, sometimes I believed as many as six impossible things before breakfast."
Alice in Wonderland

Utah
2 October
2100

Jennifer Beck had gone home to New York long enough to explain to her mother that she was wrapped up with college and was going out to Washington D.C. to accept and begin training for her first government job. The Seattle team had packed up her off campus apartment and shipped it to Jax Malone. When she was done with her long weekend, she met Carl MacManus who helped arrange her flight out to Utah. Strangely, he implored her not to have more than one drink on the flight and not to fall asleep. She was going to need to be able to sleep for one of her tests which would be administered shortly after her arrival.

She was in just as much awe upon arrival inside the hangar in Utah as when Matt had brought her in a few days earlier. This time she was met by P.J. Minter and Victor Figueroa who would be her lead trainers. Both men wore the desert digital Crye Precision uniforms favored by the special operations community and had applied the rank and identification badges of Air Force Master Sergeants. She wasn't sure but she thought that they had both served with Para Rescue before coming over to the Fraternity. The men grabbed her bags and led her into an elevator bound for the barracks. As soon as the bags were laid on her closet floor, they escorted her back to the elevator and to Hospital 2.

"Miss Beck if you'll have a seat here Doctor Quarrels will be right with you and she will take over for a while." Figueroa told her and stepped outside the room to leave her at what looked like an overstuffed reclining dentist chair.

"Sorry to keep you waiting. Things have been a bit hectic here today, and tonight actually." Quarrels said when she looked down at her Garmin Sport watch which was telling her that she presently needed thirty six hours of recovery after her activities. She had to repress a chuckle.

"That's okay. I'm just glad to get started. I hadn't expected that we would get right to it."

"Why waste the time right? Matt said that you were a hard charger so I thought that we would take advantage of the normal sleep rhythms and get you going."

"What am I looking at? Something like a sleep EEG?" Beck asked.

"Something a lot like that. I'm going to leave you a gown. Please, no socks just underwear with the gown. This drink is not a lot of fun to swallow. It looks gross and tastes just like a GI cocktail. We still call it the green goddess because it works miracles. You'll see. When I come back in, I will be with a male colleague, Doctor Michael Benedetti, he is one of the best. After you get into the gown sit back and get that drink in. He and I will get you set up with a bunch of probes and we'll get started."

When Quarrels returned Beck was already feeling drowsy from the drink, she had only taken a minute or so earlier. Her knees felt the cold blast of the ceiling vents and she thought that she should shave her legs soon as she watched the tiny hairs begin to rise up on goosebumps. She heard them ask questions and heard herself answer but could not focus on what it was that was said. Benedetti, a handsome and tall man slightly older than Hauer, held up a black helmet made of mesh and wires and placed it over her head while Quarrels attached black dots covered in glue with a short wire sticking into the air all over her body. She saw them on her fingers and knuckles, her kneecaps and now bare toes with their chipped blue polish and on her ankle before Benedetti told her to start counting backward from twenty. As she fought to hold onto the concept of counting, she watched the computer screen that Quarrels was watching. It showed a white spiderweb on a black screen. Beck realized that she was looking at a reading of the electrical pulses running through her brain. At the top of the screen were the words 'Wraith Check Protocol Attempt One of One' 'Initiating in 5'.

She was aware of the needle pushing through the skin of her left arm and Benedetti's handsome face but, not of pain. Then she was aware of nothing.

When she awoke, she was aware of screaming. A small child. Her back hurt when she rolled onto it. Wincing with the pain she struggled to reach behind her and became aware of the weight and the rigid frame of a rifle in her hands. *Why do I have a rifle? How?*

Smoke hung in the air above her head. She knew that as soon as she stood that she would be engulfed in it. The child screamed again. Her back shot lances of pain that made her want to let out her own violent scream. The gun was hot in her hands. She wanted to drop it but felt that to do so meant certain death. She needed to get to that child. Under the smoke, down at the floor level, she could see the round and hand shaved faces of logs. Logs that would create a cabin. This wall held a tall glass door that looked out at a pond. It was a clear and beautiful day out beyond that door. Her first instinct inside the pain that flowed from her middle back was to put a pair of rifle bullets through that glass and let air into the room. She heard her father tell her that she better not. To open that door or any other would give the fire oxygen as well.

"Mommy." The child screamed again. Beck waited no more. She was conscious, she was alive and she had to help that child. It was above her in the smoke and Beck was that child's only chance at life. With a grunt of her own she heaved herself onto her feet and felt not only the pain and the bulk of the rifle in her hands but, the weight and unruliness of a backpack that had come loose on one of the shoulder straps. She did her best to adjust it as she fumbled in the smoke for anything that would indicate a stairwell or ladder. Something that would let her access an upper floor.

"Yell again." She bellowed and coughed as smoke filled her lungs. "Yell for me again. I'm coming."

Footsteps ran along a hallway above her. They were too heavy and too fast to have come from a child. She found the railing scalding hot on the palm of her hand sticking through the torn leather of her glove. Rocking her arm back she found the wall the railing was attached to and kept her back against it as she allowed her feet to move sideways to climb the stairs and listen for movement or the child's voice to come back again. *Take a breath, Decide and Act. Now.*

Through the smoke on the second floor, she could see the fire eating at the shell walls of the cabin and working their way up through the floor. The fire was now beyond the abilities of a fire extinguisher and would take the cabin before anyone could get equipment to it. The only thing that Beck could do was get to the child and anyone else to get them out. More footsteps came at her. Some from behind and some at her left side. She put the back of her fist into a wall on her right and checked her left to make sure she was in a hall and not facing an exposed overlook down into the living room. *Get the fuck out of the funnel. You are inside a fatal funnel and need to move.*

Where? Move Where?

"Momma." The scream came again. Followed by uncontrolled coughing. Ahead of her and on the right. *She doesn't have much time. You might not hear her again. Get to her, now Beck!*

Beck crouched low with the barrel of her rifle up at her shoulder and her left hand high up on the fore grip. She charged up the hall and laid her foot into the wood frame next to the door knob. The bedroom had not yet filled with smoke. Fire licked at the window across the room where it ran along the outside wall. A man and a woman, both in their mid-thirties, lay in pools of blood on the floor at the foot of a queen sized bed. A little girl, maybe four years old, with pink and green plastic barrettes to hold up the little tufts of dirty blonde hair on her head knelt over what was presumably her mother. Outside the window was an inferno and a drop onto jagged rock. Back down the hall was a furnace of hungry flames and someone on the prowl. Whoever had killed this girl's parents was now stalking Beck. Doing her best to scoop the child and hold onto her with her left arm Jennifer grabbed the blanket by a corner with the hand holding the pistol grip of her rifle and twirled her whole body until it hung loosely over them.

The girl clung to Jen's neck as the woman took a last look at the window to assure herself that it was not an option. Back in the hall and staring at a wall of flames rolling up the stairwell and walls she had to fight for purchase on now molten carpet. The blanket kept the flames away from their skin but did nothing to thwart the noxious smoke assaulting her lungs with every hacking breath. Then came the stalker. The man slipped from a room across the top of the stairs to block her path. A short rifle was highlighted by the flickering flames that fought for oxygen and climbed toward the ceiling. Although the man's features were obscured by the smoke, he was framed by the firelight so that he mimicked a standard silhouette training target, albeit a moving one. *With a rifle.*

As the man charged forward raising his rifle Beck pushed her own rifle away from the security the blanket. In the time that it took to fire three rounds into the chest and head the blanket had slipped away from her so that it now only hung over the child and no longer afforded Beck any protection. As the man died at her feet the fire swept around her and melted skin and hair away from her hands and head. *Do Not Breath. Do...Not...Breath.*

She could hear only her own agonized scream as she lunged down the tunnel of fire that had been the stairwell. She ran headlong through the living room, charging for the glass door and firing until she shattered glass to gain the open air and rolled them both until he fire was gone and she was left staring at the blue sky while her skin smoldered and left sickening smoke to linger in the air around her. The coughing subsided as fresh and cold air took place of the heat and smoke. The crying stopped. Her own moans stopped and she looked down the length of her arm to see smooth and healthy skin. Beyond her fingers she focused in on a man sitting on top of an old and grey picnic table looking out over a lake surrounded by tall pines. The man had long black hair that he had tied off in a pony tail with pieces of leather. There were six long bird feathers inside a band and raised high and proud together over his head. A blue and white coat lay across his shoulders. Jen watched him not paying any attention to her but staring out at the trees across the lake. He stared beyond them to snowcapped mountains. She followed his gaze and turned behind her to find the cabin restored and unharmed. Touching the skin on her arm and face to reassure herself that although she felt pain there was no damage, she sat up and realized that the pain in her back was gone too.

"Who are you?" She asked the man as she approached the man.

"A guide." He said and turned to face her. He was far older than his hair would have made her believe. He was grandfatherly.

"Do I need a guide?"

"I would argue that we all do. You're training requires a guide, Jennifer Beck."

"I'm in training?"

"Life is training."

"How am I doing?"

"You have come this far." He blinked slowly.

"What do I need to do now?"

"You will walk to that mountain on the left." He raised a wrinkled and bent hand to point at the four mountains standing above the trees.

"I would say that that mountain is twenty miles away."

"The mountain is where it has always been. And, you are here. Everything that you need to get there is in you and in that backpack. It is five o'clock in the morning. You need to be there at midnight."

"I guess I better get started then." She said and shouldered the backpack. She did the math for the required average speed she would need and didn't like it at all.

"Do not forget who or where you are." He held out a folded waterproof map to her.

She looked at him with squinted eyes and took the map. As he had told her, the backpack contained the things that she would need to complete the trek. Holding the map up to orient it to the mountain she then took a compass reading and with a wave she set out walking to the lakeshore and jumping in to swim across the cool water to a shoreline of slick rocks. The trek wore blisters into her heels and wore her palms to bloody pulp. Her back hurt again and then, like her feet and legs, went numb. She was moving slower than she wanted to. Slower than she thought she should be to make the timeframe. She ate food from MRE's without bothering to stop to heat them and drank water from hot canteens through the early hours. In the afternoon the work turned cold. Her backpack supplied warmer clothes and gloves and felt no lighter for taking the items away. She marched on.

She wondered if it was sweat or blood that ran between her toes every time, she set a foot onto the hard and frozen ground. Then the snow came.

"It's time to pay attention J." She heard her father's voice call from her memory. "Winter is the most difficult time in nature. It doesn't care about you. It doesn't offer you a thought and it will pounce hard on any mistake that you make."

"I can do this dad."

She marched on. She recalled a series of books that she had read to a group of young kids that she volunteered to work with at a summer camp. These books, "The Way of The Warrior Kid" written by retired Navy SEAL Officer Jocko Willink had resonated with not only the kids but with her. She had found out shortly after reading the first book that the man had his own Podcast and had started listening to one a day while she worked out or played poker. One in particular had the author reading a Rudyard Kipling poem called 'Boots'. She remembered the way that the man's deep and haunting voice compelled her to listen. The emotion that ran through his words told her that this man knew exactly what those words meant firsthand.

'Boots-Boots-boots-boots-movin' up and down again.

An' there's no discharge in the war!'

She let the memory of the voice roll on in her mind as she continued to lift and drop her feet. Ice formed on the hair in her nose that she would not admit to having. The cold stung her eyes as if it would turn them solid in their sockets. She walked to keep from shivering. The mountain loomed closer. The icy climb waited for her. Taunted her.

The river was something that she now remembered seeing on the map and not caring about any more than she had cared about the moderate swim to cross the pond near the old man. The river was nothing like that pond. It was moving fast enough to keep from freezing solid. It was full of boulders and debris from broken trees upstream. It was death if handled poorly and might be death even if handled right. If she crossed it, she would be wet and cold and she would die if she stayed that way. Unlike the pond, she could not afford to leave her clothing on to cross this. She stopped at the shoreline to gauge the crossing and dropped the pack to find a large waterproof bag and an inflatable tube. Once the tube was ready, she fastened her backpack and rifle onto it and disrobed. With a deep breath she aimed at a fat pine on the opposite shore and pushed into the frigid water. She felt death wrap its frigid boney fingers around her. Hell was not a place of fire and brimstone. Hell was frozen. Hell was watching your fingers turn purple and losing the feeling in your legs even as you kicked them.

The current took her where it chose and tossed her against the boulders to swallow great gulps of ice while the water sapped her life with every second she lay in its grasp.

'Jen turn back. This isn't worth it. Go do something else.' Dean Kammen's voice called to her. 'You could have saved us. You know it's kind of your fault.'

My God it hurts.

'Boots-boots-boots....'

Hell was ice caking your eyelids and being so busy in the act of kicking to live that you couldn't clear it away. She swam. She kicked with legs that fought against her will. Death wrapped in the lie of rest beckoned her. Just drift and breath for a minute. *If I do, I'll never kick another stroke.*

Her lungs ached from the shock of the icy water and sheer exhaustion. To rest is to die. She chanted the words in time with her kicks.

'Boots-boots-boots...'

Movement stopped. She stopped. She screamed out and punched at the hard rock. She wasn't sure how many more times that she could deal with the agony of slamming into and stopping on yet another ice encrusted boulder only to have to start all over again. Another jolting hit, another swing around the rock only to be swept farther away from her target.

'And there's no discharge in the war.' Willink and Kipling's words taunted her.

Biting down on her lower lip she kicked against what she expected to be the renewed surge of the current. Round rocks met her foot on the downstroke. Fortunately, her kicks had grown so weak in her exhaustion that the sting was more from the cold than from the force. She sagged to the frozen shore with fast and shallow breaths racking her body.

"If you stay here, you'll freeze to death in minutes." Her father's soft voice called to her. "You have to get up now. You're almost there pal."

Beck picked herself up, rubbed and slapped her bare skin and climbed back into her dry clothes. She had to fight against her shivers to get her pants buttoned and her boots laced but she was already starting to come away from the frozen grip of death. The mountain loomed so close that she could no longer see its profile in the sky, it was all right in front of her and it was all up from here. There wasn't much comfort in that realization. Comfort was a word she thought was about to leave her vocabulary.

The walk was now a scrambling climb. There were seldom more than five minutes spent on anything that resembled a trail. She needed to move as fast as she could and in as straight a line as possible if she hoped to meet the timeframe. Several times her foot broke loose on a rock or a pile of brown pine nettles so that she fell sprawled out on her face, scraping her chin and at one point hard enough that she was sure she had broken her nose.

'Boots, boots, boots...movie' up an down again'

She was up and moving faster than when she got out of the water. He gloved hands grabbed for boulders and branches to steady herself as her feet tried to catch up gaining inches of altitude with each step and losing feet of it with each fall. The sun was gone and she thin moonlight through the frozen pines and the luminescent tritium dial of her compass to light her way. She intermittently grabbed at or shied away from shadows as she clawed her way upward. The gloves were shredded as were the knees of her pants so that her skin went from scuffed and painful to cold and painful to numb and back to just plain painful. Her breaths came in sharp pulls, her eyes burnt from lack of tears and exhaustion, her feet her so bad from moving that she was sure she had nothing but nearly frozen blood and pulp in her socks. She had no idea where the mountain top was anymore. There was no reference in the dark. She didn't dare look at her watch.

'But night-brings-long-strings-o' forty thousand million.'

The forest finally broke to snowpack of the ridge leading to the peak. The wind hit her before she realized that her cold and battered hands were touching ice. The first gust took her breath and the second nearly blinded her with a blast of crystals thrown into her already tired eyes. The second gust knocked her off of her feet and sent her sliding on her belly and then her back down into a boulder and the snag of a deadfall pine. There was no mistaking one of the snaps she heard as that of her own left radius as her arm got caught by a rock and a branch and could not bear the weight or tongue of her body as gravity flung her over the dead tree.

"Fuck." She screamed. *Now you're definitely gonna die up here. They'll be lucky to even find your body. Shut the fuck up with that shit.*

Jennifer Beck's body found the tears that she thought she couldn't cry any longer. Tears for her dead friends. Tears for her father. Tears for the pain and the idea that she may not be able to move forward just to run out of time and fail.

'Don't-don't-don't-don't look at what's in front of you.'

"No giving up bitch, get up." She yelled at herself and screamed as she stood up. Leaning against the boulder she bit into her lower lip as she stuffed the useless arm across her chest and into the strap of her backpack. She nearly passed out when she pinched the strap down and was sure that she began to blacked out several times as she stepped forward. It got even worse when she got back to the ridge line and stomped her thin hiking boots through the rime ice and slogged her way upward again. The wind and the snow down in her boots were worse than the river. Maybe it only feels like that because the river is over now, she told herself.

'I-'ave - marched-six-weeks -in -'Ell.......'

There was nowhere left to walk.

"MAJOR BECK." QUARRELS' voice called to her. "Good morning. How would you like to try some grape juice." The woman in a blue scrubs offered her a glass full of purple liquid and a straw aimed at her.

"Anything but water." Beck wheezed and looked over at Benedetti in jeans and a black wool sweater working to remove the sensors from her body and swabbing the glue away as he pulled them off. She was surprised to find out that her lips weren't cracked. Looking down the length of her body she quickly realized that she was neither broken nor scraped up. In a gown and thick grey hospital ankle socks she was still cold though.

"See how this goes and I'd like to get something solid into your stomach soon."

"I'm good with that. Maybe while I eat you can tell me about what the hell just happened."

"It's seven in the morning. You can have whatever you want for food but I think you might want to get your clock working correctly again. Perhaps, start with breakfast."

"Is that you agreeing to tell me what happened?"

"Of course, I'll tell you." Quarrels chuckled.

"You went through testing and training that was developed by a team of neurologists and military leaders including Doctor Benedetti, Commander Hauer and myself." Quarrels told Jennifer after she had had a chance to shower and change into scrubs of her own and now sat eating in Benedetti's office. "I'm sure that you have already surmised that you passed and will be placed on Hauer's team."

"I was hoping that that was why we were still talking. How long was I under?"

"Three days. We can usually determine a fail in the first six or eight hours. After that we are predominantly testing and teaching for the more elite units within the fraternity."

"A unit like Nine." It was more of a statement than a question.

"Exactly. The problem we had with you and had to confer with both Hauer and McGuire and the Three on, was how best to use you."

"Is there another field unit that I should be in?"

"Not so much should as could." Benedetti told her.

"In addition to Nine, who does a lot of investigative work and continued presence in tough areas, we run special programs specifically designed for eliminations."

"Assassins?"

"Exactly." Quarrels said. "These are seldom groups larger than four operators and usually work solo. Not only are you well suited to that but you would be an easy fit working with us or as a surgeon. We were concerned that we might be misusing an asset."

"I really scored that well?"

"In the top percentile in every test we had you take." Quarrels told her.

"Go ahead. Tell her." Benedetti assured Quarrels.

"Okay. So, normally when it comes to Nine, we are getting someone culled from Special Forces to begin with. What we are looking for there is where do they fail. What, if any, psychological problem could present itself. Then we do some retesting of their initiation courses. Once that threshold is met, we teach things that have been deemed necessary to their intended fields. This neurological classroom, if you will, allows us to teach in a way that one could not afford otherwise either with time or money. What you learn you see and hear and feel hundreds of thousands of times. Your brain operates at such a high rate that here in the real world we lack the ability to present things as fast as it can process them. We purposefully slow things down to account for eye movement and vocalization even though the brain does not require it. As such, we have trained you as a Marine recruit, a Recon Operator, a MARSOC Operator, a Navy Corpsman, a SEAL and Delta Operator. You know how to use every weapon manufactured and available in the field. Further, you have continued training as a military and commercial pilot with logged time in flight in multiple aircraft. You are both a trauma surgeon and a neurologist. You will receive legitimate credentials. In three days, we have given you several lifetimes of training and experience to make you the most capable in the field without having to waste the time otherwise necessary to accomplish a fraction."

"No." Beck smiled at her.

"This is where it gets tricky." Benedetti said. "You are currently in a state of being where you don't know what you know. You will experience a level of Deja vu for a while until you become accustomed to your reality. You will pick up a book knowing that you have already read it. In the first introduction of the program, we forgot to teach the brain that it had held the book and read it aloud."

"So, I could recite the Magna Carta, run an AK-47 and fly a 747?"

"You could already run an AK-47 before we met. Magna Carta sure, but you'll find far more interesting tomes, and yes there is the possibility that your unit will recover a 747 or another heavy airliner so you are able to do so quite well. As important as the AK family of weapons is, you will find that you can also make great use of a Mil-Dot and Horus style long range scope among a multitude of other things."

"You are sure that you want to go into the field?" Quarrels asked.

"I am for now." She answered without hesitation.

"If or when that changes. Let us know. We would be more than happy to have you over on this end." Benedetti told her. "Eat up. You have a real world test coming up. Sergeants Minter and Figueroa are getting set up for you."

"Can I ask a question?"

"Ask away?" Quarrels told her.

"The cabin and the old man and the hike. What were those about?"

"That was the test to get into Nine. The cabin was a test of personal sacrifice for mission; specifically saving the life of another at your own peril. The hike was a test of mental endurance. They come as a pair. It has a 99.3 percent fail rate. Most do not complete the first part and never see the second. You added the old man and you added the Rudyard Kipling poem. Neither of us were familiar with it. You kept mumbling 'Boots'. We were worried until we brought it up on conference and McGuire, Hauer and Hamilton began laughing. Matt finally told us what it was. You made adaptations within your subconscious and gave yourself the ability to win. That is beyond exceptional."

"Thank you." She had no idea who the old man was and it bothered her but, she was not going to present that to these two right now. Now she wanted to get on with things and get down to real work.

P.J. Minter and Victor Figueroa, both in their Air Force uniforms, brought her to her room where Minter informed her that she was to take one change of civilian clothing that they had laid on the bed for her. She was given her identification and wallet and moved downstairs to the motor pool. They escorted her to a black Suburban and told her to place the black eye covers over her eyes before they placed a black cloth bag over her head.

"Here are the rules." Figueroa told her. "Do not take off the cover until we tell you. If you do, you fail and we have to find out if you start over or not. When you do take that mask off you will have forty-eight hours in which to get yourself to a meeting with Matthew Hauer at the Vietnam Veteran's Memorial in D.C. You will not harm anyone. Extremely well trained people are hunting you. If you find yourself in jeopardy there is an emergency number in your wallet. Call that and you will be picked up. You have fifty dollars. Make it work for you."

An hour later she was helped out of the back of the Suburban and told that her clock had started. She stood in a puddle of filth that someone in a restaurant had thrown out the back door. By the way it stunk she was certain that it had rotted in the heat for more than a day. She turned in a full circle and realized that there were bright lights in the sky around the alley. Colored lights. The realization made her smile. It was ten p.m. local time and she had forty-eight hours. She was in Las Vegas. This game was hers.

Seattle
October 2

"The Leib Guard is a very interesting thing." Jax told Matt when he was finally able to sit down in their ad hoc control room. Shaw and Buhr listened in while they worked at their computers. "This organization began life as Streltsy, elite rifleman units established by Ivan the terrible around 1550. The leadership of Streltsy and the horsemen Pomoestnoye Voysko which began around 1482 would become the leaders of the Imperial Guard or Leib Guard under Peter the Great in 1683. The Leib Guard were sworn to protect Russia. The belief is that the organization of these life guards was dissolved in 1917 with the revolution. More than a few were executed at Ipatiev House in Yekaterinburg with the Romanov's."

"You're about to tell me that there is so much more to the story right." Matt asked.

"It wouldn't be real life and we wouldn't be talking about Russia if there wasn't." She said.

"What's it have to do with Mongolia?" Buhr asked.

"A ton. Most germane to us is the families of Aminoff and Burkowska. Akim Aminoff and Ardalion Burkowska were captains in the Leib Guard at the house Alexander Palace, birth place of Czar Nicolas the second. They are also the first commanders of Cheka following the assassination of the Romanov's. Cheka was the secret police tasked with counter-revolution activity. Cheka became GPU, NKVD and..."

"KGB and now FSB." Shaw finished.

"And both families have been involved with every step and iteration. During all of the time of the USSR they sat on fortunes. Most of it was off shore. Given their positions, they probably lived very well because not many would question them. Further, The Leib Guard have maintained a silent existence and lost none of their lands, fortunes or influence. In just the last few hours I've tied eight of them to the Bratva mafia, multiple government agencies, companies in Poland, Germany, England, Brussels, France, here, Dubai, China and Japan. They are major factors in what we know as

Oprichniki. Eight would theoretically give them a large piece of the vote in and I'm betting that there are more than eight."

"So effectively the Leib Guard is Oprichniki." Matt said.

"I think so."

"What about the Bratva?" Buhr asked.

"Not that they are Bratva but that they allow them to operate and Bratva pays a price."

"Tell me about Aminoff."

"She's an enigma. In Russia she's basically, well you."

"Okay." Matt laughed.

"Try this on then. She is born into a wealthy family with historical ties to a secret society. She lost both parents to some questionable circumstances and she now continues to run both the family business and a secret organization within a secret organization in a country that loves its secrets." Jax ticked off the points on her fingertips for him. "Any of that sound at all familiar to you." She asked as she made a playful frown and shook her head.

"Is she good?" Matt asked.

"I think that's a relative term here" Jax said. "She's better than Burkowska for sure. I just don't know. She's old school Russia and I mean back past white Russia but she's not a communist and I don't think she has any great allegiance to their president but she doesn't seem to be the defector type and I'm kind of amazed that she will talk to you or that she had any dealings with your friend Thornton."

"You said she is in a secret agency within a secret agency. What's that?"

"Obviously Leib Guard within Oprichniki but also something else within FSB. Something small and mobile."

"Where has she been?" Buhr asked.

"Everywhere but the moon." Jax said. "She has bank accounts all over the world. What sticks out for me though is that she was in very close proximity to several major raids on terror cells globally and the assignation of a Francois Zubayr in Chad as he was preparing an army to attempt a coup in the Central African Republic in April of 2020. She was ostensibly riding alongside Russian doctors treating Covid-19 patients. That is not the most interesting thing that popped up when I searched her face."

"Oh." Matt raised an eyebrow.

"Puerto Cabello Venezuela 2021, she missed the attack on an oil company CEO by about two hours. During the assignation of Eurobank Ergasias's CEO Philip Demetriou in August of 2022 she's four blocks away. And then last year she is a mile away from the assassination of Bekzod Abdullayeva in Xo 'ja Ismoil Uzbekistan. Bekzod was thought to be the head of the Islamic Movement of Uzbekistan, responsible for several bombings and murders throughout Uzbekistan and Tajikistan."

"What am I missing here. Are you saying that she orchestrated these attacks?" Buhr asked.

"Nope. She was hunting."

"Who?" Matt asked.

"Dirtbag numero uno." She passed across an 8 by 10 of a skinny olive skinned man in a shiny designer suit. His face wore the scowl of a man who hated the world. "Juan Carlos Heminez or Kazimir Ilya Ivanov or Yevgeny Milinovich."

"Carlito." Hauer spat out the word. "Terrorist and financier of terror. She was that close that many times."

"That's your in with her as far as I can see." Jax smiled.

"Okay then." Matt said. "I'm going to have a meeting with her because I think she can give us some real intel on what our Mongolia problem really looks like but I do not want to go alone."

"And where is it that we are going to meet her?" Shaw asked.

"Switzerland."

"Beaches." Shaw nearly yelled. "Bro, can you at least try to find us something with beaches, even just one time."

> Vietnam Veteran's Memorial
> Washington D.C.
> October 4
> 2155

Matthew Hauer stood on the stone walkway and faced the memorial wall thinking about his father and friends serving in the distant jungle land as he had in places like Iraq and Afghanistan. He looked around at the silent grassy area and at the random agents strolling as they kept an eye open for Beck's arrival, hoping that they could grab her before she made it to him. He had arrived at seven hoping, believing, that she would be cocky enough to show up early to prove herself to him. She had yet to show. As nine o'clock approached he had begun catching himself peeking at his watch to find that only a few minutes had passed and began pacing as he stared out into the park as far as the light would allow. An old and broken vet in a pair of tattered coats and beat up Vietnam Veterans cap asked if he had any change he could spare. In all of the times he had visited the memorial no-one had ever approached him to panhandle. He thought that no matter how bad off one of these soldiers were the they would hold this place so sacred that they would not do so here. Still, the guy had to be in his late seventies and he stunk of vomit and cheap alcohol, maybe this man and pride had parted company and he just needed someone to show some compassion. He passed the man the four hundred dollar bills that he had and said "Welcome Home."

"This isn't good." Shaw said over the radio and flashed a light from the Three Soldiers Statue.

"We haven't picked up anything and we lost her ten minutes after she stepped out of the casino." Buhr told him as he walked up to stand next to him.

"Shit." Matt sighed. "Get Jax to start running a facial recognition check on her. What the hell happened?"

"Hey. Sorry to bug you." The old vet walked closer again. "One of you feds happen to smoke?" The stench was somehow worse.

"No. Sorry. Remember I gave you some money?" Hauer raised his eyebrows as if to make a point. He was focused on the possibility that something bad had happened to Beck and more than agitated that this guy, Vet or not, was still asking for things. "That should be able to buy you some things like that."

"Maybe I'll have to buy a watch too. You happen to know what time it is."

"Almost ten." Buhr told him.

"Oh good. I guess I still have time then."

"Time for what?"

"Time to let you think about the fact that I've been here watching you the whole time you've been in the park."

"I do remember."

"And nobody ever thought that I might be Jennifer Beck." The old man took the hat off and pulled several pins from the dyed hair to let what had looked like dirty grey fall into a cascade of stylish locks. The dirt covered face smiled up at him and she pulled the fake teeth out to give him a real smile.

"Oh shit." Buhr laughed. "That is awesome. Outstanding."

"Nice work. We have one last meeting for you. You are not riding in my car smelling like that though. Kev, get her out to the house and make sure she gets a shower before she kills my horses. Incredible." He smiled at her and shook his head.

Hauer Mansion
Maryland
2340

"TONIGHT, IS THE NIGHT that you feel what jet lag is all about. Your life is about to get extremely busy." Matt told Beck after she had had time to shower and found a duplicate of the black suit, she had tailored for her first visit with McGuire. Carl McManus walked her out to the garage where Matt waited for her in his own suit. "Although we are a rather young unit within the Fraternity, we are sticklers for tradition. So come on in and enjoy your moment."

"This isn't necessary. I just want to get to work."

"Don't worry about work. There will always plenty of it. When this mission is done there will be another one right behind it. Trust me. Take the breath while there is time to take it"

Inside the garage all of the lights and neon signs had been turned on while all of her team mates were gathered waiting for her. Most of them held bottles of beer and stood near the mixture of exotic and classic cars. Mitchell McGuire met her at the door and was the first to shake her hand. Hamilton, Delaney and Ashworth left a conversation with Jax and Shaw to greet her.

"I heard there was quite a performance this evening." Ian Ashworth spoke up and shook her hand. "Fantastic. Shall we folks?"

"We're just waiting on B and Carl." Matt said.

"Kevin went to help." Mitch said.

"Of course, he did. He's probably stealing my whiskey in the cellar."

"Nah. Whiskey I can get anytime, it's the Cognac that I have to steal." Buhr chuckled as he crept up behind the man.

McManus and B pushed carts of champagne and cognac bottles with ice buckets and glasses. Buhr pushed a cart that held several wooden boxes with a green box resting atop each. Once in the center of the gathering they stepped away from the carts and looked to Hauer.

"This is the company who knows who you are and what you are about to be a part of." Matt spoke up and all chatter ended. "There are other agents that you will run into and there are associates that you will interact with inside of the fraternity. This is your team. Carl and B are extensions that I afford to my team and they have known about this Fraternity longer than I have been alive. There are some traditions that will be met here tonight that go back to the very beginning and there are some that I have added. Jennifer Beck comes before us tonight as a sister and a warrior among a family of warriors. She has crossed the gauntlet that was set before her and performed as near to flawlessly as I have ever heard of. We will begin this with something from the beginning and something I have added." He looked to the three and they nodded agreement. Ashworth stepped forward and handed Beck a silver key chain with the Greek letters Delta, Sigma and Omega.

"Your oath is to this organization and to the preservation of this great nation. Jennifer you are now a member of the Fraternity Delta Sigma Omega and you are a Wraith dedicated to hunting the evil of this world."

Beck took the key chain and swallowed hard.

"This is not only a perfectly made timepiece but it will also tell Utah where you are in the world. If you press the back of the case three times it will act as an emergency beacon." Hauer told her as he brought the green box forward. "This is a Rolex Yachtmaster. Keep it with you whenever you go downrange." He opened the box to reveal a brilliant watch in Rolex's masterful; Oystersteel and Everose Gold. The gesture choked her for words and she gave a tearful smile as he placed the band over her wrist.

"No lasers or rocket launchers?" She smiled.

"Not so much."

"We have a team of craftsman at Sig Sauer who have no problem tuning things for us. We have adopted the M17 or Sig P320 handgun for the field because of the time we spend with other units. Ours is just a tad smoother and looks pretty awesome too." Buhr told her as he opened one of the wooden boxes to reveal a black P320 next to a short suppressor, a light and laser device and a row of five magazines and a black holster. "This one is yours and has been sighted in by P.J. Minter. This is built for performance."

"Don't forget that other thing." Shaw spoke up as he pointed at Matt who was on his way to the liquor cart.

"She definitely earned it." Jax prompted.

"She damned sure did." Jesse said.

"Alright. You're right. Okay 'Boots'." He smiled as he turned back to face her. "One of my traditions is to give something from this garage to everyone that comes aboard. B here is my master mechanic and runs my performance shop. You pick any vehicle here that you want and he will ensure that it runs to its full potential. I would recommend taking something that you can drive on the street."

"He's joking right?" She asked Jax.

"Some things you will find that Mister Hauer has no humor for." McManus told her.

"What did you take?" She asked Jax.

"A Porsche GT3."

She walked around the building and after a few pauses came back. Running her tongue over her teeth she thought for a moment and watched as Hauer looked around the room doing his best to guess.

"There's a Silver 1970 Plymouth GTX. I'll take that please."

"Oh man." Jesse laughed.

"Do you know what that car is all about?" Hauer smiled and cocked his chin as he scratched his ear.

"Yes. It's an homage to the 1967 GTX Silver Bullet sitting next to it. Maybe I'll just call it the 70 Bullet."

"Alright. Be careful in it. Ladies and Gentlemen, I have a pair of bottles of 1841 Veuve Clicqout Champagne recovered from a wreck that you may enjoy and of course to keep Kevin happy we have a bottle of Louis The 14th Cognac. If you want, have a cigar for the occasion." Matt told the crowd. "Jennifer Beck welcome aboard."

"You just took one of his favorite cars." Jax told her.

"Does that put me on his shit list?"

"The exact opposite. It just made you more desirable and he already can't get you off his mind."

"How would that work with him being my boss now?"

"I'll make popcorn, you go find out." Jax smiled and playfully punched her arm.

Chapter Nine

"It is amazing how complete is the delusion that beauty is goodness."
Leo Tolstoy

Seattle

Jax and Jenn presented a package of computer files that traced the ownership of Pontiff Cartage to Palm Holdings, a Delaware addressed company, owned by Senator Maureen Collins-Roth and her late husband. The chemicals were traced back to factories in Lake Charles Louisiana and Yuma Arizona. Both factories operated under the name EnviroFriend. Yet another company owned by Palm Holdings. The land where the North Cascades site sat belonged to the United States government but was on lease to Belfran Industries for research.

"Amandore Belfran was a classmate of Maureen's at Yale." Jenn told Matt, Shaw and McGuire.

"How much time do they spend together?" Shaw asked.

"He is on every D.C. party guest list. He makes it to most of them. We found out that he was closely associated with the late attorney Gabrielle Foster in Albany as well." Jax said.

Matt frowned and moved in to read through some of the fine print regarding Palm Holdings.

"The money increase began three years ago. We've managed to pick up ten accounts in the U.S., Canada, Cayman Brac, Switzerland and Belgium." Jax said. "The accounts received money through a launderer from the cartel but also major lump sums were deposited via routing from an Italian bank and another in Brazil."

"Any idea where those banks got the money?"

"It's a huge trail. You can't even follow it with your eyes. The computer chased it down over a six hour crunch which should let you see how insane the movements were. Sometimes it hit the same bank a hundred and thirty times in a day. The Brazilian bank originated in Curacao and was gathered at a hub of online transactions. None of them small. The Italian bank originated in the Deira district in The UAE."

"There are no Arab players in this network though?" Shaw asked.

"None that we have identified anywhere. And, Maureen Roth is a widely known Islamaphobe." Matt spoke up. "It's a decoy."

"Were any of these transfers done in person?" Shaw asked.

"Not at times of transfer. There is not a lot of paperwork on these accounts. But, the account in the UAE gave us the latest photo of Chu." Jenn told him. She changed screens. "He looks a lot different than he did in college. This is the day that account opened three years ago and this is Chu." They were looking at every portrait they had ever seen of Genghis Khan but with reddish brown hair, bright blue eyes and a tailored suit.

"He could have been a pro wrestler." McGuire said.

"He is." Hauer said. "Just not the entertainment kind."

"He was in Russia with Yelena Burkowska two days after this was taken." Jax said.

"What did he use to start that account?" Matt asked.

"Four hundred thousand Dirham, about a hundred grand U.S. There was a six million dollar wire transfer from Xinghu Industries of Hong Kong three hours later. The chairman of the board at Xinghu is Keong Saik. He is a General in the Chinese Secret police. Looking into Xinghu to find out why Chu would make the payroll I found out that Palm Holdings purchased Xinghu the next day."

"Six million dollar finder's fee." Shaw said. "Not a bad way to make a living."

"Diving deeper you find that Xinghu oversees five steel mills throughout China. Palm offloaded those mills to Temuchin with Saik still sitting as chairman of the board."

"Do we have a track on Saik?" Matt asked.

"We're working on him now." Jax said.

"Who is working this on the Palm end of things?" Matt asked.

"Roth has an ex-Army General working as her CEO. Holland Mattison."

"Tell me about him?" McGuire finally spoke up. "Where does he come in?"

"You know him?" Shaw asked.

"A little bit. He was looked at for a leadership role when they opened up Grey Fox. He was passed over and moved out to Fort Hood." Grey Fox was reputed to be one of America's elite Tier One units, if it even existed.

"Do you remember why?" Matt asked.

"Not exactly. Something in the psyche work up."

"So. His money doesn't jive with that of a career officer who came into the Army with little money. His wife isn't from money either." Jax told them. "Yet he has managed over the last couple of years to tuck away somewhere in the neighborhood of forty million dollars. He is struggling to make himself look like he is living within his means. If we weren't after him, the IRS would be digging a big hole in his life sooner or later. He has deposits in six banks including the one in Brazil. Five follow his career, Brazil is pretty new. All deposits are close to or match those of Roth. There's another major recipient and she managed to catch herself on camera a few times with both Mattison and Roth. A Casey Glencamp. She's very new. All of her activity is within the last seven months."

"Let me guess, once a student of the University of Vermont." Hauer said.

"That's the one." Jax smiled.

"Can you tie Mattison to Gabrielle Foster?" McGuire asked.

"They did it themselves." Jax said. "That cartel hit you told me about down in Texas. I ran their faces into the computer and let that go wild but, then I ran a back scan of all satellite passes over that grid in Texas. Unfortunately, we don't get a hit on Keong Saik or Chu but, we do get General Mattison, Senator Roth, Ms. Glencamp and Attorney Foster all a few weeks before the fire that gutted the compound." She stretched her back. "Then last month Holland Mattison retires from the Army, right before a board review for a placement at the Pentagon was slated."

Hauer sat back and twirled his pen while he looked from the computers and his crew to McGuire who leaned forward as he worked things out in his mind.

"That Brazilian bank money is all from online banking?" McGuire asked.

"Yes."

"Any way to track the depositors?"

"I'm working on that too." Jax told him. "There are quite a few depositors. This all happened after the Cartel disappeared."

"I think that you have two cases against the Senator and company." McGuire said.

"Yeah?" Hauer asked.

"I would be very interested to know what the transaction was to get those deposits."

"How much are they on average?" Shaw asked.

"Ten thousand at the bottom and up to a couple of million."

Zermatt
Switzerland

HAUER ENTERED THE DIM cafe looking like a seasoned mountaineer in his black sweater, tan Crye tactical pants and La Sportiva Makalu boots that Luke Webb had sold him on giving a try. They had proven to be one of the most rugged and comfortable things he had ever put on his feet. Even in late morning, the cafe was busy with tourists. Despite the crowd he was able to pick the strikingly beautiful Karina Arinoff out. Dressed in a grey suit, she sat facing the window with her head held high so that her long white neck greeted the cool air dancing along the ancient stone walkway to make its way into windows that would soon be closed for the ski season. In her right hand she held the glass handle of a mug containing one of his favorite drinks. Her left she let rest flat on the table exposing fingers fit to play the piano but also telling the world that she was not married. Hauer watched her scan the room like the professionals he had seen the world over. He smiled and made his way to her.

"I've heard that they made the best Schumli Pflumli in Zermatt." He said when he caught her eye. The drink was a mix of plum schnapps and coffee topped with whipped cream and loved by skiers and mountaineers alike.

"In all of Switzerland. Please sit." Her accent was

"Thank you for meeting."

"I think this is of benefit to both of us."

"We can hope."

"Our friend tells me that you have something to tell me regarding a train accident."

"Not so much the accident as one of the passengers that you might have an interest in."

"Would you like one?" She pointed at the drink.

"Please."

"A passenger?" She asked as she politely motioned to their waiter.

"Several passengers on that train were listed as lost."

"That is correct. There was no trace of them."

"There was a great deal of gold that went missing as well."

"Also correct."

"I found the passengers."

She laughed. Then she stared at him when she realized that he was not lying to her.

"How is that possible? There were many experts searching for them and they came up with nothing."

"I have to believe that that train made an unscheduled and undeclared stop for some time. In that time the missing people and the gold and whatever else is missing were offloaded. There was a storm that night. Sneznaya Burya, you call it. An ice blizzard. After that drop, maybe an hour after, that train was sabotaged. I believe that the searchers performed a cover up."

Again, she began to laugh and shook her head.

"The search party was OMON and Spetznaz. Above reproach. All valued for their loyalty."

It was Matt's turn to restrain laughter. The last thing that he wanted to do right now was offend this woman. "I believe they were. I just believe that they had loyalties to someone or something other than Moscow. This is beginning to make sense to me. Hopefully to you as well. One of those passengers was a Colonel in Spetznaz. I would wager that most of the men in that search party had served with him. Maybe he even paid them. He definitely used that commonality to sell the story."

"Who would look harder and be more believed?" She nodded and turned to her drink. "Who is alive?"

"All of them. Most importantly I was hoping that you could tell me about Yelena Burkowska."

The name instantly struck a chord. She looked down at the black face of Hauer's Rolex Submariner and out to the hikers walking the ancient street before the onset of winter. Winter. That's what Hauer realized that he saw in this woman's eyes. It had not been there when he first saw her. Now the eyes held frozen death. The Russians use winter as a weapon, Thornton's words echoed in his memory. There had been some bad business between her and Burkowska. Her hatred was personal. It was deeper than a love for country. There was betrayal and deceit and he was sitting with the victim. This victim though was a wolf and not the sheep that she had been mistaken for. Revenge was playing out behind those eyes.

"She lives?" Karina finally asked.

"I saw her two hours ago. On camera, not in person. I haven't done that yet."

"Our friend…" She said and turned back to the lake. She was unsure of how to continue.

"Yes?"

"Our friend told you who I am. I'm sure he did. The two of you are of the same team. I am not. Even though we serve the same purpose we fly different flags. He told you much about me, but I was not given very much about you. For that I had to look."

"He actually didn't tell me much about you. Only that you were the person to talk to about her and her lifestyle. Her contacts."

"Our friend organized this meeting. He gave us names to use. We can use those names, but I am curious about Mister Hauer."

Matt grinned at her.

"Okay."

"I am FSB. I am also old Russia. I belong to a Russia that I have never truly known. The Germans call the suffering Fernweh, or far sickness. I'm not sure that you can understand that. Communists have made it impossible to have that which I should have. There are some of us who try to carry on in the dark. It has survived for quite some time. Some would say that we have taken things back and are playing communist to keep the people comfortable and the world unstable, but we are not there yet."

"Oprichniki and Leib Guard. This is why you agreed to Switzerland."

"Part of it. I know who you are Mister Hauer. I just do not understand why you are here. Why you would have the knowledge about where she is? Your Navy says that you are retired. Even if you had not done so, SEALs are not secret agents from everything that we know. And you are not with the CIA."

"Maybe America has Oprichniki too." He said and gave her a grin.

To that she lit a cigarette and smiled at him.

"No, your country is too young for that. You are too happy for that to be the case." She curled her lip. "So, you will not ask me as our friend did once to work for you?"

"No. I don't play that end of the game."

"What end is it you play then?"

"Ultimus Optimo."

"The final option." She smiled and sat back. It was a beautiful smile but paired with deadly cold eyes. Eyes that Matt knew would have called to him like a Siren if he had not already been interested in Jenn Beck. "That is not your only Latin either is it?"

"Not even close."

She leaned forward and took a long drag of her cigarette. Hauer could see that she was younger than he had thought at first. Although she held herself with the elegance of a lady, she was only beginning to see her thirties. He saw too that she had dyed her hair black. The roots were red. They were too short yet to tell how red but, it was there none the less.

"You are driven by what, by revenge, by taking the fight to the terrorists? War for profit? What?"

"Maybe all of that. Maybe none of the above. Maybe; so that others may live."

"Very noble." She flicked the air. "I often find that I am driven by revenge. Whether it is my own or someone else's doesn't seem to matter. Generally, it is revenge for the homeland. 'It is difficult to fight against anger; for a man will buy revenge with his soul.' Heraclitus said that."

"I don't think he was completely off the mark. 'There is nothing wrong with revenge. The wrong has already been done, or there would be no need to even the score.' Ashly Lorenzanna said that."

"He quotes an angry prostitute, how very American." She stifled a laugh.

"Her vocation doesn't make her any less correct."

"WHAT DO YOU WANT TO know about her?"

"I need to know about anyone that wasn't Russian that she had dealings with, especially in the last couple of years before the train. Our friend is of the belief that you might be the one to best tell me that."

"She was a woman with many acquaintances and few friends. I was supposed to be one of those friends. More than friends."

"How so?" Hauer asked. "Lovers?"

"No." She laughed again. This time from pure comedy rather than disbelief. "I don't go that way. She didn't either until recently. No, We were more like family." She became serious again and put out the cigarette.

"Same organization?"

"Yes. The old one."

"I heard it said that that organization has its new life in every secret police organization in Russia."

"That would be a bit of a misunderstanding. We are in those places because we need to be. You would say keeping the pulse. But we are not those organizations. Because of the positions we hold it allows us to meet without suspicion."

"I understand."

"Burkowska can trace her family back to an Infantry Colonel guarding The Romanov's. He was ordered to take his family and some of the friends of the Romanov's to Finland and later into Canada. When Russia was under fear of Nazi invasion her Grandparents returned and fought alongside communists. Her grandfather was a hero and became KGB. Her father became a Doctor and she was swept into school as soon as she was tested. Their seats at the tables were established long ago. She had the ear of the Kremlin."

"And you?"

"I sit near the head of the tables."

"Your history goes back farther than hers."

"It does."

He sipped his drink and waited.

"My family was picked for Oprichnina by Ivan himself. My ancestor was a Wolfshead Cossack. A man trusted by Ivan to keep the others from being too vile in their approach to gaining order. Today I represent that order. She and I were friends from childhood. She had never presented a question in her loyalties to Russia. Until the foreigners came."

"Can you tell me about them?"

"One you must know. A horrible and deceptive woman. At first, we thought that she was an intelligence plant but she is something worse." Karina toyed with another cigarette and noticed that Hauer did not smoke so chose her drink instead. "You Americans have pushed cigarettes out of your lives. It's a shame. It has character and mystery and ..."

"Cancer." Matt gave her a smile.

"Probably true. This woman came from nearly nothing but has sold whatever soul she believed that she had to gain money and power. She has used her office in your government to transport and pedal narcotics and now people. Not the sneaking agents into countries kind but the slave labor and sex slave kind of traffic. She spent too much time in company with Burkowska. She and Yelena were friends since University in Canada along with a Mongol who prefers to call himself Temuchin. He made two visits to Russia before being barred entry. Maureen Collins-Roth was in Moscow last week. Now that you have come, I believe that one or both have something to do with Yelana's disappearance. Especially since she is alive. Where is Yelena?"

"I'm afraid I can't tell you that."

"Matthew Hauer. You have nothing to fear from me."

"She hasn't lied to you yet." Brett Shaw whispered into a microphone attached to headgear where he sat at a small computer and laser scope staring at Karina's face from a building five blocks away. "She is a Colonel in the FSB and she is a broker and founder of Love Vest, a high price bridal match making service. The three attended the University of Alberta in Edmonton together for a year."

The transmission was received in a thin and clear earpiece that sent vibrations into Matt's skull which were perceived as sound and could not be overheard.

"Maybe not. I can't have you arriving at her location, even in the area, before I solve a larger problem for not only our countries but the world."

"We can follow Maureen and see where that leads. Perhaps we follow Temuchin, the man who used to be Chu."

"One I think is a bad end for now and the other is presenting a challenge at this point."

"You are a strange man to me. Interesting in a way that men are not in our time. They are all so very predictable. The appetites of men will be their undoing. You though, you walk a different path, a better path, but also a most dangerous one."

"I like the danger. It lets me know I'm right."

"I believe that there is much truth in that idea. This thing you are following, it is bad for all of us?"

"So bad that we cannot afford to have a glitch."

"If Yelena is involved there is money and power at play for her, but she is bringing Nuclear ability to that table."

"That's what I was afraid of." Matt frowned. "I wonder if despite the fact that we only just met if I might curry favor with you?"

"Perhaps we can make a trade."

"I wouldn't have it any other way."

"I want to see Yelena. I would prefer alive if possible."

"I can make that happen."

"A bit of advice if I may."

"Please."

"Any of the others. Not so much the minister but, the Spetznaz. Do not blink with them."

"Shaposhnikov is not from O?"

"Absolutely not. You had a favor?"

"Beyond what you have already done I would ask a personal favor. Could you tell me where the lock to this key might be." He produced a tarnished bronze barrel key and passed it over to her.

She paled and swallowed hard and eventually lit the cigarette she had set aside.

"How did you come by this?"

"I found it tucked gently inside an egg."

"A Faberge' egg. A baby blue one?"

"Yes." He smiled and nodded.

"That egg has been missing for a long time. Where did you find it?"

"A cartel kingpin had it. He didn't need it anymore."

"I am not a fan of guesswork. I much prefer hard facts. That being said, I would logically bet that Yelena gave it to Maureen and Maureen gave it to the cartel."

"I would be interested in returning the egg to old Russia but I would like to turn the lock that this key belongs to."

"If you so choose, the egg should be returned anonymously. The lock I can find. That poses a problem for you. I can help you but, it could be dangerous. I gather that you do not have time for that now. Perhaps after I have seen Yelena."

"Unfortunately, I don't." "So that you don't feel like you have left here empty handed I'd like to give you this." He slid an envelope across the table. It looked like a birthday card but held a thumb drive inside the card.

"What is this?"

"That is the passings of a man you know as Yevginy Milinovich, Juan Carlos Heminez and Kazamir Ilya Ivanov and who we had initially known as Carlito. A Cuban/Russian terrorist financier. His itinerary as we know it for the next two weeks is on there. It would be appropriate for you, for Russia, to handle this."

"This is confirmed?"

"Even by our friend."

"It is a shame that we can't take in the opera. Perhaps dinner?"

"Please don't take this as an insult but I have a hunting trip and I will have to take a raincheck."

"We're playing with the Russian's now?" Buhr asked Shaw in the dark room where they were set up in their observation post behind screens they had dropped from the windows.

"It looks like it."

"The world is upside down."

"Tell me when it hasn't been." Jesse said without looking away from the scope on his Sword International MK18 rifle while he stared at Karina's chin knowing that he had to allow space under the eve of the building to get to her if he fired.

"There are two sights breaking gear down right now." Jax spoke over everyone's ear pieces from her station in Utah. "I just fried that gear." She told them as she watched the Hooligan blimps computers send laser pulses into the city. Thousands of cell phone calls were lost long enough for the user to look down at a blank screen before breathing a sigh of relief and moving along, complaining about service. Nothing that the Russians had recorded of Matt's meeting was retained. Only a set of film photographs were captured to be reviewed later. They would be completely reliant on Karina.

"She never lied. She's a solid potential asset." Shaw declared.

"Maybe." Jax said. "Big maybe."

Maryland

Mitch McGuire and Matt Hauer boarded a Marine Corps Blackhawk on Hauer's back lawn and flew to a meeting with President Brian Connolly while Jax briefed Beck on all that they had gathered while she was away. The crew of the chopper remained silent while they hugged the trees and speed inland. Hauer tapped McGuire's leg pulling him away from watching the lights of the cities pass by and held up two fingers. McGuire nodded and yawned. The meeting would be at Camp David.

They were set down on a grass pad where they were met by a pair of Marines with a golf cart who brought them first to a small cabin where they were met by a pair of Secret Service agents who they both knew from prior service and several visits during the administration. Here they were relieved of their firearms. McGuire unloaded and handed over a black Cabot 1911 pistol known as the Ultimate Bedside. The two agents admired the Damascus slide of the master crafted weapon while Hauer produced and made safe his own firearms. He laid out a custom Sig P320 and his own Cabot Apocalypse 1911, a pistol created with a Damascus slide on a brushed stainless steel frame. The weapon sported a co-witnessed red dot sight and barrel threaded to accept a suppressor. It was also worth more than three weeks salary for the agents. As they looked over the handguns, he laid out a pair of knives, a small working knife and larger fighting knife. When he was done, he took a step back.

"We are going to proceed downstairs now." The lead agent said after locking the weapons in a safe and guiding them into a back room where an elevator was hidden behind closed doors.

Another agent and a pair of armed Marines met them in a short white tiled corridor guarding a stainless steel door that slid to the left allowing them inside a room made to mimic the interior of the cabins a hundred or more feet above them on terra firma. An exhausted looking grey haired Brian Connolly met them just inside the door and pointed at the bottle of A Midwinter Nights Dram whiskey from High West Distillery and bucket of ice laid out on an oak bar. Connolly, once a commander of a Stryker Brigade and single term Texas Senator, stood just an inch shorter than Hauer but looked at if he was letting the weight of running the country push him down. Despite dressing in a suit for the meeting, he walked on the carpet in black dress socks as a way to relax.

"Gentleman, I apologize for the late hour."

"As do we sir." McGuire offered.

"I think we can dispense with the sir part of things. This is one of the reasons we are down here. We aren't followed, documented or recorded for posterity. You didn't sound too comfortable when we talked earlier so I figured we needed to do this in the dark."

"That's right. This one is tenuous." Mitch said.

"You mean the players?" Connolly asked.

"All of it." Hauer spoke up. "The short of it is that we have found a chemical weapon and a set of people moving to start a war in the east. Most of the players are in Mongolia with a high ranking U.S. official at the financial and manufacturing level. We are still researching whether other weapons were moved from the states or state run programs."

"Chemical Weapon?"

"Yes. We have classed it as QB Hyper Chlorine. It creates an extremely corrosive gas and means near instant death for all that come into contact. This is a video from our controlled laboratory."

Connolly watched in silence and emptied his glass before sighing and heading to pour himself another drink. Sitting back down, he watched the video again and flicked the fingers of his left hand held up next to his ear while his face reddened and he breathed through flaring nostrils.

"Damn it I wish that I still smoked. It's not presidential Ginger says." He looked toward the stainless steel ceiling and took a deep breath. "How did you find this?"

"Someone moving it around on the edges of North Cascades National Park in Washington decided to kill some people to keep it hidden. We took a look and found more of it in Mongolia. The CIA dumped a deep cover agent on us and we've been digging hard." McGuire told him.

"Who over there has it? Is this a rouge state?"

"No. This would play out as terror strikes to create war. We believe they are looking to spark a Chinese-Russian conflict and make a power grab once it has gotten traction." Matt said.

"Who is this person stateside?"

"Maureen Collins-Roth" Hauer told him and checked his watch before standing up to make drinks for himself and McGuire. "She has a lengthy history of contact with several of the other key players. She owns all of the places manufacturing the weapon."

"Senator Collins-Roth. You are kidding right? Don't answer that. What the fuck?"

"Unfortunately, it is the truth. Realistically, if it hadn't been for this, we would probably be talking to you about her in another month anyway." McGuire told him.

"For what?"

"She's been involved in narcotics and sex trafficking for a while. Probably since her husband died. We recently gained information linking her to the murders of a Vermont State trooper's family and to the Cartel that he took down."

"I remember that case made some headlines. Nobody has found that Trooper either. He did some serious damage if I recall that correctly."

"They stopped looking for him." Matt told him. "You actually signed the order clearing him."

"Gotcha." Connolly said and rolled the glass in his hand watching the ice cube move. "What is your assessment on this?"

"We need to get after this before it goes any further. There are Russian defectors and stolen goods at play as well. We will have confirmation on the Chinese end of this soon."

"If one exists, I'm sure your genius Jax will find it."

"We have identified several sites and will need to take them down as close to simultaneously as possible. That means that we need some assets."

"Shit. That makes black operations nearly impossible." The President said and leaned forward.

"We can work that out but, we do need numbers." McGuire said.

"Are we talking Spec Ops guys?"

"And the 75th Rangers at this point in planning."

"All of the 75th?"

"Maybe a company in total."

"Hmm." The President stared into the glass again as he rocked it back and forth. "We are not putting these people into Russia or China?"

"Not if we can help it." Matt told him.

"I apologize again." Connolly stared at him. "I wasn't asking. There will not be U.S. troops in Russia or China."

"Brian you just watched two drops of this shit make a guinea pig disappear in moments. It was dead in a single breath. Imagine what gallons of it will do to a city. If we tell either Russia or China about this, we lose everything we have gained with them or we start the same war and find ourselves neck deep in it so that you do watch all of the 75th Ranger regiment get deployed and possibly ambushed by this shit. If I have to follow this to the Forbidden Palace, count on photos of me drinking whisky and smoking a cigar next to the Emperor. I'm not here to be an asshole, I assure you. This is the most serious problem of our time. With manufacture inside this country, you have to believe there is a real possibility of seeing it released on continent. Denver, Seattle, Los Angeles, Manhattan, at this damned gate. All gone is seconds. We are at war with this, and we need to act like it." Matt told him.

"Son of a bitch." Connolly put the drink down to intertwine his fingers and lean forward in silent prayer. "Is there any intel on U.S. activity?"

"I would have given that to you at the start." Matt told him.

"What about Collins-Roth?"

"There is a meeting between a trooper and his wife, an esteemed doctor, that I believe should take place at the beginning of her road to justice."

"Damn. I'm guessing that you have a way to facilitate that."

"I do." Hauer tapped his watch. "I own her clock."

"Do the country one favor with that."

"Name it."

"Let's not have her departure be ambiguous. No missing emails and no missing person. No Black prison."

"Check."

"Green light it. I'll have letters for you by the time the sun comes up. I think it's about two hours away at this point. And Matt, I'll sign these ones, okay?"

"Sorry about your night." McGuire said.

"Don't be sorry. Be successful."

"WHERE ARE THEY?" MCGUIRE asked Hauer when they were airborne and switched channels on their headsets.

"Who?"

"The wise men." McGuire shot back. "The triple threat." He was referring to Luke and Jessica Webb and Robert Williams. The three people responsible for the death of Cartel leader Juan Francisco Becarra.

"They just wrapped a job in Malawi and are on their way to Nebraska."

"That's done already?"

"Yup."

"Get them prepped. And start tracking. I'm going down to Dam Neck and then to Fort Liberty to rally some shooters. I'll see you in Nebraska."

Chapter Ten

"Justice for crimes against humanity must have no limitations."

Simon Wiesenthal

Holocaust Survivor and Nazi Hunter

Casa Milano Hotel
Milan Italy
0130

Juan Carlos Heminez, as he was known by his mother's family in Cuba and Costa Rica or Kazimir Ilya Ivanov as his father had named him, was a slender and handsome man who was often able to pass himself off as Mediterranean. This had allowed him to adapt his identity at will. That and the help of enough money to buy convincing identities kept him free and alive for far longer than even he knew he deserved. He learned early on to blend in with other groups of handsome people so that he would not be memorable in the event that he was nearby when one of his plots took place. This had unfortunately happened several times in his career when a shot was taken too early or when bombs had detonated before he had a chance to leave the area. There were places in the world where he would not conduct his dirty business but would come to relax and plan. Although Italy had plenty of groups that he worked alongside it was a place that he enjoyed and he did not want to cause enough trouble to be hunted here. Here he would only consult. Unbeknownst to him, his inaction had sparked a conversation within a group of mid-level players of the Red Brigade who had bolstered their resolve for conflict and change after the 2002 assassination of Marco Biagi, the economic advisor to Prime Minister Berlusconi. That conversation involved doubts of Heminez's willingness or ability to continue on in the fight. Matt Hauer had picked up on Heminez as a possible face to the name Carlito, a man rumored to be a new Jackal, a sort of pole star for the terrorist movements of the world. Matt had wondered if this man, possibly multiple men playing the role, was not state funded. *What better way to fight a war than to have the populace at large start it and fight it?*

When he had been able to establish something concrete on Carlito, he put together an action package on the playboy who enjoyed fine dining, luxury casino hotels and beautiful women. The target package of this action plan is what Hauer had handed off to Karina in Switzerland. Karina had not slept on it. The techs at Wendover Utah and the Intelligence gatherers at Fort Huachuca Arizona had kept Jax abreast of developments with regards to the tracks they kept on Carlito and Karina. When Hauer and his team left Switzerland Karina had stayed but moved her operation to Locarno. The techs watched men and women breakdown their watch stations that had nearly duplicated those used by the Wraiths. They watched while plain clothes operators gathered in a pair of hotels and Karina made phone calls and worked on her own computer. Those calls were traced and the receivers were added to the track until there was a spiderweb of calls leading to a return call to Karina. She had effectively labeled ten heads of the Oprichniki for Hauer and McGuire. She had also put out a capture order on Yelena Burkowska and a kill on sight order for the rest, labeling them as defectors and enemies of Russia.

After Karina took her call back, she left her hotel in a cab that brought her to the airport where she and her team boarded a jet under diplomatic cover. When they landed in Milan the plane was met by four blue and white Land Rover Discovery's emblazoned with tall white letters 'Polizia' of the Italian police force. These cars took them to a pair of apartment buildings two blocks from the hotel where the operators unloaded and readied their gear. Karina entered Carlito's hotel in the company of a man in a black suit who, acting as a husband or lover, clung to her arm as they walked through the casino searching out the terrorist. Now dressed as Italian RIS agents in military uniforms as well as four plain clothed operators Karina's team moved to the hotel.

Carlito, the new Jackal, tossed his meager winnings of a drunken night at the craps table to a tall blonde woman at his right and walked away with his glass held in three fingers. A pair of tall and wide men who looked more Arab than Italian turned from where they had been half involved in games of their own and followed behind him as he walked to the gilded doors of an elevator. Another man, closer to Carlito's five foot ten stature, met them at the elevator and cleared the car when it arrived before letting them in. Karina watched and called out the floor number when it stopped. One of her plainclothes operators watched through a pegged door as the men emerged and cleared the hallway before walking Carlito to his room.

"I want three girls tonight. The best. The very best. What about you Amil?" He asked the thinner of the group.

"None tonight. I will be guarding tonight. Tomorrow."

"Tomorrow, tomorrow." Carlito laughed. "I never trust tomorrow to come. Seize the night."

"Wait for the girls." Karina said as she called her team to gather on the floor for their raid.

"The plane is refueled and ready Leshi." He used the name of a Slavic forest spirit, Karina's codename.

"Good. Wait." Karina said as she changed from her party dress into military gear in a custodians closet next to her partner. "He only has three here?"

"Life scan is reading only four in the room." One of her shooters answered as he watched the feed of a fiber optic snake, he was running under the door into Carlito's suite. He had worked it from a room next door and watched as another pair of his team placed shaped charges on the wall behind him.

"The call is out for the girls. Ten minutes."

"Ten minutes."

"There are two men with the girls. They look like his men."

"Take them when the door opens." Karina said.

One man in a suit with his right hand holding the grip of a submachine gun that kept popping from under the cover of the fabric of his coat walked in the front with the girls in the middle. Another brought up the tail. This one was left handed and shorter than all of the others. He was the most professional of the bunch. His moves were more calculated and his eyes were constantly moving. When they entered the hallway, he walked with his back to the crowd headed for the door.

"Alexa has the lead." A woman came over the radio.

"Stephan has Tail." Another man spoke.

"The knock." The camera operator spoke. "One guard coming. Carlito is at the balcony. Two at the bar."

"Lotta." Karina called out. Fight.

Two muffled shots hit the men in the hallway as a single thump. The heavy suppressed bullets from the 9x39mm AMB-17 rifles struck skull and brain and left lifeless bodies sagging against the door and the women of the night helping to clear the way for the raid team charging at them as the wall between the bedroom and the suite next door was blown away to let more bulky Russian soldiers through the dusty holes and into the mix. Six shooters fired into the two deafened and stunned guards. They died without looking at their leader but still trying to figure out what had happened. Neither got a shot off or heard the thunderous roar of the pair if shotguns that fired at Carlito from close range, crumpling him nearly in half to land face down on the floor.

"Libero." They called out over the radios in whispers.

Karina stepped into the room and passed back two rubber filled bags to her shooters as she grabbed the playboy terrorist by his hair to stare at his bloodied face and look into his milky blue eyes.

"Kazamir Ilya Ivanov. You are under arrest for crimes against Russia and against humanity." She punched him in the neck with a pair of brass knuckles and cuffed him while an operator bound his ankles and thighs with heavy zip ties. Another grabbed his shoulders. The men lifted him off of the ground while the others tossed the room for computers and money. In three minutes, they were inside the waiting Polizia Land Rovers and headed for the airport.

Their jet landed several hours later in Moscow. Carlito stayed with Karina at the SVR headquarters while the others disbursed. In less than half an hour Karina and Carlito boarded a helicopter to Kirov where they ended their journey in the basement of The Church of the Holy Great Martyr and Healer Panteleimon.

Hauer sat at the monitor eating a large medium rare steak and steamed vegetables. This was the second time he had taken the video in. He raised a glass of port to his lips, paused to smell it and finished chewing and frowned at the monitor before swishing the delicious wine in his mouth. He had not expected to catch all that he had just been privileged enough to watch. Without the assets of the fraternity, he would have none of that ability and might be lucky to catch glimpses of the hotel footage at best. He savored that power as much as he appreciated the wine that had once sat at the bottom of the ocean and been retrieved during a treasure hunt. A bottle whose brother had sold for over forty thousand dollars at auction.

"Codename Leschi." He said finally.

"Apropos." McGuire answered. "I believe that our friend would be impressed with the entire performance."

"But I don't think we have seen the end of act one." Shaw added.

"Doubtful." Jenn said. "Leshi is a Slavic folktale. A spirit that protects the woods. What do you think that gives us?"

"Her family traces its lineage back to power in northern Russia under the Tsars. She certainly has some powerful acquaintances." Matt told them. "She really wants to talk to Yelena. Let's see what happens with the little Jackal. That should give us a clue about Burkowska's fate."

"We identified three of her shooters. They are all people we saw in Syria and Iraq. All Zaslon." Shaw said referring to a special operations unit that the world had been able to gather little information on. "This is some super-secret squad."

"See if you can, trace family histories on any of them. They have to go back too. These are all old world thinkers. Old allegiances. The Kremlin did not order this. They'll be able to claim it as a success but the trigger is somewhere else."

"That's why you gave this to her." Jen said. "Not to repay a favor but to get her to show her hand."

Matt winked at her.

"Jax. Best guess on what that plane out of Siberia was." Matt asked after he had another piece of his steak and a sip of wine.

"Spasatel." Jax told him.

"For real?"

"What is that?" Jenn asked.

"Russian for Rescuer." McGuire frowned.

"Yeah. It was mentioned in the report filed by the research ship off of Wrangel. They listed it as wreckage and produced the footage without that picture of wing you picked up on. The Kremlin has written this bird or boat or whatever it is off and ordered three more."

"So, they're making a real push for arctic research." McGuire said.

"It definitely looks that way." Jax said.

"Alright. Put that on the list of shit for future Matt Hauer to worry about. In the meantime, I need a training program for this thing and I need it fast. Then I need you to get me some plans to get the hell out of Altai."

"Hang tight. We have traffic off that patio in Altai again and some in Hovsgol." Shaw said. "Coming over now." He pointed to his monitor.

North Carolina
0200

Maureen Collins-Roth was hungover. This was not out of the norm for her. The hangovers just seemed to be more frequent and more severe lately. Moving her attention from narcotics to sex traffic over the last year had changed her schedule so that parties, out of necessity for her clients, had become a near nightly occasion. She told herself that she wasn't in her twenties anymore while she dragged her bare feet through the cold sand as she made her way to the water. Even drunk she knew that just over her shoulder two men were watching her every move. It was their job to watch. She paid them for that. They were not good men. She hadn't seen many good men in a long time. Even her late husband had turned out not to be one. From what she had borne witness to over the last year there weren't many good women left either. *You can include yourself in that calculation.*

Good men scared her. Good men would eventually stop her if she didn't stop herself. She served on the Armed Services Committee and saw the good men training. She had visited the FBI

Headquarters several times and saw the people involved in the task forces hunting for traffickers just like her. She knew how talented and practiced these people were. It worried her. She knew how evil she had become. All for money. For the feeling of power. She knew that she would be caught eventually. *Maybe I want to be caught.*

It was only a mistake or the fact that she hadn't given up that had kept her alive. She told herself as her feet stepped into the water that she would have walked away and gone back to normal and legal businesses if it hadn't been for Casey. Casey was the mastermind. The taste manipulator. She had teased at every weakness and driven her desires with morsels until she was here. She wondered if she could have gotten a gun or a knife out of the beach house and taken it out here to stand naked before God and end her guilt in the cleansing water.

"There is no forgiveness for what you have done." She whispered.

She lifted the bottle of champagne to her lips and fought to keep her balance as she tilted her head back to drink and the waves came up to caress her legs, leaving her dress stuck to her thighs when the water receded. She undid the buttons at her back and let the dress fall away with the next wave. Naked with a half a bottle of warm champagne. *Now the boys have something to watch.*

"I don't want it." She told the night. "I don't want your forgiveness." She threw the bottle to the waves. She would not be drunk or drugged again. *There was too much to do.*

"You do realize that you're naked Maureen." Mattison asked when she walked through the living room that had been made to look more like a tax office with all of the computers and desks.

"You realize you aren't my father Holland. You should be on your way to Lake Charles rather than attempting to be my baby sitter."

"I believe it is part of what had us working together. You wanted me to make sure you did not slip."

"Slip how? Please enlighten me. You are rich. Beyond what you could have accomplished in ten lifetimes as a General. You do what you want when you want. I do the same." She opened her hands and spread her arms. "The empire awaits."

"You are starting to act like a drug queen rather that a Senator and a business mogul. That image is beginning to broadcast out there. You are one bender away from becoming the drunk meme of the day."

"I just drank my last. I know. This is not what I had planned for us. There is something else on our horizon. This however is a necessary evil to attain that goal. When we arrive in Mongolia we will do so to golden palaces on earth without fear of reprisal. But here is where I am guilty. Even though we have to do this, we do not have to swim in it. Like those two you bedded last night? Go to Lake Charles and make sure things are being done right and then go home to your wife Holland."

Casey watched them on her phone screen and listened on a pair of earbuds. The cameras she had found were ridiculously small and easy to install. They picked up everything she needed. She squinted as they talked. She heard enough to know that she was alone in the world. These people had never been people she could trust. If she could have ever trusted anyone. She wondered if Maureen had not set things up in Vermont and New York to clean the road for herself. But, why kill the cartel and keep Holland? Why keep her? Why had the Senator invested so much into her before she had come up with their financial windfall? This bitch had a plan for everyone. Everyone in her life was there to move her forward. What is her plan for me? *What the fuck is in Mongolia? Why has she not said a thing about it to me?*

Keeping the microphone on, Casey changed screens to a bank and looked at her deposits for the night. She rubbed her tired eyes and moved money to yet another account. She needed to travel in the morning. Before she laid her head on the pillow again, she checked the Glock pistol beside her and set her alarm for seven. *Not nearly long enough.*

North Western Nebraska

HAUER SAT ON THE BACK porch of the lodge wrapped in a buffalo blanket with a cup of strong coffee in his hands. Thoughts of his parents, his time in the Navy, his business, Mongolia, Jenn Beck and Karina raced through his head at an uncontrollable pace. He could not make sense of some of it. Others he wanted to isolate and maintain his focus on. He stared at the frost on stalks of wheat that the thousand head of bison roaming this seven thousand acre ranch had not chewed on yet. He rubbed at the stubble on his chin and watched antelope prick their ears as they stood up to greet the day. The sun was rising. Tiny meadowlarks with their broad yellow breasts flittered about between the lodge and the enormous barns collecting the bits and strands that they could to sustain them for another day. They cared about none of his troubles. None of his loves, his hates, his losses. They only knew peace. Because he could worry about all that they didn't, because he could love or hate, he owed them their peace. He chose to allow his head to run, else it drive him mad. He let the bitter coffee sit in his mouth the way a smoker would hold a drag that they would relish for a moment of silent peace. There would be no knowing when the next one would come.

As if to put an exclamation on the last thought, the antelope shot their heads high and bolted away to the west. The birds climbed higher in the air and flew away. The air pulsed now. Propellers beat the air until the ground vibrated around him. Turbine engines banished silence. The first aircraft to come into sight was a tan six engine turbo prop cargo plane that he knew as the VC-160 Eagle. The Eagle was the next step in tilt-rotor aircraft like the V-22 Osprey designed for the U.S. military as the need for a fleet of STOL/VTOL (Short Takeoff Or Landing/ Vertical Takeoff or Landing) aircraft was on the rise as the country dealt with the changes of modern war fighting. The Eagle was meant to supplement and ultimately replace the venerable C-130 Hercules Cargo plane. Although larger than the Herc, the Eagle was faster and more fuel efficient. Its size allowed it to carry more troops or a pair of main battle tanks if necessary.

This first Eagle was transitioning its wings from forward flight to vertical so that its engines were pitched vertically and began its decent to the frozen ground where Buhr and Shaw flashed lights at the pilots and waited for the passengers to unload. Front and rear ramps were lowered to allow more than one hundred men in cold weather camouflage gear haul their heavy backpacks and weapons away under the direction of the Wraiths. Six more Eagles came and left in the next twenty minutes. Jenn Beck stood behind him while the last one unloaded.

"This is where things start to get real?" She asked.

"Yeah kid. We ain't turning back now."

"Matt. I know you're busy but, you might want to take a look at some things." Jax said from the door.

"We back tracked satellite passes to the night of the train wreck in Siberia. It happened about ten miles outside of Sludjanka, a stop at the bottom of Lake Baikal. It had a scheduled stop in Sludjanka and one in Irkutsk that it obviously didn't make. It did however make a stop in the middle of nowhere about twenty minutes before it crashed. It was stopped for almost an hour between 230 a.m. and 326 a.m. local. We got several passes on that stop. As you can see there are horses and men all around the train and leading north back toward the lake."

"North?" Matt asked.

"Yeah. I thought that was weird so I spec'd out more coverage and I found this." She changed tabs to show a full screen shot of a grey airplane on the ice at the shore of Lake Baikal as horses and men gathered around it."

"Tell me that you know where that went and where the horses went." Hauer said.

"The horses broke into six directions. A lot of them went into Russia. The plane made a low level flight into western Mongolia ending close to the Chinese boarder where we catch the tail end on a lake moving into a mountain."

"That's one of the chemical sites, correct?" Jenn asked.

"The second largest concentration."

"That's an Ekranoplan right?" Matt asked. "That's the Spasatel."

"A big one. Given the wing structure I would say it's a class C." Jax said.

"Meaning that it can fly ground effect or get up higher as an airplane." Jenn said.

"When are we going to have travel plans?"

"By the end of the day I'll have multiple routes to each site worked out."

"What's the biggest thing we've taken down with Hooligans laser system?"

"We tested on a T-90 tank at a one second burst to penetrate the hull and ignite the ammo. We hit a bunker of four foot thick steel reinforced concrete under thirty feet of packed ground with a second and a half burst. We have six shots at that magnitude before a five minute reset and cool."

"Okay." He said and nodded while he looked at the screen for a moment before heading out to the barn.

More than a thousand personnel representing some of the most elite soldiers and scientists that America had defending it were seated on bleachers that were meant for cattle auctions. They had split up into their respective units and waited for someone to tell them what was next. Shaw had taken control of the gathering and had kept the noise low while waiting for Hauer to take the reins. To the crowd Matt must have looked suspicious as he took the makeshift stage in civilian clothing and took off his heavy hide coat before taking a microphone from Shaw. Several officers throughout the barn yelled out 'Attention.' The place went silent.

"Good Morning. You have been gathered at the request of the President. Some of you are recognized as being some of the best high speed low drag special operators in the world and some of you are the best scientists and chemical emergency specialists the world has ever known. We have a mission folks. One that we hope the larger population will never hear about. If we are successful only, we and the President will be aware of what has been accomplished. We will be mobilized, but I don't know when yet. It will not be weeks. I have a lifetime hero in John Paul Jones who is quoted as saying 'I wish to have no connection with any ship that does not sail fast; for I intend to go in harm's way.' Ladies and gentlemen make no mistake, we are going in harm's way. Colonel Shaw and Commander Buhr will speak with your officers and will break you into units. Get to know each other in the time that we have. Officer's review the materials you are given and we will have a conference this evening."

Hauer passed the microphone off to Shaw and waved at Jesse Randall to follow him. He forced himself to hold his head up as he walked. The sight of young faces bothered him today. Yes, he had given them strong words and yes, he would afford them incredible leadership but he was afraid of the level of combat they would face if the world went bad. He caught sight of Luke Webb as he descended the steps from the stage. He cocked his head directing the man to join him.

"Jesse." Matt spoke up once they were back inside the lodge and in Matt's office. "I want you to take Kim back into Mongolia as a lead element. I see this prick being at one of two places. I want you at one of them. Who do you want with you?"

"I'll take Kevin."

"Done. Kim is wrapping up at Wendover. Kevin is helping Brett right now. Bounce in say an hour?"

"You got it. See you on the other side."

"Damn right. Steaks on me." Hauer gave the man a hard hug.

Luke Webb sat back in his leather chair facing Matt for the first time in a month. He had let his once high and tight State Trooper haircut grow out into a couple inches of shaggy brown locks and let a couple days of scruff build on his face but his serious eyes were ever present. Hauer pushed himself away from the desk and took a breath as he steeled himself to deliver the news he had for the man.

"Luke, I wanted to talk to you first. I think that this is not for me to give to Jessica."

"I can respect that. What's going on?"

"I'm working a case that holds some deadly shit. A big piece of that led me back to a person of some power in the states. This is a big mission we are undertaking as you can see from the assets, we just pulled in. It's a bit beyond our normal ops. This particular target only recently came on our radar and as I've dug into their life, I realized that they crossed paths with your tragedy. In fact, they were fundamental in it. If my plan is to work, this target has to be taken simultaneously with several others that are stretched across a big map. Your team has been incredible in the field and I think it's justice to give this to you. There would be one caveat."

"What is that?"

"We need to be able to question them and then we need to make their death look like suicide or something other than murder. Quite a bit cleaner than that job in Albany."

Webb flexed his right hand and took a breath.

"Thanks for coming to me. Am I wrong in the assumption that this person is highly placed in our government?"

"Pretty high."

"I trust your discretion on this. I won't lie. I just want to bleed them out but, I'll facilitate everything that we need."

"I'll have a trace on this for you today."

"You sure you don't need me anywhere else?"

"For now, this is the path we're going to take."

Chapter Eleven

"The world is a dangerous place to live; not because of the people who are evil, but because of the people who don't do anything about it."

Albert Einstein
Theoretical Physicist and Nobel Prize Winner

Altai Mountains

Yelena Burkowska sat at the top of a bolder fifteen feet above the rocky shore of the lake. She watched the villagers of the urdo milling about their encampment and the horsemen and camel drivers coming in from the mountains. She wasn't sure if this was the same group of nomads that she had watched ride out weeks before or if it was another circuit. With Temuchin she could not be certain how many people he would allow to know where this place was.

It was cold today. There was snow in the higher mountains and she was sure it would be down here soon. When it did come, she knew it would be cold here in a way that she had never truly known. Colder even than the night she left Siberia. She knew too that she would be stuck inside for months. She envied the people in the Yurts. They seemed hardy enough to tolerate the winter and unlike their purely nomadic ancestors they would have food and fuel supplied by Temuchin to survive the winter. A winter that would change the way they lived their lives forever.

She watched the men of the caravan greeted by loved ones and friends as they unloaded their cargoes of food and weapons. It was mostly small arms this time. She couldn't tell what kind of guns and didn't care. She had the only gun she ever wanted to have sitting in a holster under her thick coat and had no intention of needing more. Her weapons would end entire countries and she didn't have to get messy in their usage. There were men around her for the messy work. Men who took joy in it. Purely psychopathic men that she realized were necessary for the world to witness true change. Long ago she had learned that she was attracted to the brutality of such men. She had also been smart enough to notice that they were attracted to her. The fact that their attraction was a weakness that she could bend to her own desires was a tool she learned to wield at a young age. And Yelena Burkowska desired much in this life.

She took a satellite phone from her deep pockets and waited for a signal. Once it was there, she checked bank accounts in Peru and Switzerland to reassure herself that her money was safe. She then searched the web for traces of her name. When she found nothing new, she killed the power to the phone and laid it back in her pocket to watch the men from the caravan feed a pair of eagles wearing blinders as another pair pulled the hides of a half dozen wolves from the backs of their horses.

"Your throne does not quite suit you Tsarina." The man spoke from below her feet. "It is already extremely cold."

"I wanted some fresh air Dmitry. There is only so much time I can spend in a box within a box feeling like a nesting doll." She told the big man beneath her as she scrambled off of the boulder.

"With your work complete we have only to wait it would seem."

"I don't know how long I am willing to wait. How long for the plane?"

"A week or more." He said. "The storms are coming. There will be snow here tomorrow." He admired her small frame even under her thick coat. "You won't want to be out here for more than minutes when that starts. Even when the plane is ready, we have to wait for Temuchin to begin before we make our move."

"Can we get far enough away?"

"Of course. That is why we chose this machine."

"It's only good to us if it works." She said. "How is everyone?"

"The men and your doctors seem good. The Minister is miserable as usual."

"When it is time Dmitry, his misery should end. He and the doctors, have served their purpose."

"More room on the plane." He said and looked across the lake at the base of a tall sandstone mountain. Where the water met the cliff there was an enormous door. Behind that door he knew was their escape plan. It had gotten them out of Siberia and there was no reason it should not get them out of here as well.

"WHAT WOULD IT HURT to shoot them both right now?" Keong Saik asked the much taller man standing at his left while they watched the Russians below them. From their recessed patio dug into the mountain centuries before they were born the two men had a view of the whole upper valley for miles.

"Because they are still useful." Temuchin answered without looking away from the Russians. "As long as they are useful, they will live. I hope that she remains useful beyond her ability to sit on a throne in Russia. Shaposhnikov will not live outside of Mongolia."

"Very good."

"She will be the only one from that group that does live beyond the winter."

"Do you trust her to hold her end of the bargain once she takes power?"

"No. I don't trust anyone Keong. Trust is for fools and children. She will take power in a nation like all other nations that we allow to exist. One lacking the power to stand against us. The world will understand that soon enough. Much as your sniper rifle there holds Shaposhnikov's life in its teeth the world does not yet realize that it is at the mercy of Mongolia." He clapped his enormous hands together and smiled down the thousand yards at the little specks of people around the lake below him and walked back inside of his fortress.

"Did you get a glimpse of him or just get voices?" Matt asked Jax as he took a seat next to her and her monitor.

"We have one hundred percent on the two Russians and a great side face hit at Saik. It's pretty solid on Chu. He's grown a thick beard but, the system still put his bone structure together. Him being seven feet tall didn't hurt the math either. That's him."

"We have all of the players accounted for then." Shaw declared.

"What was she doing on that rock?" Matt asked.

"Checking her bank statement." Jax said.

"There is dissention in the ranks." Shaw smiled. "That's a tool we can use."

"I wonder if we'll have time to capitalize on it."

"What is the most remote site that has a trace of the chemical?" Matt asked.

"Right now, there is a caravan hauling artillery shells across the border into China. They look like they are headed to a site that could target Beijing." Jax said.

"How big is the caravan?" Matt asked.

"Eighteen men. Fifty horses." She told him.

"How close to ready are we Colonel?"

"We can move the teams to staging points within the hour. They are ready to infiltrate within a day."

"Where is Jesse's team right now?"

"Digging hides to overlook the Hovsgol site." Shaw told him.

"Let's mobilize to the pre-stage site now." Matt told them. "As soon as we are there, I want you to fry communications on that caravan and then I want you to make it dust." He told Jax.

"Can do."

"Can we get a drone into that mountain?"

"We don't have anything close enough that is that small to avoid detection. And we don't know that it would be able to signal back from within the mountain. That thing has super high iron content.

And we have to imagine they have electronic shielding. This asshole mimics so much of Bin Laden that it makes my skin crawl."

"If you have to get a second and third Hooligan covering that please do. I want constant coverage on these people."

"Matt." Jen turned in her chair. "Mac has something he wants to discuss with you. In private."

"Shit." Shaw pushed his seat back. "I'm gonna take a walk."

"What's up?" Jennifer asked Jax as the men walked away. Shaw stepped outside to walk in the Nebraska prairie in the night sky and Matt moved upstairs to his room.

"The last time Mac called for a private meeting we had a mission scrubbed and we were within minutes of launch. People we could have saved died. Brett took that mission hard."

"He's worried that'll happen with this thing?"

Jax just nodded.

"Load it all up we are moving to Utah now." Matt said when he came back into the room ten minutes later.

"You gonna fill us in?"

"Yeah. We are gearing up. And we just found out how these people are making their money. It ain't good and we are hoping an old team guy with some nasty friends is down for the job."

"Oh boy." Shaw said and start breaking down equipment.

Sneads Ferry
North Carolina

Joel Conrad had two missions to accomplish. After his night with Maureen Roth his mind was clear on the track that his life had to take from here, if he could salvage it. There was nothing on his computers of phones to tie him to anything in Mongolia other than that he had been Kim's handler. Unless someone in Roth's pool of friends dropped his name, he was not likely to fall with them. If they did fall, his life simply diverted back to a position at the CIA and whatever he chose to do. He did still have the traffic he worked on the side through Casey Glencamp. A side hustle that Maureen had no idea that he was deeply involved in. One that she could not know.

He had to clear his head of all of these thoughts if he was going to achieve the mission ahead of him. The sun was still a few hours from coming up when he clipped himself to the hull of the G&S 51-foot fishing boat that belonged to ex-Navy Seal Chief Petty Officer Kendall Pierce. Kendall was a creature of habit now that he was back in civilian life and his war was over. After two failed marriages in his ten years in the Teams Pierce hadn't wanted to try that road again and dedicated his time to chartering his boat throughout the week. Tuesdays were typically his day off and today just so happened to be a Tuesday. Day off or not Ken was on the water before the sun rose. The pattern that Conrad saw was that his old teammate would power out to the Intracoastal Waterway and cruise until stopping for lunch at a pub in Surf City. There would be no lunch today for Pierce, or any other day.

Conrad chose a heavier dry suit for the dive, knowing that the water would be far colder than he wanted to attempt handling for the time he needed in a wetsuit. He hated that its bulk would slow him down and hoped that he would be able to maintain the element of surprise for the duration of this mission. Any deviation from his plan was abject failure in his mind. He knew that he could easily kill Ken several ways, including shooting him. That was not a course he wanted to take because it made everything way too complicated. There was only one way that he believed could make it look like anything other than the murder that it was. Flexing his arms and legs, he slowed his breathing to make the best use of his twin 80 cubic foot tanks. If Pierce kept to his habit, he would be aboard and firing up the engines in five minutes and would be underway in fifteen maximum.

Ken Pierce pulled into the crushed stone and seashell lot of the marina parked near his boat and killed the ignition on his new Jeep

Rubicon. The boat was work in his mind and the Jeep was the one luxury he had afforded himself in the last few years. He just didn't buy stuff he didn't need. Even the Oakley sunglasses he almost forgot on the dash were nearly twenty years old. With a small backpack and a pair of beat up tan canvas flip flops in tow he left the Jeep and let himself through the gate to the docks and his boat.

The engines started without issue as he should expect from his investment and Kendal Pierces time on earth began to wind down. By the time he had tossed the mooring lines to the dock the fuel pumps had pumped fuel into a pool under the pilot house. A line that Conrad had run through the boat knowing that it would burn away in the fire sprayed fuel throughout the front of the cabin. As Pierce pushed the sleek white vessel out into the flow of the New River Conrad released his carabiner that held him to the hull and dropped away. A small hotplate that Conrad left one in the galley was licked by the first wafts of gasoline fumes and then the liquid itself and exploded in predictable fashion. At thirty feet below the surface Conrad felt none of the over pressure but saw the orange flash. The engines kept going and kept pumping gasoline into the inferno. There was no way for Pierce to survive.

Conrad kicked hard into the tide of the river and allowed it to carry him toward the waterway and away from Camp Lejeune on the opposite side of the river. He stayed under water long after he passed the wreckage and only surfaced after he had shed his diving gear and could climb into the long red kayak tied up alongside someone sport fisher. Once aboard the tiny boat he ran the small electric outboard and pretended to paddle his way through sunrise until he was near Topsail beach where he ditched the kayak and found his car in the lot of one of the last cheap motels left on the beach.

He was able to search Pierce's home before the locals arrived. There was nothing to indicate that the ex-SEAL had taken any interest in Conrad or any of his associates. Kendall Pierce had been a useless kill. That left him with one suspect. Matt Hauer.

Nebraska

"MATT YOU'RE NOT GONNA like this." Jax called out from across the big living room where Matt sat with his laptop.

"It honestly can't be any worse than all of this crap we've got going on in Mongolia."

"It's part of the same problem. It's Avery and Roth and the whole ball of wax." She told him as she approached.

"Fire away."

"Roth is the link to Mongolia but she's got a bunch of little pawns including Avery. Avery, Roth and Belfran are all linked to one guy in D.C. He shows up again for me twice with Belfran in Burkina Faso two years ago. This is where we pick up Avery in company with this group."

"Do we know who it is?"

"That's the part you won't like." She frowned. "It's an ex-Navy Seal named Joel Conrad. He works for CIA now."

Hauer moved the laptop to the side and sat up while twisting his lips in thought. As his face hardened, he shook his head and sighed through his nose. He flexed the fingers of both hands before clenching them into fists. In a moment he relaxed and looked back over to her and to Shaw who had joined the conversation.

"Someone should figure out how the hell Conrad even got into the Agency for one. The guy was fired from the Teams and subsequently separated from service after complaints in Iraq. Now you're telling that he is attached to a spec ops guy turned terrorist and to Roth?"

"It gets worse." Shaw spoke up. "He was Tan Ting Kim's handler. We have to assume his rapid departure from Mongolia garnered some attention. Conrad may be a piece of shit, but he's an intelligent piece of shit."

"The worst kind." Matt shook his head. "How the hell did we not know this? Do we have a track on him?"

"He's in D.C. as of five minutes ago."

"We can't act on him without alerting all of the others and we aren't ready to move on anything yet." Jax told him.

"Perfect. I need someone to keep an eye on him for a bit." Matt said. "How does this affect Kim's status?"

"Doctor Quarrels gives him a solid pass. To him Conrad was just a contact." Shaw told him. "Kim is dedicated to this."

Altai Mountains

"SEND THE MANGUDAI OUT to the camps. Begin making the preparations. Give the camps at the border no orders until it is time to launch. I want no defectors. The Mangudai are to maintain order." Temuchin spoke. "Keong it is time for you to retrieve your wife and your chosen staff. In one week I will close the doors and gather in the caravans to the lake. These doors will not open again until summer. Your airplane is ready."

"It is well then Temuchin. After next week I can return to my name."

"Indeed. The nine tails will celebrate your return."

"Until then."

"If you cannot make it you must go to the fields in Africa."

"Yes." The man hugged the giant before bowing and leaving the upper floors of the palace.

Temuchin stretched to his full height so that his enormous back let out a series of cracks and squinted his eyes at the passing of the General that he hoped he could count on. None of these people he had around him could he call friend. Not a true friend. He had not had one since he was a child and that boy died before they had reached their teens. He had not allowed himself to grow close to another person after that. Said was the only one that he held out hope for, even then it was the other man who would have to prove himself. Temuchin sighed through his nose as the realization that the General had left the confines of paradise to retrieve his wife, it was obvious that the man's loyalties were somewhere other than the Khanate.

Twenty minutes later a Chinese Shaanxi Y-9 turbo prop transport left the grassy fields of the Altai valley as the snow began to come down. It flew low until crossing into China and declared itself as having taken off from a military outpost near the Gobi desert. Its destination was Beijing.

"Son of a bitch." McGuire yelled out.

"Okay. We have a timeline. Jax, can we train anywhere besides here?"

"That could be dangerous. We just aren't there yet. You really need to be under the eye of Benedetti and Quarrels for that."

"Alright. You can run things from here when we leave. Stay here unless we call for you. I need your brain right here."

"Okay, okay. I promise."

"Good. How soon can you get that training scheme?"

"Probably by the time you finish figuring out your gun collection."

"Get on it then cause we are going to get our hunting licenses. After you two wake up you need to meet up with the Altai team and be ready for the go call." He told Shaw and Beck.

"I want to know how deep this thing goes into China and what he knows about Roth's other programs."

"Like Africa." Shaw said.

"Like Africa. Namely slave labor in Africa."

Chapter Twelve

"It is an unfortunate fact that we can secure peace only by preparing for war."

John F. Kennedy

35th President of the United States

Utah
13 October

"IT JUST KEEPS GETTING better." Shaw mumbled after hearing the playback.

"It sounds like we have a deadline." Malone offered.

"You three load out for Altai." Hauer addressed Beck, Shaw and Benedetti. "Hopefully I'll catch up with you in Pakistan. Otherwise, you'll leave my gear at the LZ."

"Where are you going?" Beck asked.

"To get Saik."

"Alone?" She frowned.

"I need you three at Altai. It is still the priority." Hauer told her.

"What's your load out?" Shaw asked.

"Ski's, sled, field gear, LMT MARS-H set up for sniping. There's a couple in my locker. CQB-Honey Badger, SIG 320, 5 pounds of C-4, caps, Det cord and eight M-26 grenades."

"The MARS-H. You Really are hunting bear." Beck said.

"7.62 rarely fails to stop a hundred and eighty pound man." Benedetti offered.

"Fair enough." Beck nodded. "What happens if you miss the jump?"

"I'll have to make a secondary." Hauer gave her a smile. "Oh, and Sarn' Major be sure to pack the climbing racks. I'm sure that nobody has bolted our pitches."

"Aye, aye sir." Shaw shook his head and left the room.

Maryland

Carl MacManus led Deke and Angela Hassen through the mansion to the library and into Matt's office and armory where Mitch McGuire and James McCarthy, waited at the desk for them. Deke was still getting used to wearing and exercising with his new prosthetic right leg but would not accept the wheelchair once he left the hospital. He used crouches but tried to focus his efforts on using the leg. The work made him sweat.

Both men stood to greet them when they entered and held their chairs back once Carl had closed the door to their meeting.

"This is a rather informal setting for some formal conversation. It does allow a level of privacy that the rest of the house and the hospital could not afford us." MacManus told them.

"How are the two of you?" Mitch asked.

"Good considering." Deke answered.

"Like a fish out of water. But everyone has been exceptional. Of course, we are grateful to Matt but, to all of you as well. Thank you."

"It's an honor." James told her.

"I can't speak for Matt on specifics but he is beside himself that he can't be here right now." Mitch told them. "Part of that is my fault and part of that is because Matt put himself in a role in the world which often takes him away. To that point, he has chosen, wisely, to surround himself with a close network of people he can rely on with little or no input from him to handle things while he is away." Mitch told them. "Since he lost his mother and father it has fallen on the three of us to look out for him and to keep the businesses staffed with people who could lead them in the right directions."

"Matthew has agreed that Mitchell already has a herculean task before him with the profession that they share. James and I have selected and hired several CEO's and managers in the last few years but they have lacked the ability to maintain the values and the forward vision of Matt and choose their own way. We need someone who will look out for those things and add to the equation. But, also help us look out for him as well."

"Matt wants both of you to consider running everything." James spoke up. "We would all act as a board but the two of you would be the chairmen. You would be the ones traveling to each of the offices and facilities to keep the pulse. The five of us are the closest thing that he has to family and it would mean the world to him and to us to have the two of you driving things."

"How does that work exactly?" Deke asked.

"For now, you would take up residence here. There is a suite we will redecorate to your choosing. Staying at the mansion is not mandatory. You will have all staff, properties and transportation at your disposal. You would meet all of the leadership at each facility and begin to act as their compass." Carl told him. "We meet weekly at the least, preferably here."

"What do you think babe?" Angela asked.

"This is to happen with minimal input from Matt?" Deke asked.

"Often zero. His words are that you would act as if it were him speaking. I can't divulge his other work but, I can tell you that things just changed dramatically and he will be busier than he has been. Hauer holdings running smoothly will allow us to help maintain his sanity. With five of us we should be able to retain our own as well." Mitch told him.

"It's this or South America." Deke told Angela.

"You guys are only on ice until Matt is done with this job. You are not in witness protection." Mitch told them.

"There is a place in Brazil as well, yes. I think you may remember visiting." Carl told him. "But that is not the life you want."

"We're sold." Angela told them. "When do we start?"

"Straight away."

North Carolina

CASEY GLENCAMP SAT at the kitchen table in her pajamas and socks drinking coffee with too much sugar and creamer while she rubbed her eyes looking at the night setting on the beach and opened her laptop. Tony Aiser sat to the side of the table out of the way of her view of the beach pondering whether or not to poke the bear by confronting her about how she was living life. He chose to leave it alone and wait for her to get herself together and engage him before he said anything. He lit a cigarette and sipped at his own coffee. Casey adjusted herself and took one of his cigarettes and with a look at his brass zippo and a silent nod from the man she flicked it open and held the edge of the nerve restoring death sentence and inhaled deeply. Her headache, the hangover, was not going to go away because she had a cigarette or even a cup of too sweet coffee but she would be able to think clearly. It seemed that all she had been able to do lately was think. None of it had been clear. She knew that. But she also knew that she might not be paranoid if she was dealing with Maureen Roth. There were few reasons for her to trust the Senator. Of those reasons, she decided that there were none that were not strategic moves by the woman. Something was wrong. She checked her three bank accounts. Another drag of the cigarette was the cover for a sigh of relief that everything of hers was in order. She told herself that she needed to stop the partying for a while to give her head and body a break. It was driving her crazy. Why would Maureen turn on her? She had made Maureen richer than she could have dreamed. *Because she didn't do it herself. She can't handle the thought of you having control.*

Casey did have control. She had established the network that paid them for their dark activities. Because she had she knew where the money went. She had access to both of their bank accounts. So, she checked them. The cigarette was now smoked in frustration. An anger and frustration that she could not contain or hide from

Tony. Tony Aiser had known for all of his adult life not to trust anyone. He was loyal to Casey because she paid him, more money and more often than he had expected. The other two he had no desire to be loyal to. The General had insured his employment but his position in the world offered him nothing. He would have respected the man more if he had maintained an allegiance to his country. He had nothing but disdain for him. Especially knowing the man's fantasy world. He had watched all three of them fall into a world of depravity in a short amount of time as people became a commodity to them. Money had become nothing more than a number and every new sick thought was acted on. He knew the first night he saw the General leave the room with young boys that he could kill all of them. Casey included. Maybe her first. He told himself that they were too connected to power to simply shoot them and walk away. Something would come for him if he did. For him to run from this was going to take a lot of money. He would likely have to kill the other men working with them as well. There were a bunch of big ifs. His exit plan was constantly being revised. But there was a dollar figure that he would need to support not only a life but a life style. As that number drew nearer, he remained doubtful of the outcome. Watching Casey tense up at her computer screen he knew that the world was about to change and wondered if he should just shoot her in the side of the head now and walk away.

"What did you do?" Casey whispered. Her voice sounded demonic. She spoke as she exhaled smoke which only increased the image. "You evil cunt."

Tony decided to remain silent and leave her to her work. He poured more coffee for her, cutting down the sugar and cream. He watched her shake with anger as she typed and read to type and read some more. It seemed to go faster each time she did until she growled and pushed the computer away.

"Do you have men who are like you that you can get together quickly?"

"Some yeah." He said and lit another cigarette as he cracked the patio door open.

"You can train men to fight like you did?"

"No problem. It's better if they have any experience."

"It would seem that my associates have cut me out of a very lucrative enterprise. One I'm not sure I would have wanted to be involved with. They made an alliance with some people I met and did do some business with but, I was cut out."

"What now?"

"Now I shut down the world that I created for them and I disappear."

"That might not be as easy as you think Casey. If it's bad enough, what they are involved in might bring down some heavy hands. The justice department frowns pretty fucking hard on all of the shit you guys have been dealing in."

"Yeah, no shit. Wait until I tell you what I think they're up to."

"How many guys do you need?"

"I need protection and then I want to be able to fight a war."

"No, you don't."

"How the fuck do you know?"

"Because you are one of the smartest people I've ever met. Intelligent people do everything in their power to stay out of wars. Because you have already dodged a huge bullet with that guy that killed your friend in New York and because you have a chance to bust loose and shut them both down."

"How do I do that?"

"We walk away now. Then when we are away from this house you run your back channel that you just did to ventilate their accounts and you end them."

"What if I got them together again and we killed them?"

"Sounds great but, there are way too many moving pieces to that puzzle. The Senator is a devious bitch who has the defense that you see which is already a hell of a gunfight but because of how deceptive she is you can count on double what you see set up outside. We would never get a mile from that hit." He told her. "Can you dump intel on them without it sticking to you?"

"Maybe."

"Think about that then. Get us a way out of the country for now. Pack so that we can roll out in five minutes flat."

"I have a way out."

"Where?"

"Saint Augustine."

Wendover Utah

Jax Malone sat in her office watching the tags on the bank accounts and tracking the feedback to a wi-fi router at Senator Roth's beach house in North Carolina. She turned the laptop and the cell phones in the house into listening devices. From the electronic feeds she was able to watch Casey Glencamp on her own cameras as she frantically moved about the house to collect things she would escape with. With the camera feed she was able to identify Anthony Aiser and relayed all of the information to Hauer and McGuire.

"Did our Texan friend accept the offer?" Matt asked.

"He did." McGuire said.

"Get him to Saint Augustine please. I want Luke to intercept our young mastermind."

"I have eyes on Ms. Roth."

"You want to pounce with Luke on that I'm assuming." Matt said.

"As soon as you are in Mongolia."

"I'm almost to Beijing now."

Richmond Hill
Georgia
0150

Casey slept as Tony pulled the Selenite Grey Mercedes AMG GT 63S off of I-95 and into the truck stop for gas and coffee. He fueled the thirsty grand tourer with a credit card that was immediately thrown away and paid for the coffee and carton of cigarettes with cash. He was completely unaware of the blimp watching him from a hundred thousand feet up, the helicopter hovering five hundred yards away and two hundred feet above or of the three heavily modified black Dodge Challengers Hellcats coming his way on I-95 south. He looked at the fog hanging low in the pines and at the lights of the idling trucks in the lot and streaking along the highway and got back in the car. Lighting a cigarette as he sped up the onramp, he checked the radar detector and seeing all green lights he sped up to ninety and turned on the radio. He couldn't help himself and stole a glance at Casey's cleavage through the wide top of her white t-shirt. He cursed her for ever having slept with him. Or was it more accurately his fault. Either way she was a weakness for him now. It was made worse because he couldn't tell if she was a tease in a playful or hurtful way. Usually, it was worse than this. Usually, she wore short skirts and would let more be revealed. He had to fight that weakness now. She had come to him with this problem and she was relying on him to get them both through it. He moved her hoodie over to cover her chest and she curled herself into a tighter ball in her slumber. *Stay focused or die.*

With the press of a button Jax Malone sent a laser pulse from the Hooligan blimp that shut the car off. The lights and the engine died at the same time for Tony Aiser. He was only able to steer and use his breaks to get the car off of the highway. The Challengers came in with their lights off. With nothing coming north and nothing ahead of them on the highway he found himself wrapped in fog in the dark.

His night vision goggles were in his backpack in the backseat exactly where they would do him no good.

"Wake up Casey we have a problem."

"What?" She bitched. "What the fuck now?"

"The car is dead. We're walking."

As soon as the car stopped, he threw his door open and moved for the rear door. He had enough time to hear the screaming whistle of superchargers and the barely muffled growl of high strung American V8's before a 275 grain solid copper 338 Norma Magnum bullet entered the left brow ridge just above his eye as he tensed up and looked for the sound while drawing his pistol. The pistol cleared only enough of the holster to fall away, hitting the ground right before his lifeless body fell beside it. The Challengers came to a stop and shadows surrounded Casey's side of the car ripping her out and onto the loose gravel in the breakdown lane to frisk her.

"Who the fuck are you? I want my lawyer. I own your fucking badges." She screamed as they stripped away the pistol, she hadn't even processed the need to grab for before it was too late.

"The next time you speak it will be when I tell you to. Tell me that you understand that." The woman told her as she pressed what Casey thought must be the barrel of a gun into her mouth.

"I understand." She mumbled around the now wet pistol.

"Guys. Awesome work. We'll take the car and you tail us." Luke Webb told the Strike team. "Get her in the back."

"It's jammed up with bags." Ex-Army sniper Robbie Williams said.

"Get them into the other cars then. We arrive in this and Miss Glencamp and I have some things to talk about." She told him.

"Fair enough."

Doctor Jessica Webb sat next to Glencamp in the back of the car while Luke drove and Robbie brought up his laptop to talk with Jax. Glencamp sat in her seatbelt with her hands zipped and cuffed behind her. It was one of the most uncomfortable positions she had ever found herself in. The pain of her wrists and tailbone was enough to make her teeth cut into her lower lip in the fight against sobbing. It was only going to get worse, she thought. Even in the dim blue light coming from the gauges she could see that these people were professional killers and they wanted something from her.

"How much did she give you for this?" She asked. "I can give you more. I can give you millions."

"You already have dear." Jessica brought her closed hand down on Casey's left thigh so hard that the girl did not feel the needle puncture skin or dig into her muscle. "I told you not to speak if I didn't tell you to. Any infraction of that rule will be met with pain. You have not felt pain yet."

Casey watched the man at the wheel and saw the sets of headlights in the mirror behind them. She knew that she was done. Whatever life she had known before and whatever she thought she had been running to were now things of fantasy. Every time a white line on the highway flicked under the car, she was a step further into the deep dark hole of her future. This understanding, more than the pain, brought on her tears. She would cry but, she would not give this woman the satisfaction of hearing her sob.

"I'm going to say names and you are going to tell me yes or no."

"Fuck you bitch."

"This needle in your leg contains a concoction of alcohol and chemicals that will first cause your muscles to burn in pain. The agony is said to be much like having your bones pulled apart. Doses larger than a few milliliters will cause atrophy over time. It is irreversible. The administration of this much chemical would cause enough pain to lose consciousness. Enough pain potentially kill you. I will inject some of this into you the next time you fail to answer correctly and I will continue to wake you back up so that we can proceed. Try not to urinate or defecate on my new leather seats."

"Yes."

"Good. You are beginning to understand. Maureen Collin-Roth, this should be an easy start."

"Yes."

"Good. General Holland Mattison."

"Yes."

"Beals. What was his name? Randy Beals."

Casey sat up hard enough for the cuffs to dig into her wrists with an audible crunch. Her lip quivered more from the memory of his death than from the pain, but the pain made her eyes clamp shut before she looked over at the woman still drenched in the darkness.

"I'll take that as a yes. How about Thorenson Oliver?"

"Yes."

"Did you kill Thor?" Luke asked.

"Yes."

"You beat me to that one." Luke told her. "I'm a little jealous."

"Who the fuck are you people?" She asked before she could stop herself.

The drip of chemical entered her muscle and it felt like a razor cutting into her and leaving salt granules as it dragged its way through flesh. Spots appeared in her vision and she heard herself involuntarily cry out.

"I only touched the plunger sweetheart. I really am quite serious about the infractions Miss Glencamp. That is my Husband Luke Webb and I am Doctor Jessica Webb. Your friends killed our family, so in turn we have killed most of your friends. Associates really wouldn't you say? You don't really have friends do you?"

"No."

"I know. I know you didn't have anything to do with the killings. You didn't even know about them. I didn't understand it all either, until the last few. But you were involved with the world that destroyed our lives. You are in a strange place where you know too much. Even worse for you is what you have done since. I will let you know that it was me that plunged the needle into Attorney Foster in Albany and me that administered the chemicals not all that different than what is in you right now. What I gave her was far more toxic obviously."

"Yes."

"Yes what?"

"I knew her."

"We know that now. We might have been able to help you then had we known. You might not have gone so far down your hole. But, there really isn't much helping that. Now your price for participation is a question of life or death. You are going to help us, there is no question of that. How much I have to push you for that help is going to dictate what happens to you. That is where our leniency for your involvement in our pain ends. Don't forget that we did kill many people who had no direct involvement. You are simply one of them."

"Yes."

"Good girl. Tell me the name of the boat in Saint Augustine."

"'Princesse Violante' at The William Pope Duvall Yacht Harbor." She sighed. "Amandore Belfran set it up."

"Who the fuck is William Pope Duvall?" Luke asked.

"First Governor of Florida Territory." Robbie told him.

"How the hell do you know this shit?"

"I get bored and read a lot."

"You get that Jax?" Luke asked.

"Got it. You guys get to the airport. Reggie can escort her back here. The Texas team is going after the yacht. I need you guys to hustle to Tahoe. You have an important meeting."

"Roger that Jax. Thank you." Luke told her.

"Tell me the access numbers to your accounts and to those of the men on the yacht." Jessica Webb told Casey.

"There are sixty for me and I don't know all of them for the men on the yacht. I'll give you what I do know."

William Pope Duvall Yacht Harbor
Saint Augustine, Florida

Five minutes after Casey Glencamp had uttered the name of the yacht Andrea Jackson Malone identified the sleek blue Azimut Grande Trideck sitting in the water forty yards from the main docks of the club. This information made the man from Texas smile. Having the vessel away from the docks and any innocents made his job easier and made his boarding of the vessel all the more a surprise to his targets. Five minutes after confirmation Jax gave him a life count and a rough layout of the vessel. While he waited for her details, the crews of three stealth SB-1S Defiant helicopters made their aircraft ready for flight and The Texan's team made themselves ready for an airborne ship raid.

On the deck of the Princess Violante none of the six men in grey suits holding short Zastava M21 rifles heard or saw the helicopters sweep in from the Atlantic side. They were, even the ones stationed to watch the sea, paying attention to the shore and the party that was still well under way as the Americans were resisting the passing of warm weather. These men were trying to admire the exposed breasts of the rich women ashore who had had more than enough intoxicants to lash out against the world that kept them locked up to keep up pretenses. They would never be like the sex slaves and whores kept below decks with their bosses. They were a level of sex that these men could not pay for and would never have been able to earn. It made them all the more thirsty for it. Even if they had not been distracted by their desires, they never would not have heard the inbound helicopters. Two of the Defiant's turned broadside to the luxury yacht eighty yards away and six suppressed Sword International MK-18 Mjolnir rifles spat tiny flashes of fire that were lost on anyone on shore. The heavy three hundred grain hollow points struck each man at the base of his skull and ended their fight. Although the bullets left the skull they ran out of momentum and landed in the water where they posed no threat to innocent life. As the bodies of the guard force hit the deck so too did the black soles of LALO boarding shoes of the assault team who ran for predesignated targets. With less than thirty shots fired from the time they hit the deck until they owned the ship The Texan's team killed four more guards and took two Serbian mobsters into custody. They liberated thirteen young women and sixteen men under the age of twenty five. Most of them were of African American or Spanish descent and as one of the mobsters confessed, they were destined for work in a mine in Africa after having been traded for sex. They had trauma that they would need counseling to get through but, they would not die among the missing and they would have a chance at a real life again. After years of living on the edge hunting down terrorists and preparing for war, this was the mission that big red headed Texan felt was why he had been put on earth. He also knew that there was much more to do. *Revel in the victories.*

From a handmade humidor he removed a box of long cigars and passed them around, watching his team while he used an old brass trench lighter his great grandfather had brought home from World War One to put a flame near the hand rolled leaves and inhaled the fumes of triumph. He kept the heel of his boot dug into the stomach of the larger Serbian tied up under him. The first ashes landed in the mobster's eyes as the first helicopter hovered to load the liberated.

"Tell me about Belfran and tell me where in Africa." The Texan growled.

"We make the trade in Ghana. From there they go to Burkina Faso to the mines."

"Who buys them?"

"Chinese. Sometimes Russian."

Chapter Thirteen

"There are no great men, only great challenges, which ordinary men like you and me are forced by circumstances to meet."
Admiral William F. "Bull" Halsey Jr.

Lake Hovsgol
Mongolia

"Guys I have some kind of honcho down here that Kim says is a Mangudai. He's got people load shells into Lada trucks and onto horses. What's the payload look like?" Jesse Randall spoke softly into his microphone to Jax Malone back in the bunker in Wendover.

"It's chlorine Jesse." She told him.

"I think the schedule got bumped up."

"We are still three hours out from staging." Shaw said.

"Well Mister Murphy just crashed that party. Dude we can't let this much stuff move." Buhr spoke up as he woke up and got himself situated on the Mk-48 machine-gun that would cover them while Kim and Jesse engaged targets with the heavy hitting sniper rifles.

"Guys, Matt is unreachable." Jax told them.

"We need to make a decision here."

"Anything we do now has to be definitive. We cannot risk alerting Temuchin."

"Tell me what you're thinking Jax." McGuire entered the conversation and headed for her office.

"Jesse hold on target. I need to talk to Mac."

When she had told him what her intentions were he only asked if it could work. She said that it could, especially with two Hooligans tasked to the site. To that he nodded his approval and sat in a leather desk chair watching her monitors and waiting for someone to bring them fresh coffee.

"Okay Jesse." Jax came back across the radio. "I am going to try something. When I tell you, I want all of you to close your eyes and keep your heads in the dirt. When I tell you that you're clear I want you to engage your targets. Brett, head for site Charlie direct. I will alert Matt to the change." Jax told them. She moved her chair to the left and scanned a monitor before tapping keys. There was nothing to see here except for a red bar on a Hooligan readout letting her know that a communications laser more powerful than a solar flare was jamming communications into and out of the area of the Altai mountains camp. With that active she moved back to the center of her massive desk and zoomed in on the warehouse area where the Mongol soldiers were loading trucks with chemical weapons. The warehouse was attached to an enormous beautiful wooden palace that must have been several hundred years old. She gave thought to how many lives were down there and quickly refocused to how many innocent lives would be effected if she did not act.

"Gentlemen close your eyes now. I will tell you when to reopen them. Firing now." Jax pushed a red button kept to the right side of the key board and shrouded by a metal flap that she had to lift to access as a failsafe.

From one hundred thousand feet above the lake a violet colored 1 million watt gas laser sliced through the sky, the concrete roof of the warehouse, the barrels of chlorine and the truck they were loaded on to dig a ten foot hole in the ground under them. As the laser pulsed at ultra high frequency it made a thwack sound that was mistaken as thunder from over a hundred miles away. Jax moved the laser as it cut so that the building caught fire and artillery shells began to detonate. As it moved away, the laser allowed the chemical compounds to mix and turn gaseous. That gas almost instantly ignited in a fireball that created a vacuum pulling snow and dirt from around the hole Jesse and his team had dug close to a thousand yards from the camp. In less than a minute the camp and its occupants were gone. In another thirty seconds the heat from the laser burnt away all residue of the chlorine bomb.

"Hovsgol team you can open your eyes again. There are targets crashed in a truck north of your position at 015. 1500 yards. They are very likely blind. They had a load of ordnance, non-chemical."

"Got em." Jesse said. He chewed twice on his gum as he brought the cold comb of his rifle stock into his cheek and set his sight on the first target. "Front bumper." He took a deep breath and began to let out.

"Rear door." Kim said and took his own breath.

The Tubbs rifles Jesse had been instrumental in sourcing for the Fraternity were chambered in 20 millimeter and carried a staged barrel thirty seven inches long before meeting massive suppressors. The rifles still made a thunderclap when they fired but they were not deafening. They were also some of the most accurate weapons Jesse had ever fired. The custom machined explosive bullets sliced through the air and were still supersonic when they hit their targets half a second after leaving the barrel. The snipers had already loaded fresh rounds and acquired secondary targets. Men who had been momentarily blinded and stunned by the destruction of the camp watched their comrades dismembered in a mist of bodily fluid right before they lost their own lives.

"I'm dropping a Raufus on the truck." Jesse said.

"Roger that. Put that fucker in space." Buhr told them.

The Raufus round is an explosive anti material bullet made in Sweden and generally loaded for the larger 50 caliber Browning machine gun round. When the Fraternities Special Operations had selected the 20 millimeter for use in sniping, they had reached out to the company for a duplication of the load and now had a precision explosive device in the hands of precision marksmen. The heavy rounds were able to pierce the cases of the artillery shells in the back of the truck and let the charges daisy chain, destroying all weapons on board.

"Hovsgol team you are clear. Disengage and head for Exfil One." Jax told them.

"Moving now." Buhr told her. The team gathered their equipment and ran two miles to a gathering of boulders where they had stashed their vehicle under camouflaged netting.

"You want to drive?" Jesse asked Buhr.

"Yeah. I didn't get to shoot anything. I think I'll do some diving."

The Glickenhaus SCG Boot revved to life belching thunder through its dual exhausts. The Boot racer had been built as an homage to the actor Steve McQueen's foray into Baja racing and proved itself to be a capable off-road truck. Kevin flipped switches for night vision only headlights and the long rack of Baja style lights on the roof that lit up the world for the operators but for no-one not wearing goggles. Once Kim was strapped into the seat allowing him to man a roof mounted M134D minigun he let Buhr know he was good to go and they moved out in a blast of exhaust from the high-strung V8 powering the little Baja racer.

Beijing China

Matt Hauer had entered the city of Beijing through Daxing Airport where he was delivered by commercial airliner after rapid transit to Korea. He was met at the airport by a pair of CIA agents, acting as diplomats, who swept him through customs and out to a silver Great Wall Haval H6 Sport, a knock off Hummer, that belonged to the agency. After taking their numbers he checked that the bag he had asked for was in place on the passenger seat. Once he had checked the status of Beretta and Chinese QSZ-92 pistols and the Chinese military QBZ-191 assault rifle and attending magazines he ran his finger across the blade of a black Extrema Ratio Mamba knife and sheathed the Italian blade before holstering the pistols.

"Jax. I'm in Beijing. Where is Saik?"

"Matt. We had to take down the Hovsgol site. The team headed for extract five minutes ago. Saik is at an apartment above the Wei Loo restaurant at the corner of Roushi and Xianyukou. He just got there."

"Keep an eye out if you can please."

It took twenty minutes to get away from the airport and north into the city so that he was parked close enough to the building and walked in the shadows until he found the right door. Keong Saik and a short young woman with her head bowed low came down a narrow and broken set of stairs toward the darkened street. The Chinese Colonel kept his right hand in his jacket pocket and his left clamped over the wrist of his wife behind him. His head moved constantly as he scanned for threats. He never saw Matt.

"Don't move." Matt growled from behind as the fingers and thumb of his left hand clamped around the side of Saik's neck and squeezed toward each other through skin and muscle. The man could not speak through the instant shock of pain and winced as he tried to breath. Hauer removed the pistol from the man's right hand and stuck it into his kidney. His wife stood wide-eyed in the rain.

"I know that you speak English so keep your mouth shut and come with me."

"Who..."

"Don't speak. Just walk."

Hauer moved the couple to the car and restrained Saik's wife after he zip-tied the man's hands behind him and sat him in the passenger seat.

"Why?"

"Temuchin." Hauer said as he began to close the door.

"You are one of Holland's men, or another Russian. I have not betrayed Temuchin. Or are you British? I thought that you people would have learned to leave this alone. The Khan should not have killed that agent. It is a most horrible thing."

"I'm none of those." Hauer managed to say before the passenger door was shoved into his shoulder. The attacker moved swiftly and made nearly no sound until he exhaled as he drove his weight into the door. Hauer shoved back instinctively and saw the black lines of the submachinegun before he saw the mans face. Matt's left hand flew down to clamp over the foregrip of the little weapon while his right hand smashed upward into the base of the attacker's nose. The crunch of the man's nasal cartilage and facial bone was felt more than heard. His lifeless body flopped against the car and sagged to the ground as the second attacker rushed forward, this one with his gun already on the way up. Having no idea of the condition of the little submachinegun he had just acquired Hauer chose to throw it at the attacker's face while he drew his own pistol. The compact Sig Sauer P365 X-Macro spat two rounds through the short suppressor. The heavy 147 grain bullets drove into the mans face as Hauer pushed the killer's gun away, a third bullet in the back of the skull acted as insurance. Though the weapon was suppressed it still created enough noise echoing down the rainy street to make Hauer want to expedite his exit. Still, mixed with the echoes of violence were the heavy footsteps of yet another attacker closing in on them from an alley across the street. This one already had his weapon firing as he left the narrow sidewalk. Where the pistol had created thumps as reports this submachine gun made a deafening chatter as its bolt chugged away at the rounds in its magazine. The knock off Humvee suffered the worst of the barrage as bullets shattered the back passenger window and riddled the doors. Matt glanced at the already dead attackers next to him and shuffled his way along the truck, first behind the engine block and then slid across the bumper and grill until he could see the attacker rushing at him. In that instant the SEAL's hands rose with his Sig and as he exhaled, he fired three controlled pairs of shots from the man's waistline up to his chin. Hauer snapped photos of each man's face with his phone and sent them to Jax as he gathered the weapons which he deposited onto the passenger floorboard before pulling away into the night.

"Khampa." The General said as Matt drove into the rain.

"What is that?"

"Tibetan Nomad Warriors. Temuchin has promised them the return of their homeland from China."

"Another promise he has no intention of keeping."

"Not likely." Keong agreed. "You are not here to execute me?"

"No."

"Then why sir? How do you know me? You knew how to find us. Only Temuchin knew where I was. He sent the Khampa. Who sent you?"

"Don't concern yourself with who I work for. I know about Temuchin and I know about the gas, the weapons. I know about the Russians and I've seen what a nine tails ordu looks like. I'm going to end it."

"Fascinating isn't it. As an officer I can truly appreciate the modernized tuman. Ten thousand men on horses with machine-guns. There will be no long sieges as it was in history. Can you imagine the changes for China? For the world? You won't stop it. The world does not want you to stop it."

"He's planning to gas cities. Your own people."

"Many cities. He will use nuclear weapons as well. Some must fall so others can grow. It is life."

"Where are the nukes going?"

"Moscow. To repay Ivan."

"Ivan?"

"Ivan Grodzni. The Terrible. He ran the Mongol out of Russia in 1555. Because of him and the Dynasty and the flooding of the Yellow river the Mongol way and the Khan's died away."

"You're telling me that he wants to nuke people five hundred years later?"

"It is a plan for the first wave yes."

"How much of these plans do you know?"

"I believe all. I have been there since the beginning. If you understand Mongol history, I am a Tar-Khan. I am entitled to access to the pavilions, the spoils of war and can essentially do no wrong." Saik told him. "By the code, the Yassa, I am to be forgiven the death punishment nine times."

"I think your hit squad would prove otherwise. Be that as it may I think that you should know that I know about the ordus in Altai, Hovsgol, Lhasa Tibet, Gobi And Kashmir."

"I see. These camps are special. They all have chemical weapons. These are starting points where Mangudai, our God-belonging suicide squadrons are prepared for the initial strikes. Other soldiers will come and form ordus and Tumans in the coming days. This will be the horde. Altai and Hovsgol are our Ordubaligh, court cities, pavilions if you will."

"What is so special about Altai. Why not Tibet?"

"Altai is a sacred place for the Mongol. It has been so since before Genghis."

"You are the Chief Financial Officer for the legitimate business of Temuchin Steel. What about the horde?"

"Because of my time with the infantry I would have leadership in the horde. As Tar-Khan I would ride with ten Tuman."

"A hundred thousand horses. How many are there?"

"Five hundred thousand right now."

"Tell me. Where is he planning to strike?"

"Moscow, Shanghai, and Beijing will get the devastation strikes. Bases will follow if the military does not follow orders. Then he will dispose of all leadership heads throughout Asia. From here he will push north and west. What you call Eurasia would be Temuchin's in one year."

"I beg to differ."

"Sir. I will freely admit that you frighten me. But I am one man. What would you do against five hundred thousand that will grow to millions? How many can you kill?"

"Tell me about Holland Mattison and his employer."

"They have a man named Avery. A mercenary. That is an insult to the profession. He is a hired killer with a company of equally vulgar rapists and murderers. They are adept. All highly qualified. The person paying them right now is very powerful in America."

"By person you mean woman. We're talking about Maureen Collins-Roth."

"Yes. The American Senator. She controls a large company, a law firm in New York and arms dealerships."

"Illegal arms dealerships."

"Quite so. We used her to broker the purchase of tanks, helicopters, howitzers and of course chemicals."

"And where did the nukes come from?"

"The Russians."

"You were going to run, weren't you?"

"How could I not? You are a very astute man. I tried to alert my country of this man's plans. I tried to alert the world through the British agent but no-one believes it. Or they don't care. I'm tired of it all. I'm tired of the communism of China and the radical world domination ideals of people like Temuchin. I have a video to send to the State Security before I was to leave the country and I would have disappeared. At this point I am afraid that even the secret police have Mongol sleepers in the mix."

"That's realistic. Who can you reach directly in Chinese leadership?"

"My superior, General Chuang."

"I can go a little higher up the chain." Matt told him.

They were only a mile from the airport when three sets of red and blue flashing lights appeared in the road behind them. Hauer looked in the mirror and adjusted his grip on his Beretta pistol, waiting as he stepped harder on the gas pedal.

"Do not stop Matt. Those guys that attacked are Khampa, but they were also at least trained by the Harakat Ul-Mujahidden in Pakistan and Kashmir. The HUM has links to Chinese Uyghur Liberation Organization. These guys are playing the cops tonight. There has been no police radio traffic regarding your vehicle. We're picking up cell phones now."

"Clear my way in then."

"You have six Chinese soldiers at the gate and our guys talking with them. You're good to go."

The rear window shattered, and a hole appeared in the center of the windshield before they heard the rifle shots. More bursts followed rapidly behind it. Hauer pushed Saik's wife down farther than she was already and turned long enough to fire his magazine dry into the voids under the approaching vehicles flashing strobe lights. He was reloading the pistol when he rolled through the guard station and onto the runway where Jax told him their plane was. Agents grabbed the Saik's from the vehicle and tossed them into the cabin of the waiting Bombardier Global 6000 jet that began moving while Hauer was still closing the door.

At the gate, the six Chinese soldiers, thinking they were defending a high ranking official fleeing from a gang attack in stolen police vehicles opened fire until the vehicles stopped moving. Eight Chinese men and two women would be pulled out of the wreckage, all dead, to be identified as members of ULO and the New People's Movement of Beijing. Before Hauer touched back down at OSAN airbase in South Korea seven sights of the NMP were raided by Chinese police and military who confiscated a four hundred rifles, four tons of explosives, and brought another forty terrorists into custody after killing five others. While the Saik's were escorted to an Airbus A350 headed back to the U.S. Hauer climbed aboard a black XB-88 Demon and found his gear waiting for him. He was already starting to get changed when the SCRAM Jet lifted off, never having officially been on Republic of Korea soil.

"What's the real stall speed on this bird." Matt asked the pilot.

"We touch one fifty and we drop like a rock." The pilot told him. "We land at one eighty. This thing may as well be a bus in mud under two bucks."

"Good enough." Matt said.

"Your team is on the ground now." Ashworth's voice came over the airwaves. "Is it of the utmost import that you be on this mission Commander Hauer?"

"Yes, sir it is. I believe that that site is the most important of the lot. I need confirmation that this is the head of the beast."

"I'll back him on it, Ian. I trust his instinct." McGuire said.

"So do I. I'm just trying to swallow all of this. A person I had long considered to be one of America's great assets is a threat and we are dancing with these devils trying to keep them unawares while we prepare for war. It is killing me. Mister Hauer I am sorry to have hindered you. Do whatever you need to from here out. And, Godspeed young man."

"Understood."

"Matt." Jax cut back in. "You are going to be jumping into a blizzard. Your team is already in whiteout conditions."

"Outstanding. Nice to know that Mister Murphy decided to show up for the party." Hauer grumbled in reference to Murphy's Law.

"Matt." She continued. "I think we found a fair solution to the other strikes."

"I completely agree." He said after hearing her out.

"Commander, I'm assuming you have never HAHO'd from a bomb bay before, never mind dropped in a glider." The Demon's relief pilot asked as they helped him into the darkened confines of the bomb bay where the stealth glider waited.

"Nope. I've never jumped above 30 grand either." Hauer told him as he felt his way along the Kevlar and carbon fiber glider until he printed himself and felt the belly mounted sled holding his gear. Once confident that the load would hold up to flight, he made his way forward to the cockpit and began climbing inside.

"In ten minutes, we are going to slow to two hundred knots and pull up. You will drop out and slide into the slipstream in a nose up attitude. As soon as that light goes green you will want to have you controls pushed straight into the dash. Have a good flight."

"You too."

Under the protective jump suit, he wore a grey and white winter assault suit over his thermal suit and body armor. All of this was making him sweat in the seventy degree cabin. Once the doors were shut, he placed his combat glasses over his eyes and adjusted the oxygen mask and Team Wendy Exfil ballistic helmet around them. When the light flashed green, he switched on his heated oxygen tanks and switched on the power for his jump board reminiscent of dive boards he had used in the Teams. This board, attached to a harness on his chest, gave him gauges for altitude, GPS, standard compass, temperature and his oxygen level. As backup he wore a more traditional gauge cluster on his wrist. All of this was backup to the glider's navigation package in the dash and was ready just in case he had to bail out of the glider. Murphy's law came into play far too often in combat and he needed every bit of help while he was alone. Redundancy was a key rule of survival in the special operations world.

After running through a pre-flight checklist, he forced himself to take deep slow breaths. This was not his first solo jump at high altitude at night but, it was his maiden flight in the Owl and no less dangerous than an open air jump. The waiting was the worst. The frustration and painful boredom was often worse on soldiers than the fast violence of combat. Many times, in his career he had been put on RMF, rapid mobility force, a state of readiness which had him sitting around in full gear ready to move at a moment's notice, several times for days on end, only to be stood down. It had been more emotionally and mentally taxing than most operations. He believed that a large percentage of resignations came directly from this type of stress.

"Pop up, pop up, pop up." The pilots voice called as he flared the aircraft in a slight nose up attitude to dramatically slow them down. "Door, door, door." He yelled over the radio and the frozen night opened to pull Hauer into its ready maw.

Already pushing hard on the control Hauer felt the glider jolt as the air slammed into its fuselage and again as the tailwind of the Demon's large wings buffeted in the worst turbulence he had ever experienced. The Owl pitched and yawed to the left before rising back toward the bigger jet. The shaking and pulling had Hauer wrenching at and pushing the control wheel as if he were in the gym fighting with a bench press and row machine simultaneously. The noise of the Demon's jets and the howl of the wind was enough to make one's bowels clench. The sweat ran freely down his face and across his chest under all of the layers of clothing he was bundled into. His breathing came in short sharp rasps as he fought with G-forces he had not been fully prepared for.

"Wolf is Clear." Hauer yelled unnecessarily as silence replaced the howling assault he had just endured. He watched the shape of the stealth aircraft and its faint blue exhaust fade as he fell. He regained control of the aircraft and his breathing as he watched the forward airspeed indicator drop steady out at 200 knots. He was in a slight nose down angle and ready for the glider to stretch its wings. Once they were extended, he leveled out his flightpath and slowed the craft to 180 knots before beginning his turn toward the Altai Mountains site. "Good Jump. Thanks for the ride, Mister Hall."

"Anytime Commander."

"Utah. Wolf is on Attack One. Good Jump."

"Roger that Wolf. What's it like up there? You are higher up than Everest right now." Jax said.

"Cold and snowy." He told her as he watched the rime ice form over the sled and his suit. "I have a nice tailwind. I'm falling at about ten feet a minute. It's a hundred and five below zero up here. Just another day."

"We offered you a ride." Shaw came over the net.

"No complaint. The view is outstanding."

"The beacon is coming on now." Shaw told him.

On his radar Hauer watched a green dot flash out of the black screen and lined his nose up with it. "Distance is two hundred and ten miles. Shut it down for now. How's my drop zone?"

"Choice. You have a natural field about nine hundred yards long and a hundred feet wide. You'll be two miles from the mountain."

"Matt, Kurt Thoma here." The voice cut in.

"Go ahead Kurt."

"Matt. The VNE on the Owl is 500 knots. Don't forget this please." VNE was Velocity Never to Exceed.

"I wasn't expecting it to be that high."

"Maybe don't approach it."

"You could have warned me about how severe the drop was."

"You wouldn't have appreciated it."

"We need to get that into the training protocol. And this sucker wants to yaw."

"That was just the turbulence off of the Demon."

Chapter Fourteen

"Justice delayed is justice denied."
William E. Gladstone
British Prime Minister

Washington D.C.

Ian Ashworth steered his dark blue Audi S8 into his space in the underground garage glad that he had taken the opportunity to drive himself to work today. He left the tan leather driving gloves over the center console, pocketed his fraternity key fob and with his faded brown attaché case in hand strolled toward the elevator. Using the tinted back window of a big car as a mirror he straightened his tie and lit a cigar before moving on.

Robert Hamilton and Joseph Delany, both in pinstriped suits, were already sharing their morning coffee when Ashworth entered their private library overlooking the fountain in Robert Latham Owen Park by eleven floors.

"I spoke with McGuire this morning. Mister Hauer and his teams are on the ground and hunting. Buhr and Randall proved successful at Hovsgol." Delany spoke. "Care for coffee?"

"This will be my third cup of the morning. I'll pour." Ashworth said. "I had the pleasure of speaking with Miss Malone at length this morning. She was running a large number of Hooligan blimps while we spoke. What an amazing and strange mind. M.I.T. alumni are an interesting breed of human. We discussed two things at length that we should bring to bear here."

"What exactly?" Hamilton sat up.

"Firstly, I believe we need to consider the situation of Senator Roth and how to deal with her. The would be captors of this once great woman are more angry with her than would be normal in our operation. I believe they are professional but, I believe they will need guidance on her disposal."

"Is elimination an absolute necessity, are we not able to simply contain her in a dark facility?" Delany asked.

"Given her background with Central Intelligence she could and probably would further compromise the country if given the chance.

If somehow, she did escape who knows what ends she would go to in the interest of exacting her revenge." Ashworth took his seat.

"McGuire has suggested that following questioning she should suffer a natural cause." Hamilton offered.

"Given Doctor Webb's background and prior performance I would say that is within her wheelhouse."

"We need to get ahead of this one." Hamilton said. "These choreographed takedowns are underway. If she feels cut off, she will go to ground."

"I'll make it so." Ashworth said and reached for his phone. "We all agree?"

Both men raised their hands.

"Execute." He spoke into the phone once the connection was made.

"What is our next order of business then?" Delany asked.

"Expansion." Ashworth told him. "I think that given the turmoil we have seen in the world over the last few years that we need to and can double our tactical presence. Especially with the end of conflict in Afghanistan and Iraq. The pool of candidates has not been this vast since the end of World War Two."

"I agree. The last few years have demonstrated the need." Hamilton told him. "I would amend to that a restructuring with input from McGuire and Hauer. I see a growing need for smaller, highly mobile and adept teams like the Webb's. I should think that they exemplify the model we should build on. Modern day Jedburgh Teams if you will." He said in reference to the teams of men and women used by the Office of Strategic Services in Europe during World War Two.

"Call in McGuire and Hauer as soon as Mongolia is resolved then." Delany said.

Altai

USING THE STORM AND darkness as cover Hauer and his crew worked their way past the tent village and it guards. To the west of the village was the lake and the mountain jutting up into the sky as a sheer granite slab. An unnamed majestic peak of ice and snow and grey rock. It was this natural cathedral that held the most interest for Matt. The village was insignificant despite the chemical weapons they had identified in its many tents. It had made him wonder why the warlord had given up the fortress at Hovsgol to be in the middle of nowhere. That move alone told Hauer that this place had enormous significance in the future of the Tribe of the Nine-tails.

"It looks worse from the ground." Shaw said as he scanned the jagged granite cliffs. "What the hell is so special about this?"

"Secret lair shit." Hauer whispered back.

"Possibly another lab." Benedetti said.

"I bet that and much much more."

"How are we going to do this?" Benedetti asked.

"First we're going to send in the mice and the owls." He pointed to his drag sled full of miniature drones. "They can map the place while we pull a lot of deep snow traversing, then a tough off width, not quite a chimney, probably 5.14b vertical, after a hundred feet of that there's a hundred and ten foot crack, fist sized. It's a jam fest. We need big cams for protection." Shaw said. "Two hundred feet off the deck we go horizontal on a fifteen foot overhang. One hell of a climb."

"You sure do know what you're talking about for a guy that doesn't like climbing." Beck said.

"I can climb. I just don't get a kick out of it." Shaw said.

"We don't have three days anymore and we aren't summiting." Hauer said. "I'll lead. Sergeant Major you're on belay."

"Why aren't we summiting?" Benedetti asked.

"Back door." Matt said.

"Oh, right the back door." Shaw shook his head. "Should have thought of that."

"I'll bet my Bentley's that there are a few back doors, the lake, a tunnel out below the camp and then upstairs where we're going."

"Why up though?" Benedetti asked.

"There are skylights and vents, right?" Beck said as the thought hit her.

"That's what I'm thinking." He smiled. "We tried checking the mountain on infra-red but no dice. I did however find some wicked thermals rising from the rocks as the cold weather started. Not uncommon during the daylight but at 2 a.m. sort of bizarre."

"We have four hours before daybreak." Beck told them.

"Let's haul some ass."

By the time the sun broke over the horizon the team had scrambled up the frozen granite slab until they could access what they had initially thought were air vents cut into the mountain. There were easier routes up but none that would not have left them exposed to view from the camp leading to their summary execution.

"Whoever the jackass was that said there were no straight lines in nature neglected to look up." Shaw said as Beck climbed past him into the hand carved cave.

"It's beautiful." Beck replied as she used a pair of binoculars to scan the valley several hundred feet below.

"Your legs are jacking like a sewing machine and you are acting like you're in heaven. You two were made for each other." Shaw smiled and shook his head.

"I think so too. Thanks." She gave the man a slug on his shoulder.

North Cascades

0530

Although the facility was under surveillance of a Hooligan blimp, Brian Tindall had decided to post a patrol near the access road. Lt. Angel Diaz, a former Marine, and Bob Hughes an ex-Air Force Para Rescue Sergeant had only an hour earlier relieved another pair of shooters. They sat in their cold weather gear sipping coffee in an old Dodge pickup truck watching the snow come down and pile up on the road. The access road had yet to see a plow despite three strong storms that had left over five feet on the gravel. The men shared a surprised look when the green Jeep Gladiator steered off of the unplowed main road and up the path.

"Diaz to One. Are you seeing this Jeep?"

"Roger that. One person inbound." The tech in Utah spoke back.

It took concentrated effort and nearly half an hour for the driver to muscle the truck up the five miles of snowy backroad. Three guards and a German Shepard, all in white suits, met the vehicle at the gate.

"You went through a hell of a lot of trouble to get here pal." The K-9 guard spoke in a thick South African accent to the driver until the window rolled down. "Ah…" He started when he recognized the face inside.

"Don't say my name. Just get the person at the top of that paper and put that dog in the kennel mate." He held out the paper for the guard.

"Ya. Come. I will get them."

The name on the paper read 'Roger Avery.'

Avery was asleep when the Afrikaner guard knocked at his door. In the dark he tied his boots, checked the luminous hands on his Nite MX-10 watch, a watch reputed to be favored by the British SAS and therefore something that he had to have. His left hand rested on his Browning Hi-Power pistol he answered the door. With a finger over his lips the K9 guard passed Avery the note. Avery read it and winced involuntarily.

"Grab your shit now. We need to move." Avery followed his own advice and grabbed a backpack kept at the end of his bed and a rifle that had leaned against it. Lastly, he closed a padded case over his laptop computer and ran down the concrete hall.

In the dim light of the Jeep, he read the note again.

'Roger Avery

U.S. Intelligence is watching the operation. They are preparing to strike the sights in Mongolia. Keong Saik is dead. They know your names. Get out if you can. Luck M.'

The driver pulled away into the storm.

"One to Diaz."

"Go One."

"That vehicle is on its way back down. Three male occupants. Am I following at this time?"

"Roger that, Follow."

Hughes shifted in the driver's seat and moved his suppressed Mark-18 carbine into a vertical mount at the dash. Diaz looked over at his own rifle next to it and waited while Hughes steered the truck into town where they parked at a grocery store while they watched for the Jeep to come off the mountain.

"How did you find out Trevor? And thank you for coming." Avery spoke when they were nearly done with the horrible access road.

"One of the General's people at CIA picked up the traffic on Saik and saw that the Mongolian investigation had been taken over by the FBI after that State trooper died. Turns out the FBI has nothing on this. The General decided we should pull out."

"Conrad was money well spent after all." The K9 guard spoke up from the back seat.

"Exactly right mister Kench." Avery said. "I thought he would be a loose end."

"Probably still is." Trevor told him as he got onto the still unplowed main road. "The first priority here is to get to a safe house."

"There is no such place. Let's assume that now. Get food and coffee and drive on Mister Longley."

"What happens to the op?" Kench asked.

"We fold and walk away. "Avery told him. "We have already been paid. We disappear and go back on the market."

"One to Diaz." The tech buzzed in the shooters ear again after Hughes began his tail.

"Go One."

"As I said, there are three males in that vehicle. I think we picked up some good intel that is under review. I'm going to lose them shortly on the Hooligan. Follow and I will get other teams onto this."

"Roger that one. It appears we are running steady east. Probably going for Coeur d'Alene." Diaz told the tech.

"I'll get you a relay there."

"In this weather that's about six hours away. We have sixty gallons of gas. We're okay."

"They have three drivers. Unless they are going to Canada, they are headed for points east."

Chapter Fifteen

"The rifle itself has no moral stature, since it has no will of its own. Naturally, it may be used by evil men for evil purposes, but there are more good men than evil, and while the later cannot be persuaded to the path of righteousness by propaganda, they may certainly be corrected by good men with rifles."

Lt. Colonel Jeff Cooper USMC
Legendary Instructor of Combat Arms

Utah

"MCGUIRE." MITCH GROWLED into his cell phone once he had seen that he had only been asleep for an hour before being robbed.

"Boss." Jax spoke on the other end. "We have a problem."

"Fire away Miss Malone."

"Roth knows. She doesn't know who, but she has been tipped off by an Agent Conrad out of Langley. Further, he tipped off the lead

Avery out at the Cascades sight. Avery was picked up by an ex-SAS guy turned Merc, Trevor Longley. They left the site with a South African shooter named Markus Kench. Two Wraiths from Alpha are following them now."

"Shit. What's the status on Matt?"

"Inside the mountain now."

"None of their comms got through to Temuchin?"

"Nothing."

"Good. Keep a tail on Avery. I want to see where he goes. Do we have a track on Roth still?"

"And one on Mattison."

"Clear them now. And get me a flight out to meet with the Senator."

North Cascades

"YOU GUYS OKAY IN THIS soup?" A white clad Brian Tindall asked a pair of pilots checking their OH-6 "Little bird" helicopters. The snow was coming down hard and fast in a steady blow out of the northwest so that it stung at any exposed skin.

"No sweat Colonel. We're good to go." The pilot told him as he turned his attention from the six 'little birds' to the three heavily armed Defiant's that Tindall's team had made the flight from Seattle to their staging point in. The strike team was now rallying in a field six miles inside of the national park.

Diaz and Hughes had caught a flight back from Idaho. Both were now loaded for bear and strapping into jump-seats mounted on the sides of the light helicopters.

"Com's check." Tindall called out. "All systems up."

Everyone involved endured the long check in as the cold sapped at their bodies.

"Snipers up."

"Long in position two one hundred yards north northwest of compound."

"Heath in position four ninety yards dead north."

Both men were tested products of the U.S. Army school of Sniping. They had cut their teeth together in Afghanistan and Iraq while attached to Ranger units and later with Delta Force. Tindall knew he could count on each of them when he needed them most.

"Chem team stand by. Strike Alpha saddle up. Utah Copy?"

"Roger that. Alpha is a green light. Good hunting." The voice of the male tech in Utah called back.

Tindal locked himself into the forward left jump seat with a thick Velcro strap and pointed his white and grey Mark 11 rifle to the side as he slapped the pilot on the shoulder. In a moment he was weightless as the bird took to the air. Through the green light of his night vision gear Tindal watched the other helicopters mimic the movements of his lead chopper. His heartbeat moved up a notch as they sped up and just barely cleared the tops of snow encrusted pines as they raced for the target.

"Gunships on station." Rachel Brown called out.

"Hang tight." Tindall told her, glad that his request for a pair of ACV-22 Spooky II's were on sight. Like their predecessors the AC-130 and the C-47 Puff's, the ACV could pour on suppressive fire in volume from its four 7.62mm Miniguns, two 20mm Vulcan cannons, a 30mm chain gun like that on the Apache gunship and twin racks holding 16 Hellfire misses. Unlike the old AC-130, the ACV could hover on station like a helicopter rather than have to circle the area.

"Electro pulse in six, five, four, three, two, one. Lights out." The Utah tech called out as he fired a laser cutting off the power grid at the compound.

"Roger that Utah. Strike is a go." Tindall called back.

The people on the ground at the compound were in the dark. They had no lights, no electric fences or doors, no radios, no computers and no night vision. Even their cars and digital watches would no longer work.

Tindall's rifle found a target as soon as the helicopter cleared the tree line. The Velcro strap came off with a hard tug, a second later the running-back was on the ground twenty feet behind a sentry who never heard him coming. Two pulls of the trigger sent 168 grain match grade hollow points into the man's skull. Behind him on his left two more shots rang out. On his right a short burst of light machine-gun fire came from Yeaton and his sawed off MK-46. Tindal did not wait to see the result of the gunfire from his fire team. If they stopped shooting that meant their targets were no longer a threat.

The assault teams rolled into the open hangar of the main plant where they met armed targets and dropped them. There were two cargo trailers loaded with logs like what had been shipped to the Mongols. Tindal suspected that they were chock full of chlorine and had no desire to pop them open. His hand forced, he had to push hard to get out of the bay and avoid a standoff. Three more men were fumbling in the darkened stairwell going into a basement on his left. This appeared to be the only direction to go. The Mk-11 was on his shoulder and kicking as the soldiers fell to the floor. In a smooth motion he dropped the empty magazine and slapped home a fresh one as he swept the weapons of the fallen aside with his left foot. Outside of this building he could hear the cacophony of muffled gunfire knowing that this was his team working through the other buildings.

"Tower south east, heavy weapons. View obscured." Longo called over the radio.

"Wait one." Brown answered.

For a full five seconds the night was lit up by six red lines in the sky like laser beams as multi barrel weapons spat lead. The rapid fire made the snowflakes appear to stand still in their fall.

"Tower down." Brown spoke again when the roar of her weapons stopped and the night returned to darkness.

"Nice job Rachel." The Hooligan controller spoke. "Mass flight. Twenty-six with arms dead west into the park. Looks like a tunnel. Hang on. They are trying to flank."

"Got em." The night was rocked aging with manmade thunder.

Three flights of steel stairs put Tindall's fire team in a machine shop and laboratory fifty feet below the forest floor. The colonel had done his best to keep track of the radio calls and estimated that nearly eighty enemy combatants had died since he had left the helicopter. From all of the intelligence they had gathered pre-assault he knew that there should not be many more lurking.

"Team Two. Barracks clear. Moving to lab north side."

"Roger that Coleman." Tindall told his second in command.

"Team three has the armory. Barracks two and the motor pool are clear." Diaz told him.

"Outer perimeter is clear." Longo Spoke up.

"Chem Weapons Team move in." Tindall ordered. "Simpson bring the Little Birds back to McChord. Brown loiter on station."

"No sweat boss."

"Ah Colonel." A short blonde girl looked up at him when the lights came back on. "You probably don't want to be leaning against that." Her eyes were wide as she stared at the chrome box he was leaning on. The night vision green hadn't done the shiny object justice. Now he raised his eyebrows at it and the young doctor from Lawrence Livermore National Laboratory.

"Another Chem package?" He asked her.

"No sir, those tanks are on level one and two. I think this is special. I think this is a tool box."

"A tool box." He nearly laughed.

"Used tooling for the preparation of nuclear weapons." Yeaton said and swallowed hard.

"You have experience with nuclear weapons mister...?" The young doctor asked.

"Tristan Yeaton. Yes. I was on tactical nuke response with the Teams." He told her.

"Then you understand the implications of a closed and shielded toolbox?"

"Yeah. Someone already made a bomb." He had to frown. "Guys start looking for another box. Big. It's likely lead and dull or painted. Whoever shielded this thing did a stellar job because Hooligan didn't see it." Yeaton told Tindall.

"Bro. It's up here in the motor pool." Diaz spoke in their radios.

Everyone gathered in the motor pool to look at three four wheel drive van style campers. In the back of the RV's, hidden under bunks, were long black cylinders with timer and communications packages. The timers had not been set.

"Do you see the size of this truck?" Yeaton asked no-one in particular. "It's custom made on a heavy duty dump truck or wrecker. Those bombs are damned heavy."

"What's your take Doctor Stroud?" Tindall asked the scientist from the National Lab.

"Mister Yeaton is right. These vehicles are obviously custom made to move these bombs and try to do so innocuously. I would say that they weigh a few tons each and are definitely high yield."

"What's high yield in your estimation."

"Forty or fifty kilotons."

"Bullshit."

"I shit you not. These are city killers."

"Brian, we have a missing truck." Yeaton pointed at the concrete garage floor and the rubber imprint from the dual wheels identical to the three RVs in front of them.

"Utah." Tindall called out on the radio.

"Go ahead Alpha."

"I need Malone and McGuire now."

"Mac here. Great take down brother. What's up?"

"Sir. We found three RVs loaded with Nukes. We retrieved about ten thousand gallons of the chemical QB- Hyper Chlorine. The Doc says these are high yield weapons in the neighborhood of forty to fifty kiloton. We have a missing truck sir. We have to believe there is a loose nuke. I need a NEST down here."

"Alright Brian. Hold tight there and we will get them and a Special Forces unit out to relieve you. Outstanding work Colonel."

"Thank you, sir."

"Brian, Jax here."

"Go ahead Jax."

"You are looking at nuclear devices right now?"

"Yes. I'll give you a wave." He looked to the ceiling and waved.

"Whatever they shielded that with is not registering on the scanner. I'm going to tweak the system until I can pick it up."

Missoula Montana

The room was in a rundown roadside motel just outside Missoula. The place had likely never seen anything more than mediocrity and that had probably been sixty years ago. The carpet was green and black and stunk of stale cigarettes, mildew, human sweat and who knew what else. At least the shower was hot and the delivery pizza was tolerable. Roger Avery sat at the edge of the bed closest to the front door scanning the television for any news on the site in the Cascades. There was nothing that affected him. Taking a peek through a crack in the curtains yellowed by decades of nicotine he satisfied himself that he wasn't expecting surprise company.

Leaving the bedside lamp and the television on he shouldered his new hiking backpack to give him a less militant look, pulled on his gloves and slipped out of the room and over the balcony from his second floor fire escape. In ten minutes, he was behind the wheel of a three year old grey pick-up truck with Montana plates. The envelope on the driver's seat had two thousand dollars in cash, two packs of Canadian Export A cigarettes and two new sets of identification including drivers' licenses and passports. In another two hours he was aboard a Citation private jet leaving Helena for Toronto Ontario Canada.

Trevor Longley and Markus Kench did not fare as well as their fellow Mercenary. While Avery was on his way to the airplane their doors were kicked in and two Wraiths each disarmed and restrained them. Handcuffs and leg irons were used to restrain arms and legs while thick zip ties were ratcheted around their heads to keep their mouths open and limit the noise they could make. While Avery sipped whiskey and rested his head they were hauled to hot and dark rooms inside a mountain in the Utah desert.

Lake Tahoe
Nevada

WHEN THE KELLER RESORT was built in the 1930's it was meant to attract rich clients who had managed to survive the economic catastrophe of the Great Depression and give them a place to relax at any time of the year they chose to visit. Unlike most of the resorts of the era and the modern mega hotels, the Keller had been geared toward isolation for their guests. There was indeed a main building where shows, food and gambling were available, but the rooms were kept in cottages built apart from each other with almost no visibility between them. These cottages were large enough for a family to live in or a large number of guest to be entertained in. The other amenity that Keller built into the resort was exclusivity. Guests were invited as members of an exclusive club and membership was controlled by a board. With that exclusivity came a set of laws that the state of Nevada had no control of. Anyone who complained of cigarettes smoked at gambling tables or of men and women taking company in an extramarital relationship or out and out prostitution simply found out that they were no longer a member of the club. Even with that freedom, Senator Maureen Collins-Roth had appearances to keep and conducted herself as a lady while in the main concourse of the casino. It was in her cottage, a three story Tudor brick manse built for her late husband's grandfather, that she pursued her private ventures. It was here that she was so deep into an alcohol and narcotic induced haze that she laughed when Holland Mattison told her that Conrad told him that there were agents acting on the site in Washington and that Keong Saik had been killed in Beijing. She laughed again when he told her that he had not been able to contact Temuchin. What the General could not see was that while she laughed and her company tonight, a thin man just out of his teens and a tall darkly tanned girl of the same age, laughed with her at a joke they neither knew nor cared about, she was crying. Somewhere beyond her haze she realized that all was lost. If they knew her name was involved in Temuchin's plans they had marked her for prosecution as well.

"I have to go Maureen. You should get yourself out of the country as well. You know how to find the door." He said.

"Where is she?" Roth asked.

"Who Maureen?"

"Where is Casey?" She asked and put her hand high on the girl's leg. The girl was too drugged to be offended enough to pull away at the sound of another woman's name. A woman that she herself had wanted to love and been scorned by.

"I have to think that she is dead too. The house is trashed. I don't believe that she got away and I don't see a way out for her." Mattison told her and sighed. "Good luck."

"Stupid men." She scowled as she threw the cell phone against the wall. She sneered at the thin man in front of her and climbed atop him. He thought that the woman with the dyed hair and the body she was too old to have had found a new wave of excitement for him. An excitement that he wasn't sure he was ready to meet yet. What she did have was a knife in her hand that she began plunging into his chest. "Stupid fucking men."

"Stop." The girl screamed and recoiled away from her to run. In her panic she was not aware that the lights had gone out. She was not aware of the man in the hall waiting for her but felt the stab in her chest as the probes for the stun gun dug into her skin and lightning arced through her body. She sobbed as she was restrained and gagged and dragged to a waiting van.

Another man with a stun gun drove the probes of his weapon into Maureen's neck. When her body contorted with the electric assault, she left the blood covered knife embedded in the already dead young man's heart. She was allowed to fall from the bed where she landed on her face on the tile floor. The impact fractured her orbital socket and split open her lips. She was thrown into a shower and shocked again before being handcuffed and wrapped in a blanket at the black marble dining room table where two men and a woman in black clothes waited for her in the dim lights they had restored after capture.

"I'm too intoxicated for this." She mumbled as her unseen captors sat her down. "Nothing I say is admissible and I want my lawyers."

The woman in black stood from her seat with the men and plunged a syringe into Roth before sitting back down. She stared at the older woman after she sat. If she could have helped it, if it would have done anything to unsettle the bitch, she would not have allowed her eyelids to blink. Because she could not stop them from doing what they naturally did she tried to force the blinks as a way to keep the Senator focused on her face. Focused on the hatred that seethed from her core for this worthless sack of fluid and bones that sat before her. She wanted Roth to know just how hard the mighty could fall when their time comes around.

"The chemical I just injected is any anti-narcotic ten times stronger than Narcan and an anti-alcoholic that may make you shit yourself as you sober up. I'm kind of hoping so. At the very least, I stole your high. You do like chemicals don't you Maureen?"

"It's Senator. This is supposed to scare me. You people can't do shit to me. I'll be sentenced and put in a federal prison under protection. So what? Maybe I'll even be able to escape." She thumbed at the body still being cleaned up in the other room. "And as far as that little shit, it was self-defense. He attacked my friend and I while we were in bed."

"It's not going to work that way." Mitch McGuire said as he leaned forward into the light.

"You Mitch? I thought this was FBI. Shit. This is a no brainer. Get me out of here and to a safe house. There is some major shit at play here and we may have time to get ahead of it." She perked up at the sight of him.

"You are not Aphrodite anymore; you haven't been for a long time and we aren't at the company anymore Maureen." He told her. He had not expected the reaction she had given. He had not expected the willingness to turn on her cohorts. It was then that he realized what he was dealing with.

"I want my lawyer." She yelled.

"Yeah. You said that. Just in case you haven't caught on, I don't care what you want."

"Mitch, we've known each other for a long time. I don't know who I pissed off at the company but, I'm not going to be cashiered. This better be a joke. I have actionable intel that effects the safety of the country and our allies."

"Twenty-five years Maureen. A long time. A lot of trust. That's all forfeit now. You did this. Not me." McGuire said. "You need to start telling me about an operation involving Roger Avery, A chemical weapon, a nuclear weapon and some folks in Mongolia. Don't forget to mention some names as you go. Names like Conrad."

"I have no idea what you are talking about." She sat back. Her eyes closed as the headache from a hangover she had never experienced before hit her. It brought tears back to her eyes that continued the streaks of mascara and foundation running from her face onto the polished marble.

"I've been involved in far too many interrogations voluntary and otherwise to believe that. Try again."

"Then give me the sodium penytol." She sneered. The other man and the woman laughed.

"I don't believe in it, Maureen." Mitch told her. "I would however be glad to allow this gentlemen to demonstrate how he questioned a bad detective in Vermont before that man disappeared or perhaps have the good Doctor here show you how she dealt with an old associate of yours in Albany. Gabrielle Foster Correct? I promise you that what you have forgotten in the last year or so they have not. Because you are such a diva, we do promise to save your face for last." To emphasize his meaning, he cut the end of his cigar with an Emerson Commander Combat Folder and handed the knife over to the man next to him. He lit the cigar and watched her eyes flicker as her brain attempted to work.

"You wouldn't dare." She tried to sound righteous but was already starting to crack.

"Lie again and we'll find out." He said and exhaled the pungent smoke in her direction. "Come on, you're a gambling woman. Call my bluff. You should know that, like you, I am not with the Company anymore."

Her exterior shattered. She cried freely now. Not from the headache. She would not give them the satisfaction of hearing her sob though. The tears she had no control over. She realized now that she would not leave this room without speaking the truth and that she would never see freedom again.

"I was wrong. I got greedy. I..."

"You turned on your country. You never really had an allegiance to it though, did you? You've been at this a long time. Everything was building to this. Treason. You sold a deadly chemical to terrorists and you employ assassins. You ran a drug cartel and a human trafficking chain. I know all of that. I want the fucking names." He slammed the table with both of his hands.

"Why?" She looked up with mascara streaked eyes and a quivering lip. "What does it matter?"

"Because I am going to stop them."

Now she laughed. It wasn't out of spite but, nervousness.

"Mitch these people are something we weren't ready for. They are hard corps. Temuchin built an army of men devout to one thing. Fighting them will spark a world war. It's probably already coming. Where we stand in it will define our future. Let them do their thing, then we can come to the aid of the Chinese and the Russians and build a new, bigger and stronger world alliance."

"That was your plan?"

"It has been since I was in college. My companies have several advanced combative technologies that would be valuable in a global war. Yes, I would be enormously rich. I would also be in position to take power in Washington."

"How?"

"There is a secondary plan at work."

"The nuke."

"The summit to change all summits."

"Who is the contact at the agency."

"Norm Conrad."

"Anyone else?"

"No."

"What would make Avery flee Washington?"

"He has another mission."

"And what is that?"

"The nuke."

She was on a roll now and speaking freely. He smoked his cigar and let her talk. He was already forming plans as she spoke.

"Jackson for Blue." The earpiece for McGuire's comms chirped.

"Go for Blue."

"Boss. Mattison just suicided. He stuck a forty-five in his mouth before the team hit the house. He was dead when they went in."

"Ten four." He said and smiled at Maureen as she continued to talk and cry. "Looks like General Mattison can't talk anymore. You're all out of friends tonight, Maureen."

Mitch put his hand in the air to stop the Senator twenty minutes later. She had poured out bank and phone numbers. Businesses and homes. Cars, planes and yachts located throughout the world. Associates of the underworld who already made her far more rich than she could dream of. Mitch had enough targets for ten careers in her contact list alone. It read like the downline of a pyramid scheme, every one of those contacts had a list of their own. It was enough to drive someone mad. It robbed a thinking person of the ability or willingness to trust people anymore when they looked at the network of terror that existed behind closed doors.

"Because I no longer work for the CIA and neither do you, I am in a position of judgement in a far older, far darker organization.

One you may have heard rumors of. A Fraternity with an action arm. You are in the company of members of that action arm. We promise that this will be a sterile scene. Your present reputation will remain intact. This courtesy is not for you but for the country. The girl tonight will have no memory of you or of having been here. The young man unfortunately was killed in Reno as he tried to sell himself. You should know that General Mattison shot himself in the head right after he called you. We don't even have to sterilize that one. Your friend Casey is in custody and awaiting her next lot in life." He lit another cigar and let it sink in for her.

"You aren't going to kill me." She said and tried to regain her strong attitude and standing in the world. "You can't kill me."

"I would like to introduce you to members of SEAL Team Nine. A unit that does not exist because it conducts missions that in your words it can't do. This is Mister Luke Webb and his wife Doctor Jessica Webb, formerly of Stowe Vermont. You may recall that your syndicate killed mister Webb's brother first and then killed his sister in law and niece before killing his parents and the family of his wife. You might also recall some media coverage regarding a spree of killings that tie back to you and the late General and young miss Casey Glencamp and of course Coyame. You see, you aren't the only person who employs assassins."

"Oh my God. Oh my God. No Mitch. Please. Just shoot me in the head."

"If I could I would put you in a place where you would be tortured the rest of your natural life. Unfortunately, I have neither the time nor the facility. Your solution would be too messy. Doc, You're up."

Men had replaced the bed and cleaned the house. They were only waiting now for McGuire and the Webb's to clear the dining room to cleanse that. They helped move Maureen who attempted to thrash loose of them when they set her in the bed. Doctor Webb already had a syringe in her hand injecting through the fingernail bed as Roth had done with countless heroine needles to hide the evidence of track marks.

"This is a concoction of a paralytic and a synthetic acid. It's a lot like the chlorine you sold to the Mongols actually. While it paralyzes you and it will soon, it will contract your muscles to the point of pulling themselves from your bones. You will feel everything but you will be unable to move or even scream. This is for our family and everyone you have hurt in your pathetic life. When you feel the fire, you'll know that Hell awaits." She winked at her.

"I'm sorry." Maureen slurred. "Please make her stop."

The three assassins stood at the end of her bed watching until the woman's tears stopped and her urine flooded the bed. It took twelve minutes.

Senator Maureen Collins-Roth never spoke again.

"And it'll look like an overdose?" McGuire asked.

"It is an overdose. She has so much fentanyl in her that she could make a whole hospital high. It's about the same as every toxicology screen for a fentanyl overdose I've ever looked at. The other chemicals are burnt off." Jessica Webb tossed a syringe with heroine and fentanyl residue in its barrel onto the bed next to the Senator.

Altai Mountains

Temuchin sat in the oiled saddle on the stout grey stallion on a hilltop a mile away from the village and the lights of lanterns and fires still burning against the storm. He looked to the lake and the Urdu thinking of his people still sleeping. He stared into the sky and its raging wind and flakes stinging his face to freeze on his eyelashes. He waited for the sun to fight against the blizzard, to lend light to the land. In all directions the land rolled empty for hundreds of miles. All that he could see and ride in a week had once belonged to Genghis Khan and the Mongol horde. Soon, he thought, it would be again. In days the world, his world, would change. The warning the world would receive in his actions would seal the fate of the Khanate for centuries. Mongolia would be a world superpower. The premier superpower. The shock to the modern world would cause panic. That panic would be a weapon. The modern world of luxury and convince was not ready to fight a war on his level. They may never be ready again. The accomplishments of his ancestors, even the enemies of his ancestors was unobtainable in this modern world. People were unwilling to sacrifice to the degree that the old ones had. Today's people lacked the backbone or courage to create real change. The answer was his Mongol Horde.

Lighting one of the American cowboy cigarettes that his old school friend Maureen had shipped to him, he checked the brilliant Patek Phillipe watch that she had gifted to him upon her husband's death and smiled as he tugged the reigns guiding the stallion back through the Ordu and into the tunnels of his mountain fortress. A system of natural caves in the mountain had centuries ago been widened and connected by the slaves of the Khan. In recent years heavy mining had been done so that the inner spaces of the fortress were on par with several of the arenas and giant warehouses he had seen throughout the world. In here there was space for all of the needs of his people. Modern medical facilities were of as much import as food he had realized. In answer to that there was a one hundred bed hospital and a group of talented Russian and Chinese doctors ready. Food, as the great Napoleon had said, was a deciding factor of victory. Here in the pavilion, there was enough for four Tuman and their families for four years. Along with a motor pool full of tanks and four-wheel drive Toyota trucks, Chinese FAW MV3 six-wheel drives and several of the Dongfeng EQ2050 copy of the American HUMVEE there were more than a hundred horses kept inside the mountain. Here too were stored the spoils of wars long forgotten. Gemstones, raw silver and gold by the ton. Most of it had sat here for more than nine hundred years. For now, the most important of the caverns touched the frozen lake. Massive steel blast doors closed off access to the frozen surface. Here was the armory of the western pavilion. Here too sat a nuclear arsenal.

This is where Burkowska was kept busy alongside her staff. They were already at work in the early morning. Alongside racks of rifles and machine-guns were rows of gleaming steel cased artillery shells. Most of these were conventional devices but they sat among many carrying chemicals that would kill people, crops or both. Others, more than a dozen, carried nuclear warheads that would destroy cities and in so doing cripple countries.

Satisfied with the war material, he turned his attention to the portion of the lake inside the mountain. A harbor kept clear of ice by a network of heated pipes so that a flotilla of tiny fishing boats sat on placid water next to one of his prized possessions, a monstrous grey Russian Ekranoplan. The craft had been intended to service arctic military bases but had been used by Burkowska and Shaposhnikov to facilitate their defection and a raid on Russian gold. In effect the raid was Temuchin's first strike against Moscow. The giant plane was a vehicle he would make use of as the battles moved the horde west and north. It would be his chariot for the modern world.

"Good morning, sir." Coming down from a scaffold underneath one of the right engine nacelles Dmitry Shaposhnikov greeted him in deeply accented English. This was their only language in common.

"How is the plane?"

"Temperamental. She will fly, even today if needed. Gregor is a graduate of the Polish school of Ivchenko engines. It is in the best care with his hands. We placed extra fuel tanks to extend the range to ten thousand nautical miles."

"It is armed now I see." Temuchin pointed at several long barrels pointing from open windows and cuts in the aluminum and titanium structure.

"Yes. In the observation bubble is a 14.5 mm cannon. Port and starboard we placed several 12.7 mm Machine-guns and several Russian Gatling guns. In the rear is a 23mm Gatling gun. There are also four air to air missiles under each wing. She has teeth now."

"I should say so." He offered Dmitry the rest of his pack of cigarettes. "Most excellent work."

"Gregor and his mechanics are to thank. I only told them what needed to be done."

"That is one of the finer qualities of a good commander. Being able to give the credit to the men."

"Thank you, sir."

"How is your group?"

"The soldiers are well fed and happy. They will guard this mountain against any enemy. I have placed teams as far as two miles out and when the strike day comes, I will split the main camp into four points on the compass to surround the mountain."

"Very good. Enjoy the cigarettes."

"I will, thank you."

"You are familiar with them?"

"I am. I had them in New York when I saw the big building the monkey fell from in the movie."

"I saw the same place." Temuchin smiled and walked away.

"Fucking idiot." Shaposhnikov mumbled as he turned away. He was unaware that the tall man was thinking the same about him. "Gregor." He yelled out as he climbed back up the scaffold.

"What is it Dmitry?" He asked as he wiped grease from his bare arms and hands. He only wore boots, shorts and a ripped grey t-shirt while he tinkered on the plane. He was bald and thickly built at six foot four inches tall. "Ah good smokes." He perked up when offered one.

"Gregor can you fly this?"

"Yes. Why though? Stephan and Suc Zhang are the pilots."

"When I ask you to fly, they will probably be dead." Shaposhnikov said while holding the smoke in.

"Okay Dmitry. When I put the nacelle back on, she is ready. I have just been looking busy. Only those doors are in our way."

"Those doors will not be an issue. It is good Gregor. It will not be today. You stay with the plane now. Even if I am not here you take Yelena to Africa. She will know where. Talk no more of this."

Gregor smoked his cigarette in silence. When he was done, he dropped the butt into the water

"Utah One to Wolf One." Jax's voice broke through the silence of the tunnel.

"Go ahead Utah." Matt whispered back.

"Cascades, Roth, Mattison and Glencamp are down. Mac has called Blue on the remaining sites."

"Say again blue?" Matt asked.

"Altai is yours. All other sites are Blue." She told him. He looked to the others in the group especially focusing on Benedetti who nodded at him and gave a thumbs up.

"Roger that Utah. Blue is a go. We are moving on Altai now." He told her and put his bare hands on the cold granite of the skylight tunnel thinking that it must have been hundreds of years since a laborer had done the same as they rested from their task. It may never happen again after his time here.

Shaw was using a silenced electric drill to drive three long stainless steel bolts into the roof of the five foot tall cave. Once these were in place, he hung a network of heavy gauge wires to which he locked his harness via carabiners.

"That's a nice looking plane." Shaw said as he peered over the edge of the cave cut in the ceiling a hundred feet above the roof of the Ekranoplan. "It would make a nice addition to your collection. I'm assuming you heard all of that?" He looked back at Matt who was locking himself onto a 12mm thick black rappel line with a black

D-ring rappel device that would allow him to move as fast or slow in descent as he chose.

"Yup. I was thinking the same thing Sar'n Major."

"Maybe I could borrow it for a long weekend at Catalina."

"Unbelievable." Beck shook her head. "There's dissension in the ranks down there."

"Yeah, let's not let that soap opera brew around nukes and chlorine, shall we?" Matt said. He took another peak into the void under him and beyond the fuselage of the Russian plane. After crawling through dusty and frozen tunnels of the ancient complex he had not expected to find much more than a great cavern where an amphibious plane and a camp were hidden. He was forced to choke back his surprise when he found a temple much like one from the Ming Dynasty surrounded by a lush garden and several acres of terraced grass. Small shrubs grew at the edges of the garden and along the temple blocking the harsh lines of the carved out stone walls of the cave. A waterfall cascaded from a crack high in the wall to collect in a series of pools that descended the granite face until it spilled into the lake. An enormous forty foot tall carved wooden door that must have been made from entire trees that had to be transported hundreds of miles to reach the cave sat in the carved wall behind the temple. This was surrounded with sculptures and artifacts from long forgotten cultures. All of it spoils from people vanquished by the Great Khan's. The four Wraiths stared out of the hole with tears in their eyes at the collections of hand worked silver, bronze and gold. They looked on at wooden crates spilling over with gemstones and jewelry and realized that they were in the presence of the never before witnessed Golden Horde.

"This is a national treasure." Beck whispered. "Surely this would place the holder as one of the richest nations in the world."

"Black diamonds." Shaw said. "Big ones."

THE CASCADES SANCTION

"Time to get dirty." Hauer said and looked to make sure the rest of his team had locked into their static lines and were ready to rappel. "Jax we are at the mouth of the lion. Lights out."

"Lights out."

In less than a second a pulse from the Hooligan shut off all electric lights in the complex. Under night vision Hauer plunged into the open air above the plane. Set charges shattered the mirrors inside the skylight tunnels and kept the pavilion in the dark. Anyone not wearing night vision was left with a world blacker than the night sky. In a slow controlled descent Hauer set his feet on the center of the plane's fuselage as Gregor was climbing out. The bald man never saw the man who had come to kill him. If he saw the flash from Matt's rifle his brain had not had enough time to register what he was looking at before he died. Two more men died behind him as Benedetti and Beck moved past the wings of the plane down the starboard side into the water. Once Shaw was on the ground and they were away from the water they found sentries along the walls of the temple and the armory. Like the Mongol riders of old carrying two bows as main weapons these men had pairs of old heavy barreled FN FAL rifles and AKM's. Both guards were fumbling with flashlights that they had never trained with. One was dropped twice before the user was able to turn it on. When the man did get it to work, he was only able to see Shaw's feet before Matt shot him twice. Brett's rifle spat lead in time with the team leader and they moved on. As the two Wraiths continued on a circuit of the harbor taking down sentries Benedetti grabbed up the weapons of the fallen soldiers and found the storage racks holding 55 gallon drums marked as Bio-Hazard along with the lines of artillery shells. From his backpack the Doctor produced a pair of grey boxes the size of half pint milk cartons and placed them under the racks.

"Jax, I have eyes on the weapons at Altai."

"I'm seeing everything now. You have a lot of people in there with you. There are five big floors above your heads. I have their power grid." Jax told him.

"Commander, I believe it's time to get this party started." Shaw said as he tapped Hauer's shoulder. Flashlights were charging down a ramp behind the temple and the stomping of countless boots came with them. Those boots would have rifles. Worse, Hauer needed to be up that ramp.

"Jax. Be so kind as to open those blast doors and tell our neighbors there is a block party." Matt said and placed a claymore mine at the mouth of the cave facing the ramp. Shaw did the same and moved back to the temple for cover.

"Surprise just died a miserable death." Shaw said.

With a shudder the blast doors, mounted on railroad tracks, shattered the ice that had formed on their outside surface and slid into their recesses cut into the walls. The light pouring in was blinding to the night vision goggles forcing the Wraiths to look away as Seal's from Team 3 alongside Marines from MARSOC Raiders and NEST personnel charged into the void. Farther away on the lake shore Marines of the 26th MEU were hitting the village with a barrage of unsuppressed automatic weapons fire. The noise drew more speed from the Mongols coming down the ramp.

"As soon as those claymores crack, open up into that cave." Hauer told Beck.

Six men from Team 3's Delta Platoon made it to the base of the temple with belt fed weapons before the claymore mines were detonated, each of them sending seven hundred 3.2mm tungsten balls through the air at over 1200 feet per second. The tiny projectiles cut through everything in their way for close to a hundred yards until they embedded themselves in the granite walls or simply ran out of energy and fell to the cold wet stone. After the explosion the air was filled with the moans and screams of eviscerated men welcoming death and the promise of an afterlife where the pain would stop. The strike team wasted no time charging forward. The SEALs cleared weapons away from the dying and shot those that had somehow managed to avoid the blast.

"Moving to the tunnels." Hauer said.

"Left goes up and right goes down about a hundred feet in. Down takes you to a forty by forty room. It's a dormitory." Jax told him.

"SEALs to the right." Shaw yelled.

The Wraiths ran forward and up the left ramp as they plunged back into the dark. Under Jax's guidance they swept through a floor where stables, sheep pens and chicken coops had been set up. There was constant airflow here pulling air from the lake and venting it through the skylights so that none of the animal smells lingered. More Mongols, now only in Chinese or Russian uniforms that they had barely been able to put on as they reacted to the gunfight, charged forward with flashlights and rifles at the hip. Beck was the first to respond, shooting two men at the entrance to another on the ramp before Matt and Brett could bring their own rifles into play and began the leapfrog dance of cover and movement as they engaged targets with short bursts from their hard hitting rifles. Shaw and Hauer exchanged a curious look as they saw that the rifles of their enemies had changed from the older weapons on the harbor shore to the newer QBZ-95 Bullpup rifles issued to the Chinese army.

"Mangudai." Beck told them.

"Make sure some of these rifles are collected." Matt said. "We might need them someday."

"Navy don't throw away shit." Shaw told Beck as he shook his head.

"Matt, The Marines cleared the village and gained the tunnel leading in. They are on their way in to you." Jax said over the radio.

Temuchin was undressed and looking down at the pair of young Mongolian women on his oversized bed of hides when the lights went out. Using only candles and lanterns in his room, he had not been immediately aware of a problem. When the men outside his heavy oak doors began yelling and he could see the hot white light of flashlights he knew immediately that life was changing. He picked up a satellite phone to alert all of his camps to engage their targets but found the device dead and useless. The switches to his lights would not work. The women lay silent as they stared up at him moving around to gather pants and a rifle and sword that all appeared as children's toys in the giants' hands. He rushed to the thick doors and opened one a crack to see the two guards there to protect him. A large group of Mangudai formed at the door to assist.

"What happened?"

"No one answers."

"There is a battle. We have attackers inside now." Shaposhnikov yelled as he shoved Burkowska into the room among a group of Mangudai and several of his Spetznaz fighters. He was still fastening a Russian assault vest over his snow camouflage when he entered. He carried a single AK-12 rifle and a chest full of magazines as well as a handful of night vision goggles that he handed to the giant. "If they clear that maze below, we have a fight coming."

"I heard gunshots." Burkowska said as she tried to stop herself from falling onto the bed in the tangle of naked women.

The soldiers wanted out of the room and into the fight outside the heavy doors. Most of them were standing far too close when the great carved doors were blown to chunks and splinters by breaching charges. Before the blast had ended several flash-bang grenades detonated, flooding the room in blinding light that dazed anyone not wearing night vision and permanently blinding the men who had managed to get their Chinese or Russian made goggles on. Automatic weapons fire erupted right behind the light.

Shaposhnikov, now blind and moaning, fell into Burkowska and Temuchin pushing them toward the bed. The Doctor rolled away from him and pulled the two girls off of the bed away from the attackers. Shaposhnikov tried to face where the firing was coming from but found himself lifted from the ground. His rifle fell to the ground and he realized that he was in the powerful hands of the giant. Temuchin had lost his weapons in the blast but his hands were just as deadly as any sword or rifle. Shaposhnikov knew this as he felt the berserk Mongol squeeze as he tried to bring both hands together despite the man's skull cracking between them. Dmitry lashed out with punches and kicks that did nothing to deter the larger man.

Yelena Burkowska grabbed the girls and held them down at the far edge of the bed trying to keep them away from the large men who would crush them if they fell or the bullets that still howled through the air and flashed off of the stone walls in streaking showers of sparks as they ricocheted. Shaw, Hauer and Beck caught sight of the fight between the Spetznaz Colonel and Temuchin and looked on in horror as the man with blood running from his ears and skull, probably already severely brain damaged, closed his right hand around the wooden grip of an old short barreled Smith and Wesson revolver and began firing into the chest and abdomen of the giant holding him a foot off the floor. The 44 magnum was louder than anything that had gone off except the breaching charges. Its concussion shook the room. Although hollow point lead tore holes through the man and left jagged and gushing exit wounds he maintained his grip and growled as he squeezed harder. The muscles and veins of his forearms stood against his skin and danced with the effort. Dmitry, unable to see, fired twice more as he thought his way up his attacker. The hand cannon sent a bullet into the man's heart and another into the jaw, taking off the right side of his face as it left and slammed against the ceiling. Shaposhnikov fell to the ground as the giant reached up, attempting to put his damaged head together again. Temuchin began a slow deliberate walk toward the man in the shadows under the flickering candlelight and smoke. All three Wraiths leveled their rifles and fired repeated shots into Temuchin's chest and head until he was on the ground in a puddle and moved no more. The Russian touched his eyes and the sides of his head before cursing himself and stuck the gun under his chin. He closed his blind eyes and pulled the trigger.

"Please, soldiers, don't shoot. We are unarmed." Burkowska screamed in Mandarin.

"Doctor Yelena Burkowska." Hauer yelled out.

"Yes. I am Doctor Burkowska."

"Get out here. You can help." He told her.

As soon as she stood up Beck grabbed her and cuffed her hands behind her back. "If you utter a word before you're told you will be gagged for the entirety of the ride."

The enormous Rescuer Ekranoplan affectionately dubbed the Chayka Two after the old Soviet amphibious anti-submarine plane throttled up and turned inside the confines of the cave so that it faced the open blast doors and the frozen lake. Outside, the storm continued to dump snow onto the valley and whisked at the smoke of the still burning village. Once the plane was straight Hauer looked over at Beck at his right and nodded so that they pushed the throttles of all twelve massive jet engines forward together. For a moment the thrust only kicked a wave from the lake up over the temple and its garden and surrounding walls to fall back like rain. As the howl of a million pounds of thrust raged in the confined space to the point where all on board the aircraft winced at the assault on their ears the hull began to move against the once placid lake and climbed onto the ice outside the fortress walls. After the edges cracked under the weight and the tail finally cleared the granite Hauer and Beck pushed further into the throttles and the craft scrapped over the intact ice as they gained speed. At one hundred and sixty miles per hour, the speed at which Matt had jumped from the Demon only hours earlier, they fired six rockets attached to the rear of the fuselage of the enormous plane, the ground effect craft left the surface of the earth to ride on the buffet of air between it and the frozen land under it. They looked out of the cockpit at the other aircraft that had already taken to the air extracting the assault teams and captured material.

"Wolf to Utah." Hauer said.

"Go ahead Matt." Jax told him. "We are watching you now."

"Jax we are clear of Altai, inbound Camp Vengeance. Is Mac there?"

"Go ahead tadpole." McGuire laughed. "All sites are down. We hit them with lasers and swept up with the Strike teams. We managed a broken clavicle and some scrapes. Nothing major. Hell of a job young man."

"Mac, I need a Demon at Vengeance. We can depose our guest quickly. While we do that, I would like for you to make contact with the Green Mountain boy so that we can make arrangements to enhance relations with our friend Nick."

"Is that a wise decision?"

"I would say it's the second smartest thing I've ever done."

"What's the first kid?"

"I'm about to do that now. See you in Utah. Wolf Out."

He caught Beck's attention as she stared out at the mountains as they left the grip of the storm behind. She turned to him with bright green eyes and a smile. He saw a happiness that hadn't been there when they had met. What she had done had saved many from the fate that her friends had met or worse. It wasn't enough to bring them back but it was enough for her to know that she had taken part in a solution. He motioned for her to remove her headset as he was.

"Would you do me the honor of accompanying me to dinner and a play when we wrap this up?" He asked.

"That sounds a lot like a date."

"It would be a lot like a date. Very easily confused." He smiled and blushed while hoping that she would say yes.

"I was really hoping that I wouldn't have to ask you." She said. She blushed too. It ran under her eyes. Her smile was brighter than he had seen even in the photographs when he had looked into her background. He had to take some satisfaction in the knowledge that he had created that smile. "Yes please."

Shaw looked away from the edge of the cockpit to Benedetti rolled a large black diamond in his hands and smiled before he put his feet up and closed his eyes.

Chapter Sixteen

"Revenge is an act of passion; vengeance of justice."
Samuel Johnson
English Writer

Virginia

Agent Joel Conrad began his morning as he had for the previous four years since moving to the new house. He rose at four to leave the side of the latest tanned college brunette that he had wooed with the world of stolen wealth for a glass of orange juice and a banana. After washing the glass, he hopped on a stationary bike in his basement to scroll through any of the emails on either the cell phone he wouldn't mind his boss at Langley seeing or the one that his friend Casey Glencamp had given to him. There was nothing on his open channel phone and only a smiley face on his dirty phone.

"What the fuck?" He managed to say before he saw the flash of the hands reach around his face to pull him backward off of the bike. His right hand shot to his waist, reaching for a pistol that he had routinely never carried into the sanctity of his own basement. His brain yelled 'fuck' again right before his back and head met the concrete.

"He was probably too young for you anyway Conrad." The man in the black jumpsuit told him. Two more figures in black stood behind the first. Both held suppressed weapons on him. Red lasers found his forehead and stayed there as he fought to regain composure through the shock and pain. The figure who had pulled him to the ground knelt on his chest and started pulling a hood from his face.

"Don't do that. I don't want to see your face." Joel whined knowing that it probably meant death to see his attacker.

"You really do though Joel. You were an outstanding operator. You should have been a better friend. You picked some really shitty friends this time, didn't you?" Hauer asked him.

"I fucking knew it was you after them. You don't even work for anyone though. You're just riding on daddy's legacy now. You can't be in the teams anymore either. So, there's some justice."

"Justice. We'll visit that lady in a minute."

"Go to hell Hauer."

"High roller556, that's where I live. You're about to find out."

"What?"

"That's your cute little web name, right? Tell me what your friend Keong Saik couldn't. Tell me why you never passed along the shit that Kim sent back to you and tell me about Avery. After you, he's the only one left. Tell me where he's going."

"Fuck you."

Hauer punched him in the throat. The agents body instinctively wanted to clasp his hands to his throat as if that would help him. With his hands pinned under Hauer's weight he was barely able to squirm and was left to choke as his eyes rolled back in his head.

"There's an easy way and there's a way where I start playing high school biology class meets butcher shop." Hauer pulled his Spartan Blades Nyx knife free for effect. He rested the giant blade on the disgraced man's face. "We aren't friends but you know me well enough to know that I am not playing games Joel."

"You aren't going to kill me dude, so fuck yourself."

"But I am Joel. I am." Hauer hit him again. This time in the left clavicle with the back of his palm hearing it snap as he drove down. "We we're going to hang you but now that's not looking believable. Now I have to make it look like a sex buy gone bad. No problem. We've rounded up enough of your shitbag friends to make you look as filthy as you are to the papers. We'll also be sure to dump the Department of the Navy details on you so that the Agency knows to do a far better job on future recruitment. Your parents will love that. So, what'll it be, you talk and go fast or you get hurt bad and still talk?"

"You really killed all of them?"

"What do you think?" A female voice asked from behind Hauer.

"What about the girl?" Conrad asked.

"You don't even know her name, do you?"

"No."

"She'll be drugged and moved and won't remember you. She never saw us. Tell me about Avery."

"Merc. Ex-SAS. Bigger fuck up than me but, really good at wet work. Mattison had him working for a while, did some shit down in South America and then set up security on their stateside activity. He was supposed to be their back door. He was supposed to make sure that their part of the plan was still a plan B and would still drive Roth into a power spot."

"How?"

"A legit nuclear option from what Mattison said."

"And how did you play in all of this? You created a list of potential clients for Glencamp's sex network and got to partake and you created a list of clients for weapons. What was your payoff?"

"Someone had to run agencies under a new administration."

"You really thought that would be you? With that group of friends don't you think you knew too much?"

"Do you remember a place where we howled into the night yelling 'Good Night Al Huey wherever you are'?"

"Yeah. I'll never forget it."

"I don't trust people either. I stashed some stuff on a little spot south of there. A new life. I was going to pull up stakes and then I met that girl upstairs and I stayed."

"Lie." Hauer drove the butt of the knife down on Conrad's right cheek. "You've never met a woman you gave a shit about. You stayed because there was something in it for you. Where is the nuke going?"

"Montreal G20. They were going to hit it at the same time they struck with the chemicals. It was going to throw the world in a tailspin."

"Avery?"

"Avery is so wanted right now I wouldn't be surprised if he ran the bomb in himself. Fucker took my money too."

"Money for what?"

"To kill you. I couldn't risk doing it myself and I had the cash."

"Why me and How?"

"You are one of a few people I had pegged for being involved with whoever had the tech to crack in on us. You had to go. How the fuck would I know how he would want to kill you?"

"Because you and Avery are buddies. You got him the job with Mattison. Mattison knew all about your bullshit in Iraq and knew he could buy you. If you weren't all busted up, I'd probably let you take his way out. He stuck an old forty-five in his mouth and ended it quick. But I saw your profile on that network and it makes me think that you need to know it's coming. Let's get creative with that shall we Sar'n Major?"

"Sign me up." Shaw said as he leaned in to cuff and shackle the man while Beck took her hood off and unrolled the bag to carry him out to their waiting van.

Jackson Malone followed the conversation with Conrad and prioritized a Hooligan blimp over Montreal Canada. She found the signature for the nuclear RV parked in a campground in Saint Angelique Quebec a few miles outside of Montebello five minutes after Matt left Conrad's house. Kevin Buhr, Jesse Randall and Luke Webb were inside of the cockpit of a VB-8 Demon and rolling over the sand colored runway in Utah ten minutes after that. Using the information that Doctors Benedetti and Quarrels had taken from Yelena Burkowska during her sleep interrogation Jax was able to shut down any possible way to activate the bomb through a continuous laser aboard the Hooligan. Unlike the sites with the chemicals, she was not able to destroy the weapon with a laser for fear of creating a dirty bomb event that would saturate the greater Montreal area in a toxic and radioactive nightmare. The team of Wraiths hit the ground at a Canadian Air Force base and met with U.S. and Canadian Secret Service to get to the campground where they found four men around the two tone brown recreational vehicle. These men detailed that they had been hired to wait with the RV until twelve o'clock the next day and drive to the gates of the Chateau Dufresne where they would ask for Mister Louis Slotin. None of them understood the implications of the name of the Canadian scientist sent to Los Alamos to work on the atom bombs that were dropped on Japan. There was a video feed inside the van that signaled back to a house in Jacksonville Florida. There were cameras recording traffic lights and storefronts throughout Quebec. There would have been enough collected evidence of four Arab men delivering a nuclear bomb to be released to the public in the coming days to start a renewed war in Western Asia. Even the chemical attacks could be blamed on a nation on the Sinai peninsula and serve to solidify new alliances in the world.

Members of American NEST (Nuclear Emergency Services Team) and Canadian Joint Incident Response Unit, Canadian Radiation Protection Bureau worked alongside the Canadian Army to secure the site and the truck and evacuated the campground until they could move the RV and bomb. In the middle of the night the RV was loaded aboard a ski equipped C-17 Globemaster and flown to Nunavut Provence.

Whoever had been living in the house in Jacksonville had left hours before Wraiths and the Secret Service descended on the poor neighborhood. An empty pack of Export A cigarettes was left in the kitchen sink next to the ashes of receipts for the video equipment in the RV. Neighbors told of a white man with black hair and a beard who didn't talk to anyone. He had left in a beat up old white Ford pickup truck. A BOLO (Be On the Look Out) was issued worldwide for Avery and the truck. This lead to countless stops of contractors and random people over the next two days until an abandoned 1976 Ford F250 was found behind a grocery store in Warrenton Georgia. Roger Avery's fingerprints would be identified from inside the truck. Avery though, was gone.

Narva-Joesuu
Estonia

THE GULF OF FINLAND was drenched in the blanket of night. A few ships still several miles away, cast tiny lights into the sky heavy with looming clouds that drowned out the stars. Hauer sat at the wheel of the silver Czech built Skoda Kodiaq SUV parked on the sand of the vacant beach. With his clear lensed multifunction glasses on he used the night vision setting to watch the waves slap against the dark hull of the Ekranoplan where some of the water would freeze in a thin veneer of salty ice. The Russian weatherman on the radio gave a forecast of more cold and more snow coming in from the gulf of Finland. Matt pulled his thick leather and lambswool bomber jacket tighter around him despite the heaters blowing in the car.

The luminous hands of his Rolex Submariner told him that it was 1:55 in the morning local time. Sipping coffee from a thermos he scanned up and down the beach looking for a vehicle or anyone crazy enough to walk in the subzero weather. Thornton had told him that his expected guest and the people Matt wanted her to bring along would arrive at two as asked. Matt knew that Thornton would not mislead him and hoped that his guest would not let him down in the agreement either. The Russian made AK-12 rifle, Russia's newest model, and the MP-443 Grach 9 mm pistol on his waist mimicked the equipment of the Estonian military and that of anyone coming with the guest might carry. They might buy him enough time to get away from the meet if things went bad with this meeting.

Headlights flicked on and off twice in the distance. He flicked his once in response and the car, an older heavy black UAZ Russian jeep drove onto the sand of what would be a tourist beach in a few months. Hauer counted his guest and four more men crammed into the cabin of what had to be a cold ride. She got out and slid into the leather passenger seat of the Skoda looking in the back as she did.

"Something tells me that you have people out in the cold watching us with very big rifles." She said.

"They do like their rifles. But then again, so do your Zaslon friends." To this Karina Aminoff smiled.

"One day Mister Hauer we might learn to trust each other."

"Maybe." Matt told her. "I'll do what I can beyond your casino experience to help that happen. We spoke about a Doctor if you recall."

"I do. Why are we here? Why not just come to Russia?"

"I cannot bring into Russia what you can."

"That's why I needed the pilots?"

"Very particular pilots." Matt told her.

"This is why you knew their names."

"Exactly." He smiled. "Before that I came into possession of something the Oprichniki have been looking for for a long time. I want you to have it." He passed her a padded Pelican case. "Open it."

Gingerly, she released the latches and pulled open the lid. Her face fell when she saw inside. She stared at a 10-inch tall ornate blue and gold egg sitting in black foam.

"This is the Fabergé'?" She sighed. "The Danish Jubilee."

"I told you I had it."

"It is beautiful. The organization will be pleased beyond words."

"Tell your driver to turn on his lights. I'm going to turn on mine." He waited until she was looking at the grey hull at the water line and had looked higher to see the wings and tail section of what could only be a large amphibious aircraft.

"What?"

"Those two pilots are some of the few that have been trained to fly it. I can't fly that into Russia and I can't bring Yelena Burkowska to justice in Russia. That's your job. Now can you tell me where that key I asked you about will fit?"

"Yes. It belongs to a bank in Finland. It also opens a bank vault in Sweden. Be very careful when you visit those banks. They have been watched since the Tsar deposited to them before he died. There should be a fortune in them. I believe that you have earned it. It's something that the Oprichniki would not be fully aware of but if they were they would likely agree on Matt."

"Does that mean we're friends?" Matt asked.

"I think trust is being watered here." She blushed for the first time and smiled at him. "I may have some things to send you."

"For now, send them to box 43 at 80 Post in Riga. The name is Juris Akmentins. It gets checked daily."

"Easy."

"Good. Have a safe flight."

Brett Shaw and Kevin Buhr walked away from the giant plane as Arminoff's people piled in. Matt drove the Skoda in silence back to the tree line where they waited long enough for Jesse Randall and Jenn Beck to climb in.

"Get warm and get some sleep." Hauer told them. "It's a long ride to Latvia."

"Who is Juris Akmentins?" Jenn asked.

"A good guy I once knew."

"Hey diplomat. If I had said no, would you have asked her?" Jenn asked.

"Nope. I don't like the idea of having my throat cut in my sleep."

"It's an option." She smiled and closed her eyes.

"Jealous much." Buhr chided.

"Territorial." She said and Matt had to smile.

Chapter

Seventeen

One Month Later
"Violence is man re-creating himself."
Frantz Fannon
French Psychiatrist

Pennsylvania

MATT HAUER SET THE worn leather map case back down on the floor. He was looking at a hydrographic overlay of the Sandwich Bay in Labrador Canada and the shape of a ship under the frigid waters. A single black and white photograph displayed a three masted steel hulled ship with a coal fired steam engine. The ship flew the old Russian Imperial standard flag bearing a double headed black eagle over what would be a white, blue and red banner. The Bolsheviks had banned the tri-color in 1917 so this was a ship that had been down there for a long time. A ship that he wondered if he should leave alone. From the bottom of the map case fell a single tarnished gold coin. A ten ruble gold coin minted in 1911. "Nothing ends in the Russian Empire." He heard John Thornton's words echo in his mind.

Matt had waited until things were resolved from the Mongolian affair before he left D.C. and business in Maryland to take another attempt at a break. Carl had packed the map case given to him by Thornton. Carl had done it on purpose because he knew that Hauer needed closure. He knew that he would not seek it without someone pushing him toward it. If he did not find it, he would self-destruct. Hauer hated that he was right. He hated not having complete control over himself. He felt that he should be above suffering somehow, even if that sounded foolish or crazy. Too many people depended on him to be okay. That was why when he saw the tube, he decided that he had to know whatever lay inside.

Now he had to know why his father had thought that this particular ship was important. He looked back down at the map and walked across the living room to the bar and poured a tall glass of scotch while looking at the pair of long swords that had been authenticated as early Mongol in origin that now sat under his Great Grand Father's rifle. Several new photographs of his Wraiths next to the big Ekranoplan sat among the old black and whites that adorned the mantel. He had several pieces by which to remember his Mongolian trip. As he turned, his left side erupted in pain and he lost his feet. Before he hit the ground, he heard the muffled crack of a supersonic bullet smack into the wall where he had been standing. Blinking through the pain he pressed a button on a fob in his pants shutting the lights off for the entire house. Scrambling, he retrieved the glasses he had laid on the end table where he was studying the map and gathered what he thought he might need.

The bullet had mostly impacted at the lower edge of the bullet proof vest and shattered a few ribs and likely bruised organs. The copper jacket of the bullet, already peeling back from slicing through the glass of the bay window had sheared into fragments and several of those had cut through his heavy wool sweater to stick just inside his skin where they accomplished little more than drawing blood and aggravating him.

Two things were immediately obvious to him. He was injured and he was being hunted.

"Jax." He called out over his satellite phone as he stuck earbuds into his ears and made his way along the floor toward his bedroom. A barrage of machine-gun fire shredded the entryway and kept him from venturing further. The shooter was guessing, but it was a good guess. Not being able to get into that room left him with his Cabot 1911 pistol against at least two gunmen.

"Hey Matt."

"Jax. I've been shot. I'm in the living room in Pennsylvania. I think I have two shooters stalking me."

"Shit." She said. "Okay. I'm looking at it now. You have one coming inside and... close your eyes Matt."

He immediately clamped his eyes shut and held his right elbow over them. The world still flashed red as Jax directed the Hooligan's laser to fire into the hidden machine gunner.

"Thanks, Jax."

"Response is on the way."

"Are you in here Commander Hauer?" A male Cockney accented voice asked. "Still of this world?"

Hauer moaned.

"I always wondered who'd come out on top. I cross trained with you blokes. Tough enough lot I suppose, but right arrogant. You're about the cockiest of the breed. You sit here in this mansion as if you're untouchable after all you do out there. When Maureen said she wanted you people, whoever you were dead, I could have told her forty million and I don't think she would have flinched. I couldn't believe nobody else had a bounty on you. I could have made big money. And it was easy. I thought you'd be dangerous. You really fucked her world up. You won't be in the way of mine though."

"It's Avery." Jax said in his ear.

The man became more animated in his movements as time slipped away from him. He kept his back against walls as he made his way from the basement and into the house. Hauer watched him move and waited for the right time. The glasses lit up the night for Matt but the man had night vision of his own and he had a short and stubby submachine gun ready to unleash lead. Matt let the man move and work against himself.

"Tony don't fire. I'm going into the target zone." Avery spoke.

Hauer waited in the silence and braced himself.

"Tony what's your status?" Avery asked after a moment. "Fuck it all then." "You're playing with me now Hauer is that it?"

"I've been playing with you since the snow started falling Avery. I had to know too. Who was the better hunter. Conrad must have told you about me." Hauer whispered but his voice was broadcast over speakers placed throughout the lodge. With the speakers covering his sound Hauer moved to where he wanted to be. Avery fired a burst at a shadow on the opposite end of the room from Matt. "I won't drink out of your dirty skull but I'll have scotch over your corpse while I light my cigar."

"I saw that bar. I think I'll have a drink myself." Avery made his way across the room to the bar where Hauer had been not that long ago. Where Avery now thought that he should have taken the better shot but he had wanted to get the man standing at his prizes. Matt watched him move. Watched him stalk and taunt. Avery would have driven most untrained men mad. Mad men performed foolish and desperate acts. Hauer was angry but he was not mad. Anger fed skill and drove at tactics and the tactic here was to lay out the rope for Avery to hang himself with. Avery had lost millions and had his face plastered throughout the world. He was being hunted by everyone. He was already unstable. Having no control here made it worse for him. All of his training and all of his luck was failing him. He was alone and should pull away to fight another day, but he was too crazy with the lust for the kill that he failed to realize or care that he had ventured into the wolf's den. The wolf had patience.

Hauer waited and let the man walk out where he knew that he would. Avery was a trophy hunter and he wanted to touch the trophy before he had earned it. He was surprised to see it in Matt's hands and surprised to see the wounded SEAL sitting against the fieldstone fireplace. The lights came on in the house a moment before first one barrel of the big rifle and then the other kicked off in an enormous roar that filled the house and reverberated through the shattered window to echo down the valley below. The massive kick was more than Hauer had expected but he dealt with it. The first of the elephant rounds tore through the man's abdomen and gouged a hole through his body before burying itself in the wall. The second hit Avery in the heart after pulverizing his sternum and severed the spine as it left his body. He twitched momentarily as he died on his feet and a single nine millimeter bullet tore through the sleeve and flesh of Matt's left tricep. The hunter never saw his bullet strike. Hauer took the little submachine gun and the man's pistol and made his way back to the bar to pour another drink. Before doing so he looked at the through and through wound in his arm and put a tourniquet above it. There was a marker on the top of the bar. He used it to mark down the time before pouring his drink and grabbing a cigar to return to Avery's side.

"It's done Jax."

"Are you okay?"

"Yeah. I'm gonna need a medic but I'll see you in Maryland." He sipped the drink and took a long pull from the cigar. He looked down at Avery's body and the black lines of a tattoo inside his left wrist. A spider was nestled inside a double headed eagle. Matt shivered and sneered into the night. "Jax, get ahold of Mitch and tell him to tell our old friend in the north that I found one of the tattoo's he was interested in. Get ahold of Doctor Eric Bishop at Woods Hole and ask him if he's free anytime in the next week to take a look at some maps and charts for me."

"Your treasure hunting while you're bleeding out?" She laughed nervously.

"Something like that." He tilted his head back to give the cameras on the spy balloon a smile before finishing his drink.

Acknowledgements

To God. I would not be here, and I would not have the drive in this life that I do were it not for your grace with this wretch.

To My Wife Jenni, my best friend and biggest fan. She always hears about characters as they begin to take life in my head and never seems to tire of new twists. Without her support and ability to create time where I cannot see it none of these books would exist.

To My Dad for fostering a love of airplanes, adventure, and justice. Every time I hit a spot in life when I need to dig, I recall being a very young boy looking down from a slab of granite we were climbing and I can see your face, that smile that lived in your eyes and you nod back to me and say 'go ahead.' Now 45 or so years later it still works. That effect is what I hope to provide to your grandchildren.

To Kurt Thoma, the real Kurt Thoma with the infectious laugh. Kurt may be one of the few people I know who has read more books in more genres than me. As such, when he gives praise, I know that he means it and it comes from a guy who is not shy about ending a book when it just doesn't work.

To Rae Fraumann, ever a light in the darkness. For friendship without cost. For great conversations and some of the best soul-cleansing laughter ever. I know two people equipped with the degree of empathy that you own. I get to be married to one of them and I'm blessed to have the other as a friend. 'O Captain….'

To Danny 'Very Sick' LaValle. I could not ask for a better friend. A Brother by choice if not by blood. He is one of the most talented artists I've ever met. One of the very first people to ever read my stuff and ask for more. Sick is the only person on the planet that I trust to stick a needle and ink on my skin. If you need a tattoo your destination is Very Sick tattoos in Madison Maine.

To Eric P. Bishop, author of The Body Man, Ransomed Daughter, Breach of Trust and and his latest Babylon Will Rise. Eric and I first spoke through Instagram when his debut novel hit. In the time since I have watched him develop his own publishing company, BruNoe Media and get an incredible podcast, A Tale of Two Scribes, up off the ground. Eric has been a voice of encouragement to not only me but a litany of other nascent writers. I always enjoy our conversations even when we're limited by schedules.

To Colonel (Ret.) Steven Thomas. Thank you first and foremost for signing the blank check for our country and doing so for three decades. Thank you for buying Webb and giving such an incredible review on your platform Bestthrillerbooks.com . I was speechless for a few minutes after I first read it. Ask anyone you share this list with, that is rarity in the class of Unicorns. I believe that you would tell me that you wouldn't have said it if it weren't deserved but I am truly humbled and hope that I can continue to earn that level of review.

To Jack London, Robert Ludlum, Eiji Yoshikawa, David Morrell, Clive Cussler, Tom Clancy, John Grisham, Vince Flynn, Bram Stoker, Stephen King, Dean Koontz, J.R.R. Tolkien and Terry Goodkind for putting pen to paper crafting some of the most incredible tales to infect a young man's heart with adventure, fears and ambition. For making me want to join your ranks.

To Jack Carr, Eric P. Bishop, Sam Whitfield and a growing TBR list of writers who have picked up the torch to tell tales for our time.

To the great Men and Women who stand the line in service and defense of others. Past, Present and Future.